Pasta
Mortem

Books by Ellery Adams

The Secret, Book & Scone Society

The Secret, Book & Scone Society
The Whispered Word

The Book Retreat Mysteries

Murder in the Mystery Suite
Murder in the Paperback Parlor
Murder in the Secret Garden
Murder in the Locked Library

The Charmed Pie Shoppe Mysteries

Pies and Prejudice
Peach Pies and Alibis
Pecan Pies and Homicides
Lemon Pies and Little White Lies
Breach of Crust

Antiques & Collectibles Mysteries

A Killer Collection
A Fatal Appraisal
A Deadly Dealer
A Treacherous Trader
A Devious Lot
A Killer Keepsake

More Books by Ellery Adams

Supper Club Mysteries

Carbs & Cadavers
Fit to Die
Chili con Corpses
Stiffs and Swine
The Battered Body
Black Beans & Vice
Pasta Mortem

Hope Street Church Mysteries

The Path of the Crooked
The Way of the Wicked
The Graves of the Guilty
The Root of All Evil
Fate of the Fallen

The Books by the Bay Mysteries

A Killer Plot
A Deadly Cliché
The Last Word
Written in Stone
Poisoned Prose
Lethal Letters
Writing All Wrongs
Killer Characters

Books by Rosemary Stevens

The Murder-A-Go-Go Mysteries

It's a Mod, Mod, Mod, Mod Murder
Twist and Shout Murder
Secret Agent Girl

The Beau Brummell Mysteries

Death on a Silver Tray
The Tainted Snuff Box
The Bloodied Cravat
Murder in the Pleasure Gardens

The Cats of Mayfair (Regency Romance)

A Crime of Manners
Miss Pymbroke's Rules
Lord and Master
How the Rogue Stole Christmas

Pasta Mortem

ELLERY ADAMS

AND

ROSEMARY STEVENS

BEYOND THE PAGE
PUBLISHING

Pasta Mortem
Ellery Adams and Rosemary Stevens
Copyright © 2018 by Ellery Adams and Rosemary Stevens
Cover design by Dar Albert, Wicked Smart Designs

Beyond the Page Books
are published by
Beyond the Page Publishing
www.beyondthepagepub.com

ISBN: 978-1-946069-73-3

Pasta Mortem

Chapter One

Head librarian James Henry pushed away from the table with a satisfied sigh. "Gillian, that pizza was delicious, but I've got to lose weight. My fat clothes are tight, and when Murphy photographed me for the *Star*, I had to fight the urge to hide my middle behind the library counter."

A collective groan sounded from his four friends. The supper club members sat around the table in Gillian's periwinkle blue kitchen, a platter containing the crumbs of their meal a testament to their appreciation for the tasty food.

James continued, "It's been like a line of dominoes falling, and I don't mean the pizza kind. Well, maybe that too." James paused, then ticked off events on his fingers. "That cruise Jane and I took last summer where it seemed like we had eight meals a day, the stress of Eliot starting kindergarten, Halloween's leftover candy, the huge meal Milla cooked for Thanksgiving and the leftovers, Lindy and Luis's wedding reception, and then a tidal wave of Christmas treats. I got on the scale this morning and didn't realize the contraption could count that high."

"Tell me about it," Bennett Marshall said. "Statistics show that the average American only gains one to two pounds over the holidays, but I don't believe it. Plus, I've been stopping at the 7-Eleven again, picking up food. I had to cover a box of donut holes with a priority mail package when Murphy took a picture of me in my mail truck. I leaned out the window and gave a friendly wave in my photo for the *Star* so Murphy couldn't see my gut hanging over my belt."

Gillian O'Malley, owner of the Yuppie Puppy, swung her head toward him so fast her auburn curls whirled about her face. "Bennett! Donut holes are *full* of sugar and empty calories! Do you want to be on medication for diabetes? Our bodies are *temples* and must be treated with respect."

Bennett scowled at his sweetheart. "Woman, I don't want to be on medication. But I have to do something about the stress caused by those evil canines on my route."

Lindy, a Brazilian beauty and high school art teacher, fresh from her honeymoon with high school principal Luis Chavez, chimed in.

"Stress. I can relate to that. On the one hand, I've never been happier now that Luis and I are married. But on the other hand, dealing with Luis's mother drives me straight to my stash of candy bars."

"Didn't she go back to Mexico after your wedding?" James asked.

Lindy shook her head. "I wish. Alma's been staying with us since we returned from our trip. I made the mistake of telling Luis I wanted to change things up at the house—you know, put my own creative energy to use and update the carpet, lamps, artwork, and drapes. Oh, my goodness! Turns out Alma picked out those decorations and was madder than a wet hen that I wanted to change them. Milky Way bars, here I come."

"Did Murphy take your photo too?" Lucy Hanover, dressed in her brown-and-beige sheriff's deputy uniform, asked.

"She sure did. Sitting at my desk at school. I was able to hide my midsection. And I remembered to make sure my drawer full of candy was closed tight so she couldn't see."

"Murphy made me pose in front of my Jeep. A full body shot." Lucy tugged at her shirt as if trying to smooth it over her bulging tummy. "I guess that was better than if she'd made me sit inside the vehicle. When I opened the door, Murphy would have seen all the empty fast-food wrappers and maybe even my emergency can of frosting. I'm stressed out too."

"What's bugging you, Lucy?" Bennett asked.

"Sullie, another deputy, and I are . . . well, we've been seeing a lot of each other. Exclusively." Lucy's brows furrowed. "I think. I mean, *I'm* not seeing anyone else. Sullie's so hot in his deputy's uniform, though, he gets a lot of looks from other women. It makes me edgy. I don't have a very good track record when it comes to men, but French fries and I have always had a great relationship."

James thought of his own obsession with cheese puffs. He cleared his throat. Since he and Lucy had dated before his ex-wife, Jane, and their little boy, Eliot, had come back into his life, James felt uncomfortable when Lucy mentioned her past relationships. They were friends now, thankfully, and James had seen Lucy and Sullie out together on more than one occasion. "Sullie may be attractive to other women, Lucy, but from my perspective, I think he appreciates what he has with you."

Lucy's cornflower blue eyes brightened. "You think so?"

James nodded. "Any man who feeds his lady spoonfuls of apple cobbler with vanilla ice cream in the middle of Dolly's Diner, the epicenter of Quincy's Gap, has declared himself."

Lucy reached over and gave his arm a brief squeeze. "Thanks, James. How is Jane? Eating pickles and ice cream?"

"No cravings. The baby's due at the end of February, so she has a little less than a month to go."

"She's really had a rough time of it," Lindy said. "Luis and I would love a baby, but I don't think I'd like being pregnant after seeing how Jane's suffered."

James thought of his beautiful wife, weak from being sick in the mornings, looking after an active five-year-old, and teaching her distance-learning classes at James Madison University in nearby Harrisonburg, and couldn't help but feel guilty. He knew it was irrational, but he couldn't bear to see her feeling poorly. The doctor had assured them that sometimes women were sick in the mornings all through their pregnancies. She'd said there was nothing to be concerned about as long as Jane kept down enough nutritious meals and her vitamins. James trusted the doctor, but he still worried. Jane rarely complained, which made James more determined to do all the housework, get Eliot ready for kindergarten each morning, do the grocery shopping, and make sure Snickers the dog and Miss Pickles the cat had fresh food and water. In fact, anything he could do in the way of chores, he did. Jane begged him not to coddle her, but how could he not? She was carrying their daughter and deserved to be coddled!

"Jane had a good day or I wouldn't have come tonight."

"I, for one, feel grounded and spiritually replenished by the presence of my friends. It's been too long since we've shared a meal together," Gillian declared as she moved a ceramic figure of two dolphins kissing to one side and passed around bowls of fruit salad. She took a piece of pineapple out of her own bowl and offered it to Dalai Lama, her tabby cat. He licked it first as if to test its worthiness, then snatched it from her hand and chewed happily.

The close friendship of the supper club members had strengthened over years of shared dinners, even if their waistlines hadn't always grown smaller. James looked around the table and reflected on the number of times he and his friends had worked together in the name of justice, identifying people who had committed murder. Fortunately nothing like that had happened recently, but they made a good team. Each person possessed unique gifts and abilities.

"We might not have liked Murphy taking our photos," James said and his friends murmured their agreement, "but I think it's nice that she's using her newspaper to bolster community spirit. She took Pop's photo too, one of him at his easel, and one of Milla behind the candy counter at Quincy's Whimsies."

"Nice? Murphy?" Bennett scoffed and speared a chunk of apple. "After the way she embarrassed us all by writing those mystery novels? The characters that looked and acted like us and a plot like one of our investigations? I'd say featuring us in the *Star* is the least she could do to make it up to us."

"When is this 'Spirit of Quincy's Gap' article supposed to appear?" Lucy asked with a hint of suspicion in her voice.

James chewed a piece of pear. It sounded like Lucy had doubts about Murphy's honesty as to why she'd taken all their photos. The same doubts James had been having himself. He swallowed. "She hasn't said," he admitted, anxious to change the subject. "So does anyone have an idea about a new diet?"

Gillian looked triumphant. "You've already started it!"

Four sets of puzzled expressions greeted this statement.

"I'd been thinking about losing weight again myself," Gillian said. "Even though I try to keep my chakras aligned, the stress of not being able to hold my beloved's hand in public or kiss him for fear of what some people might say —"

"Woman!"

"Everyone knows we're together, Bennett," Gillian asserted. "It's the twenty-first century! People have accepted that interracial relationships happen."

"Not in a small town in Virginia, they haven't," Bennett argued. "And they may know about us, but they don't want to see us kissin' and cuddlin'."

"How will you know unless we give them a chance?"

Bennett tugged at his mustache. "I don't want to talk about it. Let's hear about this diet."

Gillian pursed her lips, then turned to address everyone. "Tonight you've all dined on Goat Cheese and Spinach Pita Bake, or 'pizza,' as James called it. All the ingredients are acceptable on the Mediterranean diet: the pesto sauce, pita bread, tomatoes, and goat cheese. Of course, the fresh veggies are appropriate for any diet."

"What else can we eat on the Mediterranean diet?" James asked.

"The menu is huge," Gillian answered. She walked over to the granite countertop, picked up some papers and handed everyone a sheet. "Here's a list of foods. Think Greek, Italian, even Moroccan dishes. Fish, nuts, olives, hummus, low-fat cheese. You want to *exchange* unhealthy fats for healthy ones. So good for the heart and brain!"

"What about meat? I'm not going on any diet where I can't have my red meat," Bennett declared. "I don't see it on the list."

"In moderation, Bennett, but fish, eggs, poultry, some cheeses, and Greek yogurt should be our primary sources for protein. I'll do a vegetarian version of the diet myself."

James hid a grimace behind his hand as he studied the sheet. A meat and potato man, he'd never cared much for seafood unless it was drowning in a sauce that masked the taste. Since his son had decided to become a vegetarian, James had eaten a lot less meat, but he hadn't totally forsaken it. He told himself to look on the bright side. Chicken and some red meat were okay. Maybe this could work. "What about dessert?"

"Fresh fruit, James," Gillian said with a smile. "Like the fruit salad you're eating."

"All these fruits are available now? In February?" He looked at her skeptically.

"Yes! Oranges, apples, grapefruit, kiwi, bananas, pears. Go to the produce section of the grocery store, you'll be surprised. There might even be some *pomegranates*," Gillian said, excitement growing with every word. "And frozen fruits are good too."

Lucy looked downcast as she rubbed a finger on the paper, her fruit salad barely touched. "A pear isn't exactly my idea of dessert."

James exchanged a dubious look with Bennett. He had a powerful sweet tooth and knew Bennett did too.

"But you'll feel better, Lucy," Gillian assured her. "You'll look your best too, because not only will you be losing weight, you'll be eating healthy foods instead of junk. Your skin will *glow*."

"I'd like that," Lucy said. "Sullie and I will be patroling the *Hearth and Home* TV show reunion festivities down in Cardinal's Rest. A lot of the cast is expected to be there. I had a big crush on Joshie, the oldest boy, for a couple of years when I was younger. I saw pictures of him on the Internet and he's still a heartthrob."

"I'll never forget *Hearth and Home*," Bennett said. "When the show was on back in the late eighties, I used to watch it with my mom. I got the idea of being a mailman after watching the friendly Mr. Jakes deliver the mail to the Lewis family."

Gillian tilted her head. "I didn't know that's how you decided to become a mailman, Bennett. I, too, watched the show. Such positive vibes and messages of hope and goodwill. A wholesome blending of families after each suffered the pain of losing a spouse."

No one said anything for a minute. The supper club members had only recently learned that Gillian herself had lost a husband, a man she'd married when she was twenty and who had died not long after.

Bennett put his arm around Gillian. "We'll pick some events and go if you want," he said gruffly.

Gillian nodded and leaned against him.

James could sense that Gillian's heart had never forgotten her lost love, even though she had Bennett now. He said, "I remember *Hearth and Home* was on Thursday nights. Like Bennett, I watched the show with my mom. She said it reminded her of a modern version of *The Brady Bunch*. I'd like to go to a few events."

"Can we get back to talking about the diet?" Lindy asked. "What about wine, Gillian? Is that on the list? Luis likes a glass with dinner and so do I." Lindy ran her hands through her sleek black hair.

Gillian pulled away from Bennett and nodded. "Like red meat, wine is okay in moderation."

"Do we have to count calories?" Lucy asked.

"No counting calories," Gillian pronounced.

James liked that. He didn't want to have to think about numbers every time he put food in his mouth. "I'm game."

"I'm in," Bennett said.

"Me too," Lindy said.

Lucy sighed. "I need to do something. Might as well be the Mediterranean diet."

Gillian clapped her hands. "I'll find some recipes and email them to everyone tomorrow."

"Thanks, Gillian," Lucy said. "Too bad we didn't get together a few weeks ago and start the diet. I could have had that glowing skin you mentioned in the photo Murphy took. Maybe that 'Spirit of Quincy's Gap' feature she promised will be in this Sunday's edition of the *Star*."

James looked around the table at his friends and knew they were each thinking the same thing he was thinking. Had Murphy told them the truth? Had she taken photos of each of them for her newspaper? If not, what was her motivation? Murphy had shown herself to be ambitious and ruthless in getting what she wanted. She'd built herself a kingdom, or rather a queendom, with her astronomical book sales. She'd bought the town newspaper, the *Shenandoah Star Ledger*, and a big house on Main Street. No one got in the way of whatever it was that Murphy Alistair wanted. James felt a ripple of unease.

He looked at his watch. "I'd better get home to Jane and Eliot in time to read him a bedtime story."

Gillian got up. "Wait, James, I have a fruit salad for Jane for you to take home." She opened the stainless steel refrigerator, took out a brown paper bag, and handed it to him.

"Thanks, Gillian," he said and gave her a hug.

Lindy helped Gillian clear the table. Everyone else shrugged into warm coats, hats, scarves, and gloves to brace themselves against the freezing temperatures, then chuckled as they tried to wrap each other in hugs before leaving for the night.

Outside, the bitter winter air stung James's face. He looked up at the clear night sky and wondered if they'd finally get that big snowstorm the meteorologist kept promising. He waved to Lucy as she got into her Jeep, then climbed into his old Bronco and turned the key.

Nothing happened. The motor was dead.

Chapter Two

"No, no, no, not again!" James yelled and pounded the steering wheel. "I need to get home!" James saw the red taillights of Lucy's Jeep disappearing down the street. Not that she'd be able to help. It wasn't like the car's battery needed a jump. This was the third time the old Bronco had given up the ghost in the new year. The first time, for seventy-five dollars, he'd had the vehicle towed to a shop in Harrisonburg. Five hundred dollars later, the Bronco had a new fuel pump and a promise that the problem had been fixed.

Two weeks later, the car shuddered to a stop on Interstate 64 outside Richmond, where James had attended a regional library conference. He'd made a call to one of his Richmond colleagues, who recommended a shop in town. One hundred dollars for a tow plus four hundred dollars for an ignition module later, James was once again on his way with assurances that the Bronco was fixed.

Now he sat drumming his fingers on the steering wheel wondering what to do. Out of the corner of his eye he saw Gillian and Bennett come outside. They didn't have coats on and hurried to the truck door. James rolled down the window.

"What's wrong, James? Are you all right?" Gillian asked, shivering.

"The Bronco won't start."

"My man, how long are you gonna hold on to that dinosaur?" Bennett asked.

"As long as I can. Who can afford a new car nowadays? I better call a tow truck."

"Wait," Gillian said. "A young man named Ace started coming into my shop for dog food with his dog, Bacon, last summer. Bacon's the sweetest bloodhound mix, but I saw right away the poor thing had two ticks behind her ear that she kept scratching. I got rid of those with baking soda and some apple cider vinegar. Anyway—"

"Are you going to get to the point, woman? I'm freezing my butt off out here," Bennett complained.

"Go on back inside, Bennett, I'll be right there," Gillian said, her breath visible in the night air. "James, Ace is what you call a mobile mechanic. You could call him and he'd come over and get your truck started. I have his number in the house. Come inside where it's warm."

James didn't take long to think it over. A mechanic who would come to him would be faster and maybe cheaper than towing the truck to the mechanic in Harrisonburg. "Okay, thanks."

Gillian turned and hurried back to the house.

James leaned his head on the steering wheel and said, "Listen, Bronco, I don't have the money to keep getting you fixed. What am I supposed to do? I've got a pregnant wife and a son waiting for me."

Feeling like ten kinds of a fool for talking to the truck, James rewrapped his scarf around his neck. When he reached to take the key out of the ignition and join Gillian and Bennett, he turned it one more time on impulse.

To his astonishment, the Bronco started right up. "Good truck!" he cried. "I'll get you some premium gas as a treat tomorrow!"

Without turning the engine off, he got out and went to Gillian's door. She said, "Maybe the truck was cold, James."

James didn't meet her eye. Instead he looked at the polished front door fitted with leaded glass panes. "I hope so. I doubt my own judgment sometimes, Gillian, especially when it comes to an important financial matter like replacing the truck."

Gillian put her finger on James's chin and turned his face toward her. "You stop that right now, James. It's never easy making big decisions in life. Choices when large amounts of money are involved can be tricky. Give yourself credit for not rushing into anything. You know, you're not the same man as when I first met you, when all of us formed the supper club."

"Why do you say that? It's not like I've slimmed down and have rock-hard abs."

"It has nothing to do with the way you look. The changes are on the *inside*. Don't you know how much more confident you are? When we formed the club, you'd lost Jane, you'd lost your mother, and you'd given up your teaching job at William and Mary to come back to Quincy's Gap and care for your father. You were insecure and miserable. Now, you're sure of who you are and, unless I'm mistaken, you're happy about the most important things in life: love, family, friends, work."

James thought for a moment, then said, "If that's true, it's because of the love and support from my friends and Jane and Eliot."

Gillian nodded. "We all flourish when surrounded by love. Keep an open mind about your truck. Here's Ace's number in case you ever need it."

James accepted the slip of paper and tucked it into his wallet. "Thanks, Gillian." He gave her a long hug. "Tell Bennett I said good night."

He jogged back to the truck, which had him safely back at his little yellow two-story house on Hickory Hill Lane in less than ten minutes. "Jane!" he hollered up the stairs. "I'm home. I'll be up in a minute!"

"Okay," she called.

Snickers the schnauzer danced around him.

"You want to go outside, don't you? Come on, I'll let you out back where it's fenced."

James didn't have to wait long. The freezing cold had the dog scampering inside the house in minutes and curling up in his warm dog bed.

Miss Pickles, the tortoiseshell cat, turned her pink nose in his direction, waited for an ear scratch, then, once satisfied, went right back to her nap.

James hung up his coat in the hall closet, retrieved a fork from the kitchen, and ran up the stairs to the bedroom. His beautiful wife, Jane, lay propped up in bed, her walnut-brown wavy hair a dark contrast to the pale blue pillowcase. She had a warm, colorful wedding ring quilt pulled up over her belly. She'd been reading the latest Lee Child novel, but James noted with a pang of guilt that she had her cell phone at her side.

"James!" Jane cried. "I was beginning to worry about you. I thought of phoning but didn't want to disturb you if you were having a good time."

"I'm sorry, honey. We talked about a new diet and time got away from me. You should have called. Or I should have called you." James hastened to her side, a lump forming in his throat. Sometimes, he still couldn't believe that they had found one another again. Gillian was right. When Jane had left him, James had been so hurt, so lost, but the pain had vanished when she'd come back into his life with their little boy. Even though they'd both had other relationships, James had never stopped loving Jane, or she him. Now they'd remarried and were expecting a daughter. He leaned over and kissed his beautiful wife on the lips, then sat on the bed next to her. He couldn't resist placing his hand gently on her belly. He hoped to feel his daughter move, something that never failed to fill him with awe, but she was asleep. "How are you feeling?"

Jane rolled her eyes, then smiled at her husband. "I'll be glad when I don't have to hear those words every day. Our little girl hasn't given me any trouble at all, unless you count kicking me the whole time I tried to nap this afternoon. She seems to delight in waiting until I'm trying to sleep before performing somersaults. What's that you have?"

"Gillian made fruit salad and sent me home with some for you. Do you feel like eating?"

"Mmm, hand it over, mister. Sounds delicious."

James took out the yellow vintage Tupperware bowl, removed the lid, and handed it to Jane along with the fork. He reached back into the brown paper bag and found a napkin. Trust Gillian to think of everything. "Is Eliot asleep already?"

Jane swallowed a bite of banana and nodded. "It's almost nine on a school night. I had to make him go to bed at eight thirty. He wanted to show you the magic reading wand he made in class, but I told him it could wait until tomorrow."

James felt his heart plummet. He had gone to Gillian's straight from work, so he hadn't seen his son since that morning when he'd taken him to the bus. The bus stopped right on the corner outside their house, but Jane and James had decided that, at least for the first year, one of them would stay with Eliot until the bus came and meet him when the bus brought him home. Jane had met Eliot at the bus when he finished school for the day.

"A magic reading wand. I want to see that," James said. "Maybe I could look in on him. I won't wake him."

"Be sure you don't. Let him show you the wand tomorrow morning. Otherwise, he'll get excited and won't go back to sleep for hours. First, tell me about the new diet."

"Gillian came up with the Mediterranean diet."

"Oh, I've heard of that. It's supposed to be very healthy."

"No desserts."

Jane chuckled. "James Henry, you have the biggest sweet tooth in all of Quincy's Gap. I'll bet there aren't any cheese puffs on the diet either."

James paused in the act of unbuttoning his shirt. "How did you know I'd fallen off the cheese puff wagon?"

"Wives know everything," Jane said, mischief in her brown eyes. "Okay, maybe the other night when you were massaging my swollen ankles, I might have noticed that your right index finger looked orange."

James groaned.

"I'll be happy to go on the diet with you."

"You don't have to go on any diet. You're still planning on nursing, aren't you?" James asked, concerned that she'd changed her mind. "I don't want you depriving yourself."

"As I recall, the Mediterranean diet is full of tempting food choices. And of course I'm going to breastfeed our baby girl. But that doesn't give me an excuse to stuff myself with junk food." Jane squinted and pretended to think hard. "Well, maybe sometimes."

James laughed. "Sure I can't get you some pickles and ice cream?"

"Ugh!" Jane grimaced. "Neither sounds appealing."

"I thought most women craved pickles and ice cream when they were pregnant."

"I'm in the minority, then," Jane said and wrinkled her nose. "Anything else happen tonight?"

James pulled out a pair of warm flannel pajamas from the triple dresser. He really didn't want to tell Jane about the Bronco not starting. They'd already had one "discussion" about replacing the truck. James didn't want to upset his wife.

"The Bronco, James?" Jane asked.

James's eyes rounded. "How did you know?"

"I told you. Wives know everything. Now, what happened?"

"Gillian called to make sure I got home okay, didn't she?" James guessed.

Jane nodded and forked a slice of orange into her mouth.

James adopted a light tone. "The truck didn't want to start, but I talked it into behaving. Brought me home fine."

Jane rested the bowl of fruit on her rounded stomach. "James, it's time for a new vehicle. I know you said we can't afford it, and I agree that we shouldn't take money out of savings. But I'll continue my distance teaching at JMU after our daughter is born, and that brings in a small income. We'll have a tight budget, but we'll be able to handle a car payment on a used truck if we're careful."

"Jane, let's not talk about this now," he said, pulling on his pajama bottoms. "You know I don't want you to have to teach after the baby is born unless you want to."

"Which I do. I love teaching. With distance learning, all I need is my laptop to post lectures and grades. You want to wait for the Bronco to break down again?"

"Pop always says that buying a used car is buying someone else's problems."

"That's often true. We can reduce the risk if we have any potential new vehicle checked by a mechanic first."

"Please, Jane. Let's not have an argument about this now," he pleaded, buttoning the top of his pajamas. "I'll take the Bronco back to the mechanic in Harrisonburg tomorrow and tell him what happened. He'll check the truck over."

Jane put the empty Tupperware bowl on the nightstand and picked up her book. "All right, but promise me that you'll tell me what he says."

"I promise." James stepped over to the bed, leaned down, and kissed Jane on the forehead. "I love you. I'll go look in on Eliot, then make sure everything's locked up and come to bed."

James crept silently into Eliot's room. In the dim light of Eliot's Curious George nightlight and the luminous planets and stars on the cobalt blue ceiling, James could make out the top of his son's head. The rest of him was buried under thick blue covers. James listened to the sound of his son's soft breathing and smiled. Who knew that the sound of a little boy sleeping could delight his ears more than even the most beautiful music?

James picked *The Lion, the Witch, and the Wardrobe* off the floor and placed it on Eliot's bedside table without a sound. He and Jane had been taking turns reading the second book in the Chronicles of

Narnia series to Eliot. Although the stories were supposed be for ages eight and up, five-year-old Eliot had comprehended and loved *The Magician's Nephew* and begged for more. James and Jane had bought a copy of *The Lion, the Witch, and the Wardrobe* and were already halfway through reading it to Eliot. As he looked at his boy, James wished again that he'd been home to read to Eliot. Easing the door three-quarters of the way closed, James whispered, "I love you, son."

When he'd finished checking the locks and turning out lights, he returned to the bedroom. One look told him that his wife had drifted off to sleep. James switched off the lamp and slipped into bed, careful not to wake her.

Snuggled under the covers, James said a silent prayer of thanks for his family and friends and asked to be blessed with a healthy baby.

• • •

The next morning, James surprised the two best library assistants in the world, the Fitzgerald twins, by letting the guys into the library, turning up the heat, and then taking off for Harrisonburg immediately, leaving them in charge. Once there, he drank burnt coffee and resisted the siren call of the vending machine for two hours in the shop's waiting room, hoping for a positive verdict on the Bronco from the mechanic.

The man finally came into the waiting room, where James had been checking the *Star* for a feature story on Quincy's Gap with his photo. Gray-haired and short, the mechanic wore stained coveralls and wiped his hands on a dirty rag. "Mr. Henry, I can't find anything wrong with your truck. No codes coming up on the computer."

James perked up. "That's good news."

"Maybe. Sometimes on these older models, the computer doesn't throw a code. An engine cutting off or refusing to start can be hard to diagnose. She's got almost a hundred and eighty thousand miles on her. Might be good for another twenty thousand."

"Two years," James estimated.

"Like I said, might be. You bring her back if she acts up again."

James called Jane right away and told her the mechanic said nothing was wrong with the truck. Although she'd said okay, James could tell she wasn't convinced.

As he drove back to Quincy's Gap, James smiled as he remembered Eliot's excitement that morning when he showed him the magic reading wand.

"Look, Daddy!" Eliot had exclaimed, waving the wand in front of his face. "I can use it two ways. As a bookmark like this"—Eliot grabbed a Dr. Seuss book and demonstrated—"or as a pointer while I read, like this. Here, you can hold it." The child held out the wand as if bestowing James with the crown jewels.

While Eliot pulled on his navy blue sweater, James accepted the wand. Made of a Popsicle stick with a cut-out glittery foam star at the end, the wand had been painted blue. "This is neat, son. Did you glue these hearts and circles on here?"

"Those are moons, Daddy, like the ones I have on my ceiling," Eliot corrected.

"Right. I see that now." When James had bought the house, the previous occupants had glow-in-the-dark stickers on the ceiling of what became Eliot's room. James loved to cuddle in bed with his son while the two looked up at the moon, stars, and planets above and discussed Eliot's day.

Eliot talked nonstop about his kindergarten teacher, Mrs. Spalding, who was pretty and lots of fun, while James made him pancakes and finally got him out the door and on the bus. James had stood and waved at his son until the yellow bus was out of sight.

Now he parked the Bronco in front of the Shenandoah County Library. A quick glance at his watch confirmed what his stomach told him. It was almost time for lunch. Luckily, he'd had the foresight to stop at the grocery store before he left Harrisonburg and pick up a Greek-style salad with chicken. James made it past the snack machine that contained mini packages of cheese puffs without making a purchase and walked into his beloved library.

"Hey, Professor," Scott Fitzgerald called out. The twins often referred to James as "Professor" since, before he returned to Quincy's Gap, James had been a professor of English Literature at William & Mary College in Williamsburg.

James smiled and waved a greeting. He divested himself of scarf, parka, and gloves, put his salad in the break room fridge, then joined the Fitzgerald twins. They stood with Fern Dickenson at the checkout counter cutting red hearts out of construction paper.

"You sure were in a hurry this morning," Francis said, a question in his voice.

Identical twins, the Fitzgeralds were twenty-seven-year-old, long-limbed, brainy bibliophiles who wore tortoiseshell glasses. Each had a bottomless pit for a stomach. They were the best assistants in the world, in James's opinion, and he didn't know how he'd run the library without them. Over the years, they'd become his friends as well as his employees. Heck, James considered them family. Last year, the Fitzgerald twins had won a contest for creating a new video game and, with part of their winnings, had bought cruise tickets to Bermuda for James and Jane as a wedding present.

"Good morning, Fern," James greeted the pretty, auburn-haired young woman, who wore the same tortoiseshell-style glasses as Scott and Francis. A talented photographer, she worked part-time at the library and dated Scott.

"Hi, Mr. Henry."

"I had to take the truck into Harrisonburg so the mechanic could check it over," James explained.

"Again?" the twins asked in unison.

"When are you getting new wheels?" Scott asked. "That truck is as old as a PlayStation One."

"Yeah, you could get a brand-new Tesla," Francis suggested.

"Not you too," James grumbled. "The truck is fine, especially for a family. Granted, it's getting older, but a few repairs should keep it on the road. What are you up to?" he asked and motioned to the red hearts.

Fern said, "For Valentine's Day, I thought I'd make a wall tree out of paper and use the hearts as leaves. I'll keep the hearts blank in case anyone wants to write their names on them."

Scott slid Francis a look. James believed they had a silent way of communicating and he was pretty sure the two were not excited about the upcoming romantic holiday.

"That's a great idea, Fern," James said, moving behind the counter and admiring their handiwork. "Where are you thinking of putting it?"

"I thought it was time to take down my wall of photos," she said, indicating a collage of photos of library patrons. During the Christmas season, the twins had fashioned a photo booth where patrons could have their pictures taken by Fern. Later, the creative young woman had created the collage.

"Tell her that's a bad idea, Professor," Scott said, laying his scissors down on the counter. "Everyone likes seeing themselves on the library wall and they're seriously cool photos. We can put the, um, Valentine tree over near the Romance section."

"I have to agree with Scott, Fern," James said, accepting late fees from a patron and handing over their scanned books and receipts with a smile. He turned and looked at the photos on the wall, prepared to further his case, when a thought struck him. Had Murphy been in the library since Fern put up her creative display? Had she stolen Fern's idea of photographing the locals? If so, why?

At that moment, Bennett, dressed in his postal uniform, strode into the library, a magazine in his hand and a look of thunder on his face. "Excuse me," he said to the twins and Fern. "James, I need to borrow you for a minute. You better look at this. Right now. That Murphy. I knew she was up to no good!"

James and Bennett moved down the counter. James accepted a copy of *Southern Style* magazine from Bennett, his heart rate kicking up. The glossy cover had a photo of the *Hearth and Home* cast members posed in the house the show had been filmed in. They were grouped in the kitchen, smiling, under a wooden sign that read "All Because Two People Fell in Love."

"Look at the articles listed on the side," Bennett ground out.

James read aloud: "*Hearth and Home's* Thirtieth Anniversary Reunion! Bestselling Author Murphy Alistair on her new book, *Murder in the Caverns.*"

He turned the magazine over. The entire back page was the colorful cover of Murphy's new book. James knew the story would be a fantastical retelling of a murder investigation the supper club had conducted after finding a dead body at Luray Caverns a few years ago. Murphy's previous book had been equally horrible, but wildly popular. James looked at Bennett in dismay. "She's started the publicity for her new book in a big way."

"That's bad, but you missed this," Bennett said impatiently. He flipped the magazine back to its front and tapped his finger on the third feature, which read in large, red capital letters, "FIVE BEST UNDISCOVERED SMALL TOWNS YOU SHOULD BE LIVING IN!" In smaller letters underneath were the words "Including Murphy Alistair's own Quincy's Gap!"

"What?" James said, confusion turning to anxiety. "*Southern Style* has named Quincy's Gap one of the best small towns to live in?"

Bennett snatched the magazine from his hand. "Look at this." He flipped through pages and held open the magazine. In bright blue letters were the words "Quincy's Gap! Mountains! Apples! Farms! Cheap Land! Wouldn't you want to live among the friendliest people in Virginia?"

And there they all were. James, Lucy, Bennett, Gillian, and Lindy, and in a smaller shot, Jackson and Milla. Murphy had given the photos she'd taken of everyone at their jobs to *Southern Style* for the feature on Quincy's Gap and the promotion of her new book. She had never intended to use the photos in the *Star*. And she'd gotten the idea from Fern's innocent wall of photos in the library! Outrage ran through James.

Scott and Francis had snuck over behind him and had been reading over his shoulder.

"Wow, Professor, you're famous. *Southern Style* is based out of Louisville, Kentucky, but it's sold all over the country, not only in the South."

Francis said, "That TV show reunion is next week in Cardinal's Rest at the Red Bird B and B. That's twenty minutes southwest of here. Willow told me they're making extra candy at Quincy's Whimsies for tourists. I'd better call her and tell her to expect a tsunami of people coming to see the 'best undiscovered small town' as well as those celebrities."

"That Murphy," Bennett said through gritted teeth.

James quickly scanned the article. It made Quincy's Gap, population 2,026—soon to be 2,027—sound very appealing. Good schools. Low crime. Picturesque. All of which was true. James could imagine lots of people across the country reading about his town and rushing to buy up property. Hordes of people. Developers buying land and building new subdivisions, new apartments, new office buildings. When they were done, James wouldn't even recognize the town he'd grown up in, the town he loved, where he planned to raise his children. And he and his friends would have played an unwitting part in the nightmare that awaited them! Anger gripped him.

"Bennett, you're delivering this magazine today to sub-scribers?"

"Yeah, and the grocery stores and drugstores are getting it today, too. Some sort of rush deal. We need to get together and talk about this."

James nodded in agreement, his head reeling. "This calls for an emergency meeting of the supper club. I'll send out emails right away suggesting we go to Mamma Mia's restaurant for dinner."

"See you then. In the meantime, I've got a fresh box of donut holes to eat." Bennett trudged out of the library and into the cold.

James stared at the magazine. He wouldn't be the only one angered by what Murphy had done. Besides his friends, other townsfolk were bound to be up in arms over this kind of publicity for Quincy's Gap and what it might mean for all their futures.

Murphy had better watch her back.

Chapter Three

James walked into his childhood home with Jane and Eliot. The smell of cilantro, coming from a big pot heating on the stove, met his nostrils. He welcomed the warmth not only of the comfortable, homey kitchen but also of Milla's smile.

"James and Jane, come in out of that awful cold," Milla said, wiping her hands on her apron. "And there's my favorite grandson! Do you like avocado, Eliot? I'm making you a vegetarian black bean soup and chopping some on top."

"Grandma!" Eliot yelled and rushed into Milla's waiting arms. He hugged her tight. "I like everything you cook."

Milla's smile grew bigger, if possible, and her silvery blue eyes twinkled with these words of praise. "Oh, it's good to see you, little man. I'm so happy that your mom and dad brought you over."

Sitting at the kitchen table, James's father, Jackson, wearing his favorite overalls and a warm plaid shirt, said, "Don't crush the boy to death, Milla."

"Pop-Pop!" Eliot shouted. He tore himself from Milla's arms and ran to his grandfather, who lifted him onto his lap. In a stage whisper, Jackson said, "See if you can get your grandmother to give us some tortilla chips with the soup. She won't let me have any."

Eliot's brows drew together.

James exchanged a rueful glance with Milla.

Milla said, "Tortilla chips are not on your stroke prevention plan, my love."

"I already had a stroke," Jackson replied darkly.

"And you won't have another as long as you take care of yourself," Milla said cheerfully.

"You okay, Pop-Pop?" Eliot asked, his golden brown eyes big with concern.

"Fit as a fiddle," Jackson declared. "But you and I have a mission to accomplish."

"We do?" Eliot asked.

"Sure, go into the TV room and see if you can find what it is."

Eliot scrambled down and raced into the adjoining room.

"What's going on, Pop?" James asked.

"I picked up one of them Lego dinosaur sets after you called and asked us to look after the boy tonight."

Jane said, "You didn't have to do that."

"Are you kidding?" Milla said and laughed. "Jackson likes putting those things together as much as Eliot!"

"Maybe it'll take my mind off the trouble about to hit this town," Jackson said curtly. "Best undiscovered small town, hmpf. Won't be for long. Gonna be like when Home Doctor took over Henry's Hardware and Supply, a place I built from the ground up, only this will be on a bigger scale."

"Pop, that's why Jane and I asked you to watch Eliot tonight. I'm meeting with my friends to see exactly what's going on and what we can do about it. I don't want to see Quincy's Gap change either."

Jane said, "I don't know. Exposing Eliot and the new little one to a bigger group of people might be good for them in the long term."

James stayed quiet. Jane was entitled to her opinion, he was entitled to his. Keeping the peace between them meant more to him right now than trying to get her to see things his way. He wanted Eliot and his little girl to grow up in the same small town he had. What was wrong with that?

Jackson, however, felt free to speak his mind. "Jane, I've come to love you like a daughter, but you are dead wrong." He banged his fist on the table. "There's nothin' wrong with our town as it is. It's a good place to raise children. You want to take the boy to a bigger place, take him to visit Charlottesville, Richmond, or Harrisonburg, but bring him back to where he knows his neighbors and friends."

James couldn't help but agree with his father, but he said nothing.

Milla stepped into the breach. "Jane, dear, how have you been feeling?"

"Fine, thank you," Jane said.

"I know how to make homemade ice cream and could make you a batch of your favorite flavor," Milla offered.

Jane put a hand to her stomach. "That's a kind offer, Milla, but not now. Maybe another time."

"We'd better go," James said. "Thanks for taking care of Eliot."

"I'll tell him we're leaving," Jane said and went to find her son.

Milla said, "You don't have to thank us, James. He's our

grandson and we love him to pieces. He's welcome here anytime. You know that."

James stepped over and gave Milla a hug. "I'm so glad Pop found you after Mom died," he said into her dusty blonde curls. He turned to his scowling father. "Try not to worry yet, Pop."

Jackson grunted.

Jane returned. "Eliot's got the package open and half the dinosaur built already."

Jackson's chair scraped the floor as he got up. "Better get in there."

James put his hand on the doorknob. "Are we getting that big snowstorm the weatherman keeps warning us about, Pop?"

"I'll let you know when the hound next door starts howlin'. Until then, nope," Jackson said and disappeared into the other room.

"Is he okay?" James asked Milla in a low voice.

Milla walked over to them. "Cranky as ever, but I'm up to the challenge! We went to the doctor today and all Jackson's reports were excellent, so we're on track. Now, you two try to enjoy your dinner and take your time getting back. When you open the door, watch that Prince Charles doesn't get out—oh, dear, I'm sorry," she said, putting her hands to her cheeks. "Sometimes I forget he's on the Rainbow Bridge playing with other dogs and waiting for me."

Milla's beloved dog, a corgi, had passed away in his sleep shortly after Jackson and Milla were married.

"No need to apologize." Jane hugged her, then they left.

When James and Jane arrived at Mamma Mia's, they found the supper club members already seated at a big round table covered with a pristine white tablecloth. Red napkins were folded at each place. Dozens of Italian flags hung from the ceiling and colorful paintings depicting scenes around Italy hung on the walls. A recording of Maria Callas singing from *Madame Butterfly* met his ears. James thought the décor had improved for the better since the last time he'd been at the restaurant.

The supper club members greeted James and Jane, and then James said, "I hope we're not late. We had to drop Eliot off at his grandparents." He looked around. "Where's Lindy?"

Gillian, dressed in a purple cowl-necked sweater, sat next to Bennett. "It's parent-teacher night at the high school. She and Luis had to be there."

"Can we order soon?" Bennett asked. "Being angry at Murphy made me work up an appetite."

James said nothing about the donut holes. Why should he guilt Bennett when he'd been eating cheese puffs all afternoon?

Lucy had changed from her deputy's uniform and wore a fuzzy blue sweater that brought out her eyes. "I already know what I want. Hurry and decide, James, before the waitress comes back." She smiled at Jane. "How are you feeling?"

Under the table, James gripped Jane's hand. She looked up from the menu she'd been studying and said, "Fine, thank you, Lucy." Returning her gaze to the menu, she said, "I think I'll go with the chopped salad minus the house dressing. How about you, James?"

James looked at the description for the chopped salad. *Crispy prosciutto, tomatoes, blue cheese, avocado, and house dressing.* While it sounded good, James wanted something more substantial. "The Lighter Style Chicken Marsala is tempting. The word 'light' makes me think I'll be in my diet zone."

"My man," Bennett said, "you read my mind."

"Good choices," Gillian commended the two. "For myself, I'll have the stuffed mushrooms and some olives."

The waitress came and took their order. Lucy asked for a bottle of Chianti for the table, saying she needed a glass of wine after the day she'd had. After the waitress left, Lucy passed around a copy of *Southern Style*. "In case anyone hasn't seen it."

"Are you kidding?" Bennett asked. "The whole town is buzzing, not only with the Best Undiscovered Small Town label we got, but also about the *Hearth and Home* reunion."

"I'm sorry if townsfolk think that newcomers would be bad. I, for one, think new blood would be a good thing," Gillian declared. "Maybe if the town grew, you'd feel more inclined to be affectionate in public, Bennett. And don't forget that I asked you to consider shaving off your mustache."

"More people mean more mail deliveries and more evil canines," Bennett said. "I like Quincy's Gap exactly as it is. Otherwise, I wouldn't live here. And I'm not shaving my 'stache."

"I talked to Lindy right before she started her parent-teacher meetings," Lucy said into the awkward silence that had fallen. "She and Luis are concerned about the school infrastructure and whether it can handle being inundated with new children. Lindy said she likes having smaller classes and feels she has the time to help kids individually."

"That's an important point," James said. "I don't want Eliot going to an overcrowded school." He looked thoughtful for a moment. "Let's backtrack a minute to Murphy."

"She lied to us," Bennett snapped.

James nodded. "Yes, she did. I feel betrayed. Furthermore, I have a young photographer, Fern Dickenson, working at the library. She's been taking photos of patrons and arranging them in a collage on one wall. I think Murphy saw that and distorted the idea into taking photos of us at work."

Gillian looked aghast. "I can't tolerate people who infringe on others' creative endeavors."

"I can't tolerate Murphy period," Bennett said. "I guarantee you she's behind all this Best Undiscovered Small Town and it's for her own gain, not the town's."

The waitress returned with a basket of breadsticks. Lucy picked one up and used it to point at Bennett. "Exactly. Sullie and I went to a security briefing for the *Hearth and Home* reunion festivities. Guess what I found out? The editor of *Southern Style* is Joel Foster. He played the youngest boy, Sam, on *Hearth and Home*, remember? So Joel Foster had a vested interest in the magazine's cover featuring the cast members and promoting the reunion. And there's more."

"He had the cutest dimples," Gillian interrupted.

"Still has them," Lucy confirmed. "He was at the meeting. Joel's got to be in his mid-forties now, but he doesn't look a day over thirty. A real baby face. Listen to this: I asked him how the magazine had come up with Quincy's Gap as one of their best undiscovered small towns."

"What did he say?" James asked, leaning forward in his seat.

"First, he tried to tell me the towns were chosen by an independent panel consisting of travel experts. I didn't believe him so I resorted to a little white lie. I told him I knew my friend Murphy Alistair had lobbied to get the town on the list. And get this," Lucy said, making sure she had everyone's full attention. "Joel chuckled and then he winked at me and said, 'Good for

Murphy's business, that's for sure.' I wondered, which business? The newspaper? Her books? But Sheriff Huckabee called me away before I could question Joel further."

"That's what I want to know," James said. "How is Murphy benefiting from what she's done?"

Bennett nodded toward the entrance to the restaurant and lowered his voice. "Why don't we ask her? She just walked in."

As one, the supper club members turned and looked at the couple standing at the hostess station. Murphy appeared tall and sleek in a pair of skintight, black skinny jeans tucked into high-heeled black leather boots. Her bobbed hair had been colored a rich molasses brown and shone under the restaurant's soft lights. She wore a form-fitting gold sweater that was cut very low and showed off her ample assets.

"Who's that with her?" Gillian asked.

"We're about to find out," James said.

When Murphy spied their table, she made a beeline their way. Her companion, a tall, lanky man with brown hair, thin lips, and an angular face with a wide forehead, kept his hand on Murphy's lower back. He wore a white button-down shirt, khaki pants, and a navy blazer and looked around with a proprietary air.

Reaching them, Murphy's sharp gaze went directly to the copy of *Southern Style* on the table. "So you've seen the magazine. I hope you appreciate my surprise. All of you are famous!"

"Without our permission," Bennett growled. "You said the pictures were for the *Star*."

Murphy raised her index finger and shook it back and forth. "Now, now, Bennett, you signed a release form when I took your photo. Each of you did. I put the photos to better use."

"Nobody read that fine print," Bennett shot back.

"That's not my fault. What's wrong with you?" she demanded impatiently. "You all seem angry. I thought you'd be pleased to be ambassadors of our growing town, featured in a national magazine. Never mind. You'll soon change your tune. Let me introduce you to the man who's going to help Quincy's Gap grow. Everyone, this is Ray Edwards, my partner in the new Honeybee Heaven Farms Corporation."

"Partner?" James repeated.

Edwards looked at James from under thick eyebrows. "That's right. I'm a real estate developer, and this hot property"—he glanced at Murphy and wound an arm around her waist—"and I are going to make you Quincy's Gap folks rich."

"Along with ourselves, right, stud muffin?" Murphy said, a glimmer in her eye.

"You betcha," Ray Edwards confirmed.

Lucy glared at Murphy. "How are you going to do that exactly?"

"*Exactly* like this, Lucy dear," Murphy replied, scorn lacing every word. "Ray bought Buford Lydell's peach farm and the two thousand acres with it for development. I'm an investor and partner in the corporation. Quincy's Gap and the whole area will benefit from our foresight."

"But Lydell's honey and peach farm has been a popular attraction for as long as I can remember," James protested. "During the peach season in summer, Lydell has hayrides set up, a petting zoo, and a small fair. I go every year."

Gillian said, "I have a jar of Lydell's honey in my kitchen cabinet right now. *Locally* sourced honey is the best."

Edwards scoffed. "Quaint, but we won't be doing anything so small-town. My plan is to turn the farmland into a massive planned community of two apartment complexes, condos, and houses around a new man-made lake, and a shopping center. We'll have no problem selling to people from all over the country. Current businesses will thrive, which will attract more companies, bring in new restaurants." Again, he looked around Mamma Mia's with an appraising eye. "This place might want to open another location in our shopping center. They better hurry if they do. All of Quincy's Gap's properties and land are about to skyrocket in price, especially now that Murphy got Joel Foster to feature the town in *Southern Style*."

James contemplated Murphy. "All of this is about money. You don't care about Quincy's Gap. You only care about lining your pockets! Aren't you rich enough from your book sales?" He turned the magazine over so that Murphy's new cover was faceup. The supper club members looked from the image of the book's cover to Murphy with disgusted faces.

Murphy adopted a wounded expression. "When my last book

came out, it doubled tourism and brought money to shopkeepers and places like Dolly's Diner. I've done nothing that hasn't made Quincy's Gap better."

"And if you happen to make enough money to buy the whole town with this latest scheme," Bennett said, "that will be to our benefit too, right, Murphy?"

James saw a faint rise in Murphy's color. Maybe it *was* Murphy's plan to own as much of Quincy's Gap as she could!

"A big increase in population will bring crime with it," Lucy said. "Have you thought of that?"

Murphy's gaze darted over to Lucy and sharpened. "You should be happy to have your photo in a national magazine, Lucy. Maybe some man will find you attractive and get in touch. With the TV show reunion coming up, you're bound to lose Sullie to a pretty girl from Hollywood. Or, with his movie star looks, he'll dump you and move out to Los Angeles to pursue a film career."

Lucy stood. "Why you—"

Gillian put a restraining hand on her arm.

Lucy sat down but scowled at Murphy.

Murphy ignored them. "Jane, I almost didn't notice you."

Jane didn't lower herself to respond. Before James could say anything, his attention was captured as a distinguished-looking gray-haired couple entered the restaurant. James recognized Arthur Pritchard IV, the owner of Pritchard Stables. The Pritchard family had been breeding racehorses since the 1930s, the business passed down within the family through the years.

Unfortunately, Ray Edwards recognized Mr. Pritchard as well. "Mr. Pritchard, sir," he called.

The older man, dressed in a handsome tweed suit, motioned for his elegant wife to continue to their table. He strode over to stand in front of the developer.

Ray Edwards held out his hand. "Have you thought about my proposal?"

Mr. Pritchard ignored Edwards's proffered hand. "Have you thought about mine?"

Edwards rocked back on his heels. "Now, Mr. Pritchard, you don't want to be the one holding back progress, do you? Preventing a further expansion of this great town? I made you a more than fair offer for your land since it abuts the peach farm and lands I now own."

Pritchard stood unusually still. James thought the man was barely containing his fury.

"I told you, I'm not selling, and I made you a good offer for Lydell's farm."

Edwards chuckled. "Mr. Pritchard, I understand that your land has been in your family a long while, but there's a time and season for everything. This is the time to retire, let your land become the new home of many people instead of one family. Accept my offer, take your wife and the money, and go somewhere warm."

"Never," Pritchard declared. "Not only is it my nephew's inheritance, but people around the United States rely on me when it comes to purchasing horses fit for racing. Racehorses are high-strung animals. A year or more of construction noise from what you're planning will be detrimental to them in the extreme."

Edwards shrugged. "You'll have to buy 'em earplugs then. You can't stop progress."

Pritchard's face reddened. "It's not progress, it is greed! I've warned you. I will not be thwarted in this matter. You have my word on that."

"You can't stop me." Edwards took a step toward the older man. "Like I said," he sneered. "Go someplace warm. Like Hades."

Mr. Pritchard stalked back to his table.

Murphy took Ray Edwards's arm. "Come on, stud muffin, I brought a bottle of Dom Perignon over here earlier and had them chill it for us. There's no sense in spending another minute with people who don't know how lucky they are." The two walked away.

Bennett looked at their retreating backs and said, "Murphy's so cold, if she wanted to chill the champagne, she could have just put the bottle in her mouth."

"I can think of another place she could put it," Lucy fumed, sitting down.

The waitress brought their food, but although the fare was tasty, after they'd all eaten, James thought no one had really enjoyed their meal. An atmosphere of apprehension had settled over the supper club members.

James couldn't shake a feeling of dread.

Chapter Four

Over the next week, Quincy's Gap changed from a tranquil place where neighbors stopped to chat with each other, and the news of a wedding or the birth of a child could keep people talking for days, to a veritable hive of activity. Throngs of cars with out-of-state license plates—James counted three from Wisconsin—clogged the streets and roads around the town. Curious out-of-towners were everywhere he went, jamming the shops and eateries on Main Street, and not all of them were as polite as the residents of Quincy's Gap.

James took to leaving the library at lunchtime in order to keep abreast of what was going on. He tried to tell himself that most of the strangers were in the area for the *Hearth and Home* reunion, which would begin in three days, but he knew that was only partially true.

He decided to grab a salad at Dolly's Diner. Dolly would have the latest news. But despite high temperatures of around thirty-three degrees, James found he couldn't get anywhere near the diner. The line extended out the door, with people he didn't recognize standing in the cold wanting to get a taste of small-town diner food.

He drove to Joan Beechnut's office at Blue Ridge Realty, anxious to put a few questions to her. Joan, a prim blonde, had been the Realtor who'd sold him his cozy house. She was the area's leader in home sales for four years running. Today, her professional demeanor slipped.

Seeing him, she held up her hands in a defensive position. "Don't even think of asking me what your house is worth, James."

"Why would I do that?" James asked, wrinkling his brow. "I love my house and so does Jane."

Joan stared at James. "Since Quincy's Gap was featured in *Southern Style*, I've been swamped with people wanting to know how much they could profit if they sold their house. Half the time, I can't decide if they're serious about selling or not, but I still have to put in the work."

James imagined a mass exodus of the current townsfolk and grimaced. "Have you gotten any new listings?"

"Two in the last three days. And I've already sold both of them. One to a family from Maryland, the other to a couple from Detroit. See this binder?" she asked.

"That's where you keep listings for houses for sale in the area. I remember going through it with you when I was looking to buy."

Joan nodded, opened the binder, and flipped through the pages. "Every one of these is sold. I've rented all the available apartments in Mountain Valley Woods too." She closed the book with a snap. "Ordinarily, I'd be thrilled to do this much business in the middle of winter, but I'm concerned about the future of Quincy's Gap. Why, I even sold the old Hayes House and Tavern."

"You did? I thought the Shenandoah County Historical Society planned to buy it and fix up the tavern. George Washington supposedly drank there. He mentioned it in his diaries."

Joan nodded. "That was the plan, but Savannah Lowndes at SCHS told me that Hayes dragged his feet about selling. Said the Historical Society had too many rules. Then he up and died, leaving everything to his granddaughter over in Richmond. All she cared about was who offered her the most money."

"Who bought it?"

Joan's lips thinned. "That developer, Ray Edwards. The house and tavern come with ten acres of land. He'll raze everything and put up as many houses as possible."

After meeting the man, James believed that's exactly what the developer would do. "Joan, that's terrible. A loss of our county's history."

"I agree. That Edwards is a shark. You know, even with all my sales awards, he wouldn't hear of me coming on board to help him sell his new houses once they're built. The ones he's putting up in Buford Lydell's old peach farm? Edwards is bringing in some woman from his hometown in Kentucky, who'll make a killing." Joan paused. "Or maybe it's a man. Edwards said he'd yet to make a decision. All I know is that it won't be me."

James commiserated with her, then left. First the Lydell peach farm, then the Hayes place, and an offer, unlikely to be accepted as it was, for the Pritchard horse farm. If Edwards had his way, all that natural beauty and history would be gone, replaced with what James was sure would be cookie-cutter homes.

James had a sour taste in his mouth. He decided what he needed was a cup of whatever new flavor of custard Willy had come up with this week at the Custard Cottage. Making his way there, James had to drive the Bronco through the parking lot three times before a space opened up. He dashed through the cold and opened the yellow door.

All the tables were crammed with people. Customers were lined up at the counter, watching Willy scoop up custard, add their requested toppings and a spoon, and place the cup into eager hands. Willy saw James and grinned, but it was a good fifteen minutes before he could serve him.

"What will you have, friend?" Willy asked.

"Memories of Moon Pie is the flavor of the week?"

Willy leaned closer so the people behind James couldn't hear him. "I haven't had time to make up a new flavor this week. It's been nuts in here and I'm not talking about the toppings."

James nodded. "I'll take a small one," he said, thinking neither the marshmallow, the chocolate, nor the pieces of cakelike cookie were on the Mediterranean diet. He told himself the custard was his lunch and accepted the generous portion Willy fixed him.

When James pulled out his wallet, Willy waved it away. "On the house. You know, I pride myself on knowing all my customers, what custard they like with what toppings. I love creating new flavors, too. But if the rumors are true and Quincy's Gap becomes a big town, I don't know if I'll be able to keep up. I'll be grateful for the extra money, but it's kinda sad what I'm trading for it. You want anything to take home to Jane?"

"No, that's okay. Thanks." James mulled Willy's words over as he sat in the Bronco and devoured the custard. Willy had hit on exactly what he didn't like about Ray Edwards and Murphy's development scheme. An increase in business and profits would come at a high price: the personality of their little town.

Back at the library, he gave the Bronco's dashboard a pat as he pulled into his parking spot. "You've been good this week. Keep it up and you'll get more premium gas."

He stepped out of the vehicle, and to his shock heard a man's voice, then a microphone was thrust in his face. "Excuse me, what did you say?" James asked.

A fit bald man in an expensive suit said, "I'm Chuck Curtis from National News, Mr. Henry. It is Mr. Henry, isn't it? Town librarian?"

"Y-yes," James stammered, noticing the man behind Curtis held a huge, long camera propped on one shoulder, aimed right at him.

"I thought I recognized you from *Southern Style*. What's your opinion on the proposed renaming of Quincy's Gap to Quincysville in light of the town's projected growth?"

"What?" James spluttered.

Chuck Curtis turned to face the camera. "And there you have it, folks. People in this small Virginia town are reluctant to embrace change."

"I didn't say that," James protested, but as quickly as they'd appeared at his side, the news reporter and his cameraman disappeared into a white van with the National News logo on the side and drove away.

James stomped through the front door of the library. He paused at the vending machine inside. Fumbling in his pants pocket for change, he muttered, "Quincysville? What the heck? Is that Murphy's idea or Edwards's? Probably Edwards's. Murphy would rename the town Murphysville." He pressed the button that would release a little package of orange heaven. Taking the package of cheese puffs and ripping it open, he popped one puff into his mouth and savored the salty goodness as he entered the library.

"Hey, Professor," Scott called. He sat in front of a screen in the computer section.

There was no need to whisper, James realized, as a quick sweep of the library told him they had no patrons. "Hi, Scott. Where's Francis?" he asked, crunching another cheese puff.

Scott turned in his chair. "He's eating lunch in the break room. Willow made a rum cake. You've got to try it. It's intoxicating . . . well, not in that way, but it's mind-alteringly good."

James knew he shouldn't, but Willow's cakes were better than any he'd ever tasted. Francis had called his girlfriend a "cake enchantress," and the phrase was apt. "Have you been busy?"

"Not really. Been kinda dead in here. Looks like you were interviewed on National News. You're famous!"

James scoffed. "Not something I asked for. That reporter asked me how I felt about the town being renamed Quincysville. Have you heard anything about that ridiculous idea?"

"Yeah, but don't worry, Professor. It's probably fake news."

James grunted.

"Francis said you've been invited to the special VIP reception tonight for the *Hearth and Home* people over in Cardinal's Rest."

"All of us who were featured in that *Southern Style* article were."

"You going?"

James shrugged. "I thought I would. What have you been up to?"

"Francis and I emptied the shelving cart and dusted the children's section." He tilted his head toward the computer screen. "You might want to see this."

James balled up the empty bag of cheese puffs, threw it in a trash can under the computer desks, and moved to Scott's side. "What is it?"

"This is the Quincy's Gap section of the Airbnb site. Look at all the listings for rooms to rent."

"Almost three hundred dollars a night for one bedroom?" James exclaimed.

"Yeah," Scott confirmed. "And get this. They're all rented through the weekend. I hope it's because of the *Hearth and Home* reunion."

James eyed his young friend. "You don't like the idea of Quincy's Gap expanding?"

Scott shook his head no. "Francis and I like riding our bikes around town and renting Widow Lamb's garage apartment, not to mention our jobs here. If we wanted to live and work in a bigger town, we'd move to Charlottesville or Harrisonburg."

James patted his shoulder, then brushed off a few orange crumbs his fingers had left. "I can't run the library without you and Francis."

Scott punched a few keys. "Maybe you can get more news tonight at that party. If Ms. Alistair and that developer have their way, we'll need more help, or even another library. Listen to this. It was pre-taped."

The screen displayed a replay of a national morning talk show with the host interviewing Murphy. Her new book, *Murder in the Caverns*, stood prominently between them.

"Wow," James said. "Murphy really knows how to promote herself."

Scott turned up the speaker volume. Murphy's voice broadcast in the quiet library. "I want to invite everyone who craves clean living, low crime, good schools, and friendly people to come on down to Quincy's Gap and take a look at the plans for brand-new homes about to be built with mountain views. Remember, it's only in Quimby's Pass that murders occur." Murphy finished this speech with a wink at the camera, indicating her book. Quimby's Pass was a not-so-thinly-disguised Quincy's Gap in Murphy's novels. The screen switched to a commercial. Scott closed the tab.

"This isn't going away, is it, Professor? The whole planned development is going to happen. There's nothing we can do, is there?"

James heaved a sigh. "I'll try to find out more tonight, Scott, but at this point, I don't know what will stop it."

Chapter Five

Snow flurries melted on James's navy blue parka when he walked from the Bronco to the front steps of the Red Bird Bed & Breakfast. Spotlights showed off the large and imposing Victorian Painted Lady, whose rich blue color was accented with red and white gingerbread trim and a white front door. With its wings and bays facing in many directions, two round turrets, and a wide porch sporting a half dozen white rocking chairs, the B&B looked much the same as when the exterior had been used for the *Hearth and Home* show. Of course now, instead of being the fictional Lewis family home, Carol and Brian Anderson owned and ran the popular B&B. James wished Jane could be with him to see it, but she had papers to grade and opted to stay home.

The image of a male cardinal in all his red glory had been fashioned from glass and hung from a chain on the front door, a cheerful contrast against the white. It jangled as Carol Anderson opened the door to him. In her mid-sixties with gray-blonde hair cut short, she looked at James through rectangular glasses and gave him a wide smile.

"You must be Mr. Henry," she said. "Welcome to the Red Bird. Come in and let me take your coat."

"Thank you," James said. He studied the hand-crafted wood foyer with its soaring ceilings and a grand staircase. "What a beautiful home."

"Brian and I do our best to preserve it. That's been our job since we bought it from the previous owners, the Richardsons, you know. We're caretakers and love sharing the home with guests." She closed the hall closet and directed him through to the spacious living room, where a fire burned brightly in the marble fireplace.

Next to the fireplace, a tall white Christmas tree had been decorated for Valentine's Day. Wrapped in red velvet garland, trimmed with red hearts and golden arrows, the tree glowed from the light of dozens of tiny fairy lights. A matching white wreath hung over the fireplace. A red satin sash reading "LOVE" ran from side to side. On the mantel, two heavy glass cardinals, a male and female, held place of pride.

James saw Mayor Bright, Sheriff Huckabee, Lucy, Sullie and a few others seated on an inviting red plaid sofa and matching chairs. Standing around talking and drinking were several more people, including an elegant blonde who reminded James of an older Carrie Underwood, his favorite country singer.

Lucy gave him a curt nod. James wondered if Lucy was in sheriff's deputy mode in front of her superiors. Then he realized by the way she had her hands clasped tightly in front of her that his friend was anxious. James looked at Sullie and saw the cause of Lucy's anxiety: Sullie's attention was on another woman. A very attractive woman.

When she'd been on the TV show, she'd played the middle girl, Angela, but James knew from the *Southern Style* article on the cast members that he was looking at Amber Ross, YouTube beauty guru and creator of her own line of makeup brushes. James had to admit, the woman was stunning in a short, ivory-colored dress that showed off her legs. Her long brown hair contained soft blonde highlights, and when she smiled, as she did now at Sullie, her teeth gleamed white. James guessed her makeup was perfectly applied, but it was too heavy for his taste. Sullie must not think so though, James thought, as the man was almost drooling.

Over by the big bay window, James saw Joel Foster speaking with another man and an excited-looking middle-aged woman wearing a heart-shaped button on her dress that read *"Hearth and Home. Always in Our Hearts."*

James had no idea who the woman was, but Lucy had been right about Foster. He still had a baby face. James peered at the other man. Brandon Jensen, that's who he was, James realized. Brandon had played the eldest son of the Lewis clan, Josh, the serious one who helped his dad on the family farm. He'd been a teenage heartthrob and was the one Lucy had said she'd had a crush on. James looked at the two grown men and thought about how he'd carried them in his memory as teens. Funny how the passing of years could take a person by surprise.

"We're delighted to host this reception for the cast members of *Hearth and Home* and special guests," Carol continued, breaking James away from his observation of the group. "Through the living room, you'll find the formal dining room, where food and drinks are set out."

James thanked her before she hurried away to answer the door. He saw that Lucy and Sullie were drinking from champagne flutes filled with a red liquid. Thirsty and curious to try the drink, he turned toward the direction she indicated.

That's when he saw Murphy and Ray Edwards sitting in, of all things, a red leather love seat, drinking champagne and looking anything but in love. As he watched, Murphy poured the last of a bottle into her glass. Another bottle, also empty, lay on its side on the floor. From the way Murphy swayed into Edwards, James figured she was well on her way to falling-down drunk. The skirt of her silver sequined dress rode up her thigh when she suddenly reached out and repeatedly jabbed a finger in Edwards's chest, a frown on her face. One side of Edwards's mouth was turned up in a superior smirk. The two spoke in hushed tones, but clearly all was not well in paradise.

In the dining room, his host, Brian Anderson, a gray-haired man in an ivory cable-knit sweater, leaned against a marble fireplace. It twinned the one in the living room right down to the two heavy glass cardinals on the mantel. "Help yourself, Mr. Henry. There's plenty to go around."

Bennett, Gillian, and Lindy stood at the heavily laden table selecting goodies to place on red plates. The wooden table had been sectioned off into three areas. One was for the red-colored liquid in flute glasses; a small white card declared them "Cranberry Kisses Mocktail." Another section held antique glass containers marked with the names of the candies inside; James saw striped candy sticks, heart mellows, chocolate pretzels, ribbon candy, and red licorice. Finally there were pink parfait topped with granola, and old-fashioned milk bottles containing strawberry milkshakes sitting in ice. Plates of colorful skewered fruit that had been cut into heart shapes were scattered around the table, along with heart-shaped shortbread cookies, bowls of nuts, Chex mix, and chips. On the sideboard, glasses were lined up next to bottles of beer and soda.

The friends greeted one another. Bennett nodded at him. "Try one of these," he suggested.

He held up what looked like a muffin, but when James accepted it, he found it was a chocolate chip cookie that had been shaped into a muffin with a well in it. The concave part overflowed with red frosting.

"Not exactly on our diet, but who could resist?" James had just bitten into the confection when the front door slammed open, drawing everyone's attention.

Buford Lydell, wearing a field coat and jeans, stormed into the room, looked around, and then trudged past shocked faces to stand in front of Ray Edwards. The farmer emptied the contents of a manila envelope in Edwards's lap. Ashes fluttered down onto tailored gray slacks. "There's your sales contract."

Edwards lurched to his feet, shaking off the debris. "You'll pay to have these pants cleaned," he slurred.

"I'll subtract it from the money you paid me for my land," Lydell announced. "You lied. You said you'd save five hundred acres of the peach farm from development. You said you'd keep my farmhands on to look after it. Now my head man tells me you went and fired them all!"

"I told those hicks they could apply for construction jobs," Edwards said.

"That's not good enough! The contract is void because you lied. You can have your money back. I want my land."

Edwards snorted. "The deal was made. You signed off on it, Lydell. There's no going back. You people out here in this backwoods don't understand how contracts work. Guess you didn't finish the fifth grade."

Lydell's face went an alarming shade of purple. "I've got a degree in agriculture from Virginia Polytechnic Institute and State University. Now, unless you want me to tear your arm off and beat you to death with the bloody stump, you'll give me my land!"

Edwards let out a loud laugh.

Buford Lydell drew back his fist, but Sheriff Huckabee and Sullie had quietly come on the scene and restrained him. Lucy stood nearby.

"Come on, Buford," Sheriff Huckabee said. "Let's go outside."

The farmer allowed himself to be led, but before he went out the front door, he looked over his shoulder and yelled, "I'll get my land back one way or another!"

Everyone watched as Edwards continued to laugh. He half fell back down on the love seat next to Murphy.

To James's surprise, Murphy hissed something at her partner, then turned and flounced from the room, her silver sequined dress flashing as she walked past everyone and up the stairs to the bedrooms.

As one, the supper club members gravitated toward the living room and watched her go.

"Come on, partner, wait for your stud muffin!" Edwards called as he staggered behind Murphy up the stairs, gripping the wooden handrail.

Bennett whispered to James, "Looks like Edwards's 'hot property' has cooled off toward him. Won't be much going on in that bedroom tonight."

James put the other half of his frosted chocolate chip cookie in his mouth. Best keep his mouth busy. He didn't want to comment on what might be going on upstairs. Instead, his thoughts were on Buford Lydell. Could the farmer have the sales contract voided? Or was it wishful thinking that Edwards's development could go away so easily?

Swallowing the last of his cookie, James said to his friends, "I know the reception has hardly begun, but it feels over to me. I'm going home. Maybe when I wake up in the morning, I'll find that Edwards has crawled back under the rock he lives under."

"Bennett," Gillian said, "James is right. Let's go. I'm uncomfortable in this house."

"Bad juju, woman?"

Gillian nodded.

"I'll get our coats."

Lindy picked up a handful of chocolate pretzels. "I'll stay long enough to make sure Lucy is okay. I can't believe the way Sullie is mooning over that actress-turned-makeup-guru. I could kill that deputy."

James hugged her. "Try and restrain yourself. The last thing we need is a murder."

Chapter Six

The next morning, James was finishing up the hold and transfer requests when he had a powerful craving for Dolly's meat loaf and mashed potatoes. He reminded himself of how he'd already blown his diet the day before. Maybe one of Dolly's Western omelets with tomatoes, onions, and diced ham might come closer to what he was supposed to be eating on the Mediterranean diet. That is, if he could get past the crowds and into the diner.

He looked at his watch: 11:10. If he left the library now, maybe he could beat the line. Saying a hurried goodbye to Francis and Scott, James got in the Bronco and drove the short distance to Dolly's. He groaned when he saw a half dozen people standing outside the door.

Figuring he'd put his name down on the wait list, James hurried through the freezing cold, opened the door to the diner, and immediately felt the warmth envelope him. The midday sun glinted off the exotic souvenirs Dolly and Clint had brought home from their travels around the world and decorated their diner with.

Then he realized that the diner seemed louder than usual. People were talking and gesturing animatedly. Dolly saw him and came out from behind the long counter, tucking stray strands of her white hair back into her bun.

"Sakes alive, James, can you believe it?"

"Believe what?" James asked.

"I know she's not very well liked, but this! Oh, I suppose you're here for lunch. Well, you can see there's not a single space available. Lucy called, though, and asked me to hold a booth for her. After all she's been through this morning, I thought I'd better."

"Is Lucy okay?" James asked, alarmed. "What's happened?"

"I know," Dolly said, surveying her domain. "You can sit at Lucy's booth. You'll want to hear all about the murder. It's all anyone's talking about."

Dolly moved forward, but James stood rooted to the spot. "Murder!" he exclaimed, drawing the interested glances of several patrons.

James hurried after Dolly.

"Here you are," she said, giving the already clean table a quick swipe with a cloth. "I must have subconsciously known you were coming. It's your favorite booth. Sit down and tell me what you want to eat."

James sat, barely glancing at the colorful leis, small Tiki torches, and the poster of a cobalt sea bordering a strip of gleaming sand in the travel-themed booth before holding Dolly's gaze. "What murder are you talking about? And who is not very well liked?"

"Murphy, hon, who else?"

"Murphy's dead?" James gasped.

The bell over the diner door chimed. Dolly looked up. "Here comes Lucy now. She'll tell you all about it. What do you want for lunch?"

"I think I'd better have a minute," James said faintly. At the moment, he felt as if his heart had sunk into his stomach. Murphy had done some offensive things, but he certainly didn't wish her dead!

Dressed in her sheriff's deputy uniform, Lucy slid into the booth across from him. "James."

James grabbed her hand. "How did Murphy die?"

Lucy's eyes widened. "What on earth are you talking about, James? Murphy's not dead. When I left her, she was safely behind bars in jail."

James felt a flood of relief. He let go of Lucy's hand. "I thought . . . I mean, from what Dolly said . . . never mind. Why is Murphy in jail? Was there a murder? Dolly said there was."

"Come on, James. This is me. I know you. When I walked through the door and saw you sitting here, I wasn't the least bit surprised. I figured you wouldn't be able to resist hearing all the details."

"Lucy, I came here for something to eat! I don't know what's going on! Please tell me!"

Lucy cocked her head, then seemed to come to a decision. "Ray Edwards was bludgeoned to death. Murphy says she found his body when she woke up this morning. We're holding her on suspicion of murder."

James's head felt like it was spinning. Murphy was alive, thank goodness. But Ray Edwards wasn't. James remembered the argument he'd witnessed—that *everyone* had witnessed—between the two the night before at the Red Bird B&B.

Dolly appeared at the booth, catching Lucy's words. "Holding Murphy at the jail, Lucy?"

"Yes, ma'am," Lucy said in her guarded, sheriff's deputy voice. Everyone knew Dolly was the biggest gossip in town.

"Think she killed that fella who was going to ruin our town, huh?"

"Murphy found Mr. Edwards's body this morning. We're questioning her," Lucy replied. "May I have a cheeseburger and fries, Dolly? I haven't eaten all day. And coffee, please."

"Sure, hon. What about you, James?" Dolly asked. Although she carried a pencil and pad, Dolly never wrote down orders. She simply remembered them.

"Um, a Western omelet with tomatoes, no green peppers, and some coffee for me too, Dolly."

When she'd gone, James leaned forward. "Lucy, Edwards and Murphy went upstairs together last night. You saw."

"Yes, I sure did."

"They were sleeping together."

"That's right."

"You said that Murphy found Edwards's body this morning. Do you mean in their room?"

Lucy pursed her lips. "I shouldn't be giving details of an ongoing investigation. Even if it does appear to be an open-and-shut case."

James felt a moment's annoyance. "Surely you can at least fill me in on what everyone else here seems to know," he said, gesturing at the other diners.

Lucy sat stubbornly silent.

Dolly returned with two thick white coffee mugs and a pot of steaming hot coffee. She placed a cup in front of each of them, poured and said, "Sullie came by about half an hour ago for coffee and a couple of sausage biscuits to go. Said he was on his way over to Charlottesville."

"Sheriff's business, Dolly," Lucy said, adding sugar and cream to her coffee.

Dolly put a hand on her hip. "Y'all usually get your forensic work done over there, right?"

"Yes, we don't have the resources here. I think Sheriff Huckabee will be making an official statement later today. Should be the top story on the five o'clock news." Having dropped that tidbit, Lucy took a sip of the hot liquid.

"I'll be back with your orders shortly." Dolly rushed away, no doubt to pass along this latest piece of news.

James drank some coffee, then said, "Sullie taking the murder weapon over to Charlottesville?"

"Good guess."

"Fingerprints?"

Lucy nodded. "A rush job."

"What was the murder weapon?"

Lucy sighed and pushed her coffee cup to one side. She folded her arms across her chest, then said, "You'll keep this between us, at least until Sheriff Huckabee makes his statement?"

"Cross my heart."

Lucy leaned forward and lowered her voice. "Edwards was killed by a hard, sharp blow to his head. The murder weapon was one of those heavy glass cardinals that were on all the mantelpieces at the Red Bird B and B, where he and Murphy, along with the cast members of *Hearth and Home*, are staying."

"Male or female cardinal?"

"What difference—okay, it was the male bird, the red one."

"Where did Murphy find the body?"

Lucy looked away for a moment, then met his gaze. "In the king-sized bed they were sleeping in."

"Oh, no!" James exclaimed.

Lucy looked around. "Sshh. It was a mess."

James held up a hand. "Okay. I get the picture."

"So you see how there's no possibility that anyone other than Murphy could have killed him. No one else was in the room with them, James."

James huffed out a breath.

Dolly returned with their orders. Lucy tucked into her cheeseburger. James put the image of the crime out of his head and focused on Murphy's condition before she went upstairs with Edwards.

"Murphy and Edwards had been drinking heavily. You were there, Lucy." He took a big bite of his omelet and let the melted cheese linger on his tongue before swallowing.

"Yeah, I saw them argue, too, and that strengthens the case against Murphy."

"But they were so drunk. They'd been through two bottles of champagne. I can't imagine Murphy doing anything other than passing out the minute she got in bed."

"That's what she says happened. Doc put the time of death between midnight and two in the morning. Murphy and Edwards could have gone to bed and fallen into a deep sleep, but in certain amounts alcohol is a stimulant. It disrupts sleep patterns. Murphy likely woke up half sober, picked the cardinal off the mantel, hit Edwards with it—"

"And gotten back in bed with the corpse?"

"Don't be morbid. They had the largest room at the inn with an office attached. She could have done some work, or fallen asleep in a chair, anything. Then, a little after seven, she screams the house down and pretends she has no idea what happened to Edwards."

"But why? What did Murphy say when you questioned her about the argument she had with Edwards last night?"

Lucy popped a French fry in her mouth. "She didn't. The minute she realized we thought she'd murdered Edwards, she clammed up. The only person she's talked to since we took her into custody is her lawyer."

James shook his head. "It doesn't make sense. You heard their plans the other night when we were all at Mamma Mia's. Edwards and Murphy stood to make a fortune with their development corporation. Why would she kill the golden goose?"

Lucy shrugged. "Lovers' quarrel, probably. The reason will come out. Once they get the fingerprints off the bird, we'll be able to formally charge Murphy with murder."

"Surely those cardinals had been handled by many people, guests at the inn. Can forensics even get a clear print?"

"Mrs. Anderson, the innkeeper, said that she spent the last few days cleaning ahead of the *Hearth and Home* reunion. She dusted and polished everything, including the cardinals. Sheriff Huckabee thinks we'll get the killer's fingerprints."

"I can't picture Murphy as a murderer. Someone else must have gotten into that room."

"They were on the third floor. No one could have come in

through the window without a very tall ladder. Someone would have heard or noticed that."

"What about the bedroom door?"

Lucy shook her head. "Murphy admitted she locked the door before getting in bed for the night after Edwards came up to the room. James, why are you defending Murphy? She's not a nice person. Look at what she had planned for Quincy's Gap. Look at how badly she's treated the supper club members in her books. Murphy lets nothing stand in the way of what she wants. She's ruthless."

"What about Buford Lydell? You heard him threaten Edwards. Not that I want to think the farmer capable of carrying out his threats."

Lucy wiped her hands on her napkin and dropped it on her empty plate. "Buford Lydell wasn't in a locked bedroom with Edwards. No, James, this was a crime of passion. Whether Murphy killed Edwards over another woman, something about their business together, or the way he parted his hair. She's the only one who could have murdered him."

After Lucy left, James finished his cold omelet. He then ordered and absentmindedly ate a huge piece of Dolly's special buttermilk pie. He decided he'd like to see the crime scene, talk to some of the other guests, those TV actors. Sheriff Huckabee probably had a deputy on guard, maybe even the nasty Keith Donovan. He'd have to wait.

Pulling his wallet out, James thought he'd like nothing more than to call a meeting of the supper club members. He couldn't, though, before Sheriff Huckabee's statement or Lucy would find out right away. She'd consider it a betrayal. But maybe they could gather and watch the five o'clock news together in the library break room. Lucy couldn't object to that.

He dropped bills on the table and headed back out into the cold. The Bronco started up with minimal encouragement. James pointed it in the direction of Buford Lydell's peach farm.

Chapter Seven

James drove along a two-lane road and turned left at the weathered, gray wooden sign that read *Lydell's Peach Farm*. A large image of a peach, the yellow and orange colors faded over the years, was situated next to a big dark blue arrow that pointed toward the farm. As James rode down the driveway the few miles to the white farmhouse, he saw the peach orchard with trees bare of leaves.

Memories of summer visits when he was a boy flickered through his mind, the trees heavy with fruit. He could almost taste the delicious peaches, the juice running down his chin, as he and his parents laughed in the July sunshine.

All of a sudden, James felt a sharp pain the region of his heart at the thought of his mom, Constance Henry. It had been several years now since she died, leaving him and his father bereft. James never stopped missing her, never stopped wishing that she'd lived long enough to see Eliot and, soon, his new little girl. While James was happy that his father had found Milla, and James loved her dearly, no one could replace his mother in his heart. Instead, his heart had grown bigger to include Milla. When they were old enough, James would tell his children all about their grandma so that her memory would live on through them. James thought he wouldn't wait too much longer to show his mother's photograph to Eliot.

James cleared his throat and set his mind on the task at hand: finding out where Buford Lydell had gone after he'd left the Red Bird B&B last night.

He stopped the Bronco on the gravel drive next to the farmhouse. No sooner had he turned off the engine than Lydell appeared on the front porch. James waved and covered the distance to the farmhouse steps.

"Hello, Mr. Lydell. I wonder if I might speak with you a minute?" James asked.

"Better come in out of the cold," the farmer replied, rubbing his short white beard. He turned and walked stiffly back into the house. James followed.

Inside, the living room was packed high with moving boxes.

Lydell led him back toward the kitchen. "Got until the fifteenth to be out of the house before that Ray Edwards takes over. Huckabee told me last night I haven't got a chance tryin' to go back on the sale. Some people will never strain their backs totin' their brains. That's how I'm feeling about myself right now for being taken in by Edwards."

James realized that Lydell didn't know that Edwards was dead. Either that or he was as good an actor as any of the *Hearth and Home* cast.

"Edwina, James Henry's here," Lydell announced as they reached the bright white and green kitchen.

A gray-haired woman wearing a pink cardigan over a neat blouse and jeans turned from where she'd been carefully packing glassware wrapped in newspaper into a sturdy box. "James! How nice to see you. How's your father?"

"He's doing much better, thank you, Mrs. Lydell. Milla's taken good care of him."

"And your wife? She's due this month, isn't she?" Mrs. Lydell asked, her soft blue eyes filled with concern.

"Yes, ma'am. Not too much longer now." James paused, unclear as to how he should go on. He realized that he hadn't considered the fate of the land now that Edwards was dead. Had the corporation Edwards set up owned the land outright, and if so, would Murphy now be the sole owner? What would happen if she were convicted of killing Edwards? No, that simply wasn't possible, James decided. Murphy was innocent of murder at least.

The Lydells were studying him with curious eyes. "Would you like some coffee?" Mrs. Lydell asked.

"No, thank you. I came out to see if you'd heard about Ray Edwards," James fibbed.

"What about the bastard?" Buford Lydell asked.

"Buford! Language," Mrs. Lydell scolded.

"Mr. and Mrs. Lydell, did you know that Mr. Edwards died last night?" James looked right at Buford Lydell when he posed his question.

The man's eyes widened in shock. He gripped the top of a ladder-back chair. "What happened to him?"

Mrs. Lydell had moved to stand next to her husband. She

wrapped her hands around his arm and gave him a comforting squeeze.

"I have it on good authority that he was killed, Mr. and Mrs. Lydell. Sheriff Huckabee will be making a statement for the press later today. It'll be on the five o'clock news."

"Does this mean we'll get our land back?" Mrs. Lydell asked.

"I honestly don't know," James replied. "Unless there's something in the contract that specifies . . ." James stopped himself. He remembered that Lydell had burned the contract and poured the ashes into Edwards's lap. Surely there was another copy. "I suppose it depends on how Edwards's business corporation was set up."

"You say he was killed," Buford Lydell said. "How? He was drunk last night. Don't tell me he left the Red Bird and got behind the wheel of a car."

"No, sir, not that I know of. Talk in town is that Ray Edwards was murdered."

"So we weren't the only ones who hated him," Mrs. Lydell said in a voice that suddenly was as cold as the outside temperature.

James saw that she was staring off into the distance, out the window over the kitchen sink to the bare peach orchards.

"Murdered? Who did it?" the farmer asked.

"That's, um, unclear right now. I expect we'll know more when we get that statement from Sheriff Huckabee. I guess the sheriff will be questioning everyone as to where they were last night."

Mrs. Lydell turned her gaze from the window to him. "We were both here together, like every night."

"Yes, ma'am," James agreed although, for a second, he thought he saw something in Buford Lydell's expression. Something quickly covered.

James couldn't put a finger on exactly what it was, but it piqued his curiosity.

• • •

Back on the two-lane road, James used his cell phone to call Gillian. He hated driving and talking on the phone, but he didn't have much time. He asked Gillian to have the supper club members meet him at the library at four forty-five. Dodging her questions by telling her that he was driving, James disconnected the call.

And not a moment too soon, as he slowed the Bronco for a pair of riders on horseback in the nick of time. Two teenage girls guided their horses as close to the side of the road as they could so that he could pass. James looked in the rearview mirror and saw them turn into the drive of a farm.

That's when James thought of Arthur Pritchard IV. Did the racehorse breeder know of Ray Edwards's murder? Could he take him by surprise the way he'd done Buford Lydell? What excuse could he give for calling on the distinguished man?

His mind fixed on this dilemma, James turned at the forest green sign with gold letters that announced he'd arrived at Pritchard Stables, Established 1935. As he drove down the winding drive and the house came into view, James admired the red-brick, stately two-story house with the white columns and double chimneys. He felt himself growing nervous and almost turned the Bronco around.

Mrs. Pritchard answered his knock. She had on a pair of slim, camel-colored tailored slacks and a chocolate brown turtleneck sweater. Her silver hair had been styled in a short cut with bangs sweeping to one side. She didn't look particularly welcoming, but she gave him a polite smile.

"Good afternoon, Mrs. Pritchard. I hoped I might see your husband for a few minutes."

"All right, Mr. Henry. Arthur's out at the stables with the vet. You can wait in his study."

James followed her across Oriental carpets and into a wallpapered, masculine room where a fire burned brightly. A winged-back chair sat behind Pritchard's polished desk. Mrs. Pritchard gestured to a smaller chair on the other side. James sat down and she left the room.

After five minutes of waiting, James felt even more antsy. He saw a newspaper on the side of the desk and reached for it. It was the Louisville, Kentucky, *Courier-Journal*. "Probably subscribes to keep up with horse-racing news," James muttered to himself.

He'd read almost the entire paper before Mr. Pritchard entered the room and sat behind his desk. "I've heard the news, Mr. Henry. I can give you a few minutes."

James folded the newspaper and dropped it on the desk. "What news would that be, sir?"

"Don't play games with me, young man. I share an attorney with Murphy Alistair. Cyril Morton called me an hour ago and told me Edwards is dead. I also know that you and your friends have been instrumental in solving murders around Quincy's Gap in the past, but I believe the sheriff has the murderess in custody."

"Mr. Morton doesn't think so, does he?" James asked.

"I'm sure he has no opinion on the matter. It's not his job to determine whether or not someone is guilty of a crime. Morton's job is to defend his clients and keep them out of prison."

James thought about that for a moment, then said, "I wondered if you'd seen Ray Edwards after he confronted you at Mamma Mia's."

Mr. Pritchard steepled his fingers. A long moment of silence passed and James fought the urge to fidget in his seat. Then Pritchard said, "That's none of your business, but as I've nothing to hide, I'll answer your question. Edwards came here the very next day. I assume he wanted to try and persuade me to sell my land."

"You assume?" James asked, puzzled.

"I was on horseback at the time and couldn't be bothered to dismount. I've met men like Edwards before in my lifetime. I knew he wouldn't change his mind and see things my way." Pritchard paused and a slight smile appeared on his lips. "I do believe I gave Edwards a fright. I was riding Ivor, you see, and he's quite spirited."

Visions of Pritchard using the horse to trample Edwards, or at least intimidate him, flashed through James's mind. His gaze met Pritchard's, and all at once James was convinced that Pritchard knew exactly what he was thinking. What's more, the man did nothing to contradict the idea. James was certain there was more to the story, but the powerful man wasn't about to enlighten James.

Pritchard rose and James followed suit.

The older man adjusted his cuffs. "If there's nothing else . . ."

James gathered his courage. "Where were you last night, sir?"

Pritchard gave him an incredulous stare. "You overstep yourself, Mr. Henry."

James allowed himself to be ushered to the front door. He turned and gave Pritchard a final look. "What you said about Mr. Morton and his job, well, I'm sure that's true. But Sheriff Huckabee and his deputies have a job too: to uncover the truth about who killed Ray Edwards. I intend to help them in any way that I can because I don't believe Murphy Alistair is guilty of murder."

Mr. Pritchard's brows came together. "I thought you had enough to do as head librarian. If not, maybe that's an issue I should bring up with my friend at the Greenloft Club who sits on the county library system board."

At those words, James's heart fell to the ground. "We have plenty to occupy our time, thank you."

James hurried to the Bronco and seated himself behind the wheel thinking that not only had Mr. Pritchard threatened his job, he'd not answered his question as to his whereabouts the night before.

On the way back to the library, the setting sun brought a last welcome light across the fields. James wore his sunglasses to guard against the glare. He thought about what he'd said to Mr. Pritchard about Murphy. Why did he feel the need to defend her? Was it because long ago they'd been lovers? Was it impossible for him to comprehend that someone he'd once been so close to had cold-bloodedly killed another?

James had to talk to Murphy. After Sheriff Huckabee's statement, he'd go to the jail and see if Murphy was allowed visitors. Or, if this lawyer, Mr. Morton, was so efficient, maybe she'd be released and James could see her at home.

• • •

He posed the question to Lucy when the supper club members sat around the table in the library's break room. Scott and Francis had set up a laptop where they could live-stream the news. The twins promised to hold down the fort while James and his friends watched the broadcast.

Lucy said, "When I left, they were processing Murphy's release papers. She has a top-notch lawyer and, until we have more solid evidence, we can't hold Murphy."

James figured Lucy was referring to the results of the fingerprint tests on the red cardinal. "How long will it take before she can go home?"

"Might be a while," Lucy said and narrowed her eyes at him. "James Henry, you aren't going to interfere in this investigation, are you?"

"Interfere? I just want to get to the truth."

"I've been teaching all day. I'm still not sure exactly what happened," Lindy said. "Only that Ray Edwards is dead. Luis says you think Murphy killed him, Lucy."

Lucy sighed and pointed to the laptop. "Sheriff Huckabee will be on any minute, then we can talk."

Gillian had brought a ceramic container shaped like a nut. On top sat a friendly-looking ceramic squirrel. "I thought we could use a protein boost this close to dinner," Gillian said. She removed the lid and passed the bowl around. "This mix is full of heart-healthy omega-3, perfect for fighting inflammation."

James saw the contents were an appealing mix of nuts and dried fruit. He took a handful and passed the bowl to Lindy.

"Inflammation?" Bennett said. "I like that. I don't have a big gut, it's just inflamed."

"The news is on," James said and turned up the volume.

The news anchor appeared with a solemn look on his face. "Talk of a new four-lane road that would link Quincy's Gap directly to Harrisonburg was brought to an abrupt halt today. Developer Raymond Edwards of Louisville, Kentucky, whose plans to expand Quincy's Gap had been the topic of local and national news, was found dead this morning in Cardinal's Rest. We go live now to Sheriff Huckabee, who's standing by to make a statement."

The screen changed to a shot of Sheriff Huckabee inside the old brick courthouse. Beside him to his right was the United States flag. To his left, the Virginia flag. Behind him was a prominent Shenandoah County seal. Five microphones with various news outlets' logos were positioned in front of him. James assumed reporters stood off camera.

The sheriff stroked his lush, walrus-like mustache and read a prepared statement. "Good evening. At approximately seven twenty-five this morning, this department was called to the Red

Bird Bed and Breakfast in Cardinal's Rest. Upon arrival, my team and I were directed to a top-floor bedroom, where we found the body of Raymond Edwards of Kentucky. The victim of blunt-force trauma, Mr. Edwards was pronounced dead at the scene. Edwards, aged forty-seven, was the chief executive officer of the Honeybee Heaven Farms Corporation here in Shenandoah County and owned Edwards Construction in Louisville, Kentucky. The department is treating the case as an open homicide investigation. Anyone with information is encouraged to call the tip line. I'll take a few questions."

"Sheriff," a voice called out. "I've been told you've arrested Murphy Alistair for Edwards's murder."

The sheriff frowned. "That is not true. No arrest has been made."

"But she's your prime suspect, isn't she?" another voice asked.

"Ms. Alistair was brought in for questioning, but as I said, this is an open homicide investigation. We're looking at all possibilities."

"She hasn't been charged?"

"No."

James had to strain to hear the next question.

"Sheriff, we all know that Murphy Alistair and Ray Edwards were involved both personally and professionally. Can you confirm that she was staying in the room with Edwards? That they had, in fact, been seen arguing last night? Wasn't Edwards killed in the very bed they shared at the Red Bird?"

Sheriff Huckabee's mustache flared and he shook his finger at the speaker. "That is speculation, pure and simple, and I will not address it." He made as if to leave.

"Aren't the cast members of *Hearth and Home* staying at the Red Bird? Will this affect the reunion?"

"I'm confident the reunion events will still take place, but right now we're focused on this murder investigation."

"Sheriff, can you tell us who now owns the land Edwards planned to develop? With Edwards dead, who is in charge of Honeybee Heaven Farms?"

"That's a legal question I can't answer," the sheriff said and then glanced to one side. "Cyril, you want to take that?"

A thin man who looked to be in his sixties stepped forward. Gray-haired and wearing a navy suit and bow tie, he touched his glasses, then spoke in a firm, commanding voice. "I'm Cyril Morton, attorney-at-law. The ownership and structure of the Honeybee Heaven Farms Corporation is a matter of public record. To save you converging on the courthouse to look up records, I'll tell you that, with Edwards's death, the majority of the shares belong to Murphy Alistair."

Lindy gasped.

Bennett whistled.

Lucy gave James an "I told you so" look.

On-screen, the cameras were back on the news anchors, who had started talking about a developing situation in the Middle East.

James shut down the laptop and turned to the supper club members. "I want to talk to Murphy. See what she has to say."

"Why?" Bennett asked. "That woman has done us no favors."

James looked around at his friends. "Look, I know that Murphy is not well-liked."

"For good reason," Lucy said.

James nodded. "True. She lied to us about the photos she took. Her books have shown all of us in a less than advantageous light."

"She's condescending," Lindy threw in.

"And cold as a cast iron commode," Bennett finished.

"But is there anyone here," James asked, holding the gaze of each supper club member for a moment before finishing his question, "who believes Murphy picked up one of those heavy glass cardinals and bashed Edwards in the head with it? Because that's the blunt trauma Sheriff Huckabee was talking about, right, Lucy?"

"Yes," Lucy mumbled.

"In Buddha's name," Gillian said. "The anger and the evil behind that action had to be fierce. Murphy's a lot of things, but I don't think she could do it."

"Neither do I," Lindy said. "Remember how drunk she was last night?"

James raised his eyebrows at Bennett.

"I don't know. I want to hear what Murphy has to say."

"She denies killing him," Lucy told them. "She says she passed out last night, woke up this morning, and found him dead next to her. And that's all she said. She got that hot-shot lawyer down to the courthouse real fast."

"Dead next to her?" Lindy exclaimed. "Mother of God!"

"We need to do what's right," James said fervently. "Together, we're good at investigating murders. I say we put our personal feelings aside and give Murphy our help if she needs it."

Lucy pounded her fist on the table. "It's an open-and-shut case, James. As soon as we get the fingerprint results back from Charlottesville, we'll arrest her. Murphy's going to prison for a long time, if not the rest of her life."

"There are other people who wanted Edwards dead, Lucy," James said. "Buford Lydell, Arthur Pritchard, perhaps. And we haven't even considered the rest of the guests staying at the Red Bird."

"The bedroom door was locked," Lucy ground out. "Others may have had a motive, but only Murphy had the *opportunity* to kill Edwards."

James bowed his head. He didn't want to argue with Lucy, but she had made her mind up and James didn't like that. There was too much at stake.

Gillian was the first to speak. "I agree with James. We might not like Murphy, but we have to put those negative feelings aside if she needs help. This community, our town of Quincy's Gap, the place no one wanted to change, is made up of people who help one another. It's who we *are*."

"Dang, woman. When you put it that way, I don't see as we have a choice," Bennett said.

Lindy nodded. "I will help in any way I can."

Warmth spread through James. How lucky he was to have such good-hearted, honorable friends. "Lucy, where is Murphy now? I want to talk to her."

Lucy pulled out her phone. "I'll call the courthouse and find out if they've released her. But, James, I'm going with you, do you understand?"

"Sure," James agreed.

Chapter Eight

Gillian and Bennett left the library together. Lucy remained in the break room talking on her cell phone. Lindy placed a hand on James's arm. "There's something I want to talk with you about before I leave."

"Okay," James said. He looked around for Scott and Francis and saw them at the computer station. They'd watched Sheriff Huckabee's statement too and now had their heads together talking a mile a minute.

"Let's move over near the checkout counter," James said. "I can feel a cold breeze coming in from the door."

"The situation is this," Lindy began. "I'm concerned about my students. They're not reading books. I don't think they're using the school library or this one at all."

Scott and Francis approached and Lindy waved them over.

"Have the three of you noticed that high school students are coming into the library less?" Lindy asked.

Scott nodded. "For sure."

"I agree. We don't see the young ones in here as much anymore," Francis said from the great height of his late twenties.

"What do you think they're doing instead?" James asked. "Or do I want to know?"

"They're spending all their free time posting to various social media sites," Lindy replied. "Some of that's okay, but I believe it's gotten out of hand. It's like their eyeballs are glued to their phone screens. I understand it's the thing nowadays, but I think it's detrimental. Phone use is banned in class, but I can't control what they do when the bell rings."

"We need to get them reading more and interacting with one another instead of their phones," James mused.

"Exactly," Lindy said. "But how? I thought you might have a suggestion, James."

"I don't know. I'd have to think about it."

Scott and Francis exchanged a long look, then Scott nodded.

Francis spoke. "Scott and I have been tossing around an idea called Story Surprise. What we'd do is wrap a couple of dozen books in brown paper. Don't worry, Professor, we'd use grocery bags to keep the budget down."

"Then we'd write, like a hint, on the paper," Scott said, "of what the story inside is about. Kids would have fun picking out books based on that alluring tidbit."

"There would actually be two copies of each book. Like, I know we have two copies of Agatha Christie's *And Then There Were None*, so we'd include that one for sure," Francis said. "Then, we could have a Story Surprise party here at the library."

"Yeah," Scott said. "Everyone who's participated comes in and holds up their book. They match up with the other person who's read the same book. The two sit down and talk about the story. We'd have good snacks, too."

Francis nodded eagerly. "Excellent snacks are critical, dude."

Lindy hooted with laughter. "That is genius! My students will love it!"

James stopped himself from puffing out his chest with pride. "Lindy, didn't I tell you I had the best two library assistants in the world? Scott and Francis, can you start on the project right away?"

The twins beamed. "Absolutely!" They hurried down to the end of the counter, where Scott grabbed a notebook and pen. The two then darted into the fiction stacks, talking a mile a minute.

"Those are good young men," Lindy said, gathering her coat around her.

Lucy appeared. "Are you leaving, Lindy?"

"I'd better. Look how dark it is outside. I'm late getting supper on the table. Luis's mother has probably taken over the kitchen while telling her son what a second-rate wife he has."

"I hope that's not the case, but if it is, you tell him that improving young minds is worth delaying his meal," James said.

After Lindy left, James turned to Lucy. "Well?"

"Murphy was released ten minutes ago. She said she was going home to shower and change clothes. Then she's headed to the Red Bird. She wants to pick up her things from there."

James nodded. "And maybe talk to some of the actors. I'd like to question them myself. I'm going to the Red Bird."

"I'll meet you there," Lucy said. "I've got to take my patrol car in case I get called out."

A few minutes later, James sat shivering in the Bronco despite wearing his warmest jacket and wool scarf. While he let the truck warm up, he saw snowflakes begin to land on the windshield. He craned his neck and looked up at the tall light pole in the library parking lot. Against the light, he could see the snow coming down fast. Hoping this wasn't the big snowstorm the meteorologist kept predicting, James pulled out his cell phone and dialed Jane.

"Hi, sweetheart. Are you on your way home?" she answered.

James resisted the urge to ask how she was feeling. "Not exactly. Did you see Sheriff Huckabee's statement on the news?"

"Uh-huh. Excuse me a moment, James. Eliot! Don't touch the Crock-Pot! Remember how it gets hot around the top."

James could hear his son moaning in the background. "Is he all right?"

Jane chuckled. "He's fine. Wants his dinner, is all." She lowered her voice. "Now he's collapsed onto the living room rug, clutching his stomach and saying that he's going to die of hunger if he doesn't eat right now. That chili you made in the Crock-Pot this morning has the whole house smelling delicious."

"It's no-meat. I found the recipe online."

"I can't wait to dig in myself. You're spoiling me. I may have to appoint you cook after our little girl is born."

"You know I'll do anything to help out. Listen, honey, Murphy is headed for the Red Bird to get her things. I want to go down there and talk to her in person, hear what she says happened last night. I'm not at all convinced she killed Edwards."

"I know you and Murphy were close at one time."

"We were, but I've come to believe that none of my other relationships worked out because I was still in love with you."

"Oh, James Henry, I've never loved anyone besides you. I love you more every day. Go talk to Murphy and see what you can find out. I swear I think you're a police investigator in a librarian's clothes."

James couldn't help feeling proud that Jane thought so, but he knew the success he'd had with past murders was all due to team-work with the other supper club members. "Okay, if you're sure."

"Mom!" Eliot howled.

"Young man, mind your manners!" Jane told their son. "James,

I see snow coming down. Drive carefully and you can tell me all about what Murphy says when you get home."

"Can I bring you anything?" James asked.

"Like ice cream?" Jane said and laughed. "Thank you, but no."

After exchanging "I love yous," James disconnected the call and got on the road south. Pleased that the snow wasn't sticking to the roads and making them slick, he made good time. He parked next to Lucy's patrol car outside the Red Bird and walked to the front door, then glanced back to make sure the Bronco's lights were off and groaned. Deputy Keith Donovan's black Camaro was parked at an obnoxious angle on the opposite side of the parking lot. "Great," James muttered.

Inside, Donovan stood at the entrance to the living room with his legs drawn apart in a cowboy-like stance. He turned his head at James's arrival and glowered. "Looking for food? Rats try to get in places they don't belong when it's cold outside."

"I'm certain you're an expert on the subject, but I'm here to meet Lucy."

The tall redhead curled his lip. "Thought you were married now. Besides, she's over there by the sofa, mooning over Sullie. Like he cares. Can't take his eyes off Amber Ross, the makeup gal. Don't blame him. I wouldn't mind some alone time with her myself. Heck, that author, Valerie Norris, would do if Amber's not available."

James told himself that Gillian would advise him not to waste his energy on taking offense at Donovan's remarks. He looked past the aggravating deputy into the red-themed room.

In one corner, a card table had been set up. The *Hearth and Home* actors—Brandon Jensen, Joel Foster, Amber Ross, Valerie Norris, and a tubby man who James recognized as Doug Moore—sat around the table playing Monopoly and talking as they had in the show. At the end of every episode, the children and their parents would play the board game and discuss whatever life issues had cropped up during the evening's show. This always ended with conflict resolution and lessons learned combined with life-affirming and hopeful messages. James figured this grown-up photo shoot would mean a lot to fans and reunion attendees.

A photographer adjusted what looked like huge white

umbrellas with bright lights, then called out, "Okay, everyone, play the game like in the olden days and smile at one another while I get these shots."

"Woof! Woof!" Doug Moore answered.

Brandon, wearing what James thought looked like a very expensive blue sweater that complemented the actor's eyes, said, "What's Doug doing now?"

Valerie, her blonde hair up in a French twist, stylish glasses perched on the end of her nose, looked at Brandon and rolled her eyes. "Doug's got the dog piece. He said he'd only bark throughout the game."

"Woof!"

"Do I have time to check my lipstick?" Amber asked.

Joel said, "It's perfect, don't worry."

"Still the peacekeeper, eh, Joel?" Brandon remarked. He lifted his left arm and stretched so that his sleeve raised a couple of inches. A gold watch glistened in the bright light.

James wondered if Brandon was the most successful of the actors post-show and what he did for a living now. Or, maybe, since *Hearth and Home* repeats still aired on cable channels, the actors received hefty residuals.

The sound of the front door opening and closing behind him caught James's attention.

Murphy, looking far from the polished author, newspaper owner, and partner in a development scheme, took one look at Keith Donovan and Lucy and pursed her lips. She had on jeans and a white puffer coat. Her face was devoid of makeup.

Donovan turned toward her, his hand going to his gun holster as if Murphy were an armed, dangerous criminal. "Where do you think you're going?"

Lucy came forward, hands folded across her chest. "Sheriff Huckabee said she could get her things."

Totally out of character, Murphy bowed her head and waited for permission.

James said, "Hello, Murphy. I thought I'd help you pack up."

Murphy glanced at him and nodded.

"Hold the phone here," Donovan said. "Who said you could, Henry? I'm in charge of the crime scene."

James looked at Lucy.

"I did," she said. "You can leave, Donovan, now that I'm here."

"No way," the deputy snarled.

"Let James go with Murphy," Lucy said on a sigh. "She's not in our custody. We can't control who she associates with."

Thanks a lot for that glowing recommendation, James wanted to say, but he bit his tongue and walked behind Murphy up the stairs. Donovan followed. When they reached the third floor, James pulled down one end of the crime scene tape that crossed the bedroom door. Murphy turned the doorknob, switched on the light, and walked in. She held the door open long enough for James to enter, then closed it.

"I'll be right outside here," Donovan called. "Don't try anything funny, librarian. Always sniffing around my crime scenes, dang it."

"Why are you here, James?" Murphy asked. She looked around the room at the stripped bed, at the lone female cardinal on the mantelpiece, and the fingerprint dust everywhere.

James waited until her gaze rested on him again before he spoke. "I want to help. All of us do. Tell me what happened."

Murphy dropped her head into her hands and burst into tears.

Chapter Nine

James shifted awkwardly. He always shut down when a woman cried. He simply didn't know what to do. With Jane, he'd learned to hold her snug in his arms until the tears passed, but he somehow didn't think Murphy would appreciate the gesture.

Instead, he remained quiet and went into the bathroom to look for a tissue. The Victorian sink had red tulips painted in the bowl that matched the wallpaper. James found a pretty floral tissue holder, pulled the top two tissues out, and tossed them in the wastebasket. They had fingerprint dust on them. He grabbed the next two and took them out to Murphy.

She accepted them, blew her nose, and then looked at him. "I didn't kill Ray. I loved him and he loved me. We were talking about getting married."

James took a deep breath. "I'm sorry for your loss, Murphy. For what it's worth, I know you didn't kill him. We don't always agree, and you've made me angry many times, but I know you're no killer. What happened?"

Murphy stuffed the used tissues in her jeans pocket. "I don't know. I honestly don't know."

"It's okay. Tell me what you can remember."

"Right now? I'm grieving and I've got an awful headache."

James would bet she did with the combination of all the alcohol she'd consumed the night before and the horrible events of the day. "I think time is at a premium."

"You're right; they can't wait to arrest me." She took a deep breath. "Ray and I polished off two bottles of champagne. When I came upstairs, I fell into bed still in my dress." She paled and her voice dropped to a whisper. "At the jail, I saw that there were spots of blood on the shoulder of my silver dress. I wanted to take it off and throw it away, but a female deputy took it from me. They kept it for evidence."

"They're only following procedure," James soothed. "So you went to bed and fell asleep. Was Ray Edwards with you?"

Murphy nodded. "Yes. He came into the room after me. I remember locking the door, then getting into bed without changing clothes. I guess I was pretty drunk. I was cold too." She looked over at the bare bed. "There was a thick, ivory-colored comforter on the bed. I pulled it over me. That's the last thing I remember until this morning . . ."

James felt that she was seeing the scene from when she woke up in her mind's eye. Her hazel eyes widened and a hand went to her lips. He said, "Edwards was dead. What did you do?"

Murphy's voice came out in a rasp. "The comforter and pillows had blood splattered over them. Ray's skin was a bluish gray color. I knew he was dead right away. I made it to the bathroom before I threw up. When I came back out, I saw the red glass cardinal lying on the Oriental carpet on Ray's side of the bed. I ran to the bedroom door and tried to open it. For a minute, I couldn't figure out why it wouldn't open, James. I kept pulling on the doorknob, trying to get out of the room!"

"The door was locked."

"Yes. It has one of those old-fashioned keys." Murphy's gaze went to the fireplace mantel. "There it is. That's where it's kept. I must have automatically put it back there after I finally got the door open. Then I ran into the hall and started screaming. Mrs. Anderson raced upstairs to see what was the matter. She helped me walk downstairs."

"Were the other guests around?"

"A few of the TV actors, Brandon, Amber, and Joel, were sitting around the dining room table drinking coffee. I can't remember if there was anyone else. Mrs. Anderson hurried me past them to her room, which is off the kitchen. I was shaking so hard. Mr. Anderson brought me a cup of hot tea, but I couldn't hold the saucer. Then, it seemed like all of a sudden, Sheriff Huckabee, Lucy, Donovan, and Deputy Truett were surrounding me, asking me questions, but Doc Spratt said I was in shock. He gave me a pill, something to relax me. Next thing I knew, I was sitting in a jail cell still wearing that silver sequin dress. My lawyer brought me some clothes and finally got me out of there."

"They've sent the murder weapon to Charlottesville. Will your fingerprints be on it?"

Murphy shrugged. "I don't know. Probably. When Ray and I checked in, I brought several vanilla-scented candles. This was supposed to be a romantic weekend mixed with a little business.

Joel had told me that the Red Bird was booked except for this one suite. I thought it would be a nice getaway for Ray and me. See, there are two candles on the mantel. I moved that old-fashioned clock and the vase of roses to make room for the candles. I think I adjusted the position of the cardinals too."

James didn't like the sound of that. If they found Murphy's fingerprints on that cardinal, they would surely charge her with Edwards's murder.

James looked around the suite. An L shape, the main area was the bedroom with a fireplace, dresser, chair, lamp, and a door that James assumed led to the closet. The bathroom was directly opposite the bed. A set of three windows with lush red silk draperies was behind the bed, probably to provide a nice breeze in warmer months. While James saw radiators on two sides of the bedroom, he figured the Red Bird didn't have air-conditioning.

"Could someone have come through one of those windows? I know this is the third floor, but . . ."

"No, I thought of that," Murphy said, moving to the door that did prove to be a closet and opening it. She lifted a small black suitcase from the floor, hesitated, then put it at the end of the bed. "They'd need a ladder, which someone would have heard clanging against the building. As cold as it is, I think a freezing breeze would have woken me. Not to mention that anyone coming in would've had to have literally climbed over the bed." She went back to the dresser, pulled out a pair of jeans, some tops, and underwear, folded them haphazardly, and threw them in the suitcase.

James walked to the other space in the suite. A large, handsome wooden desk filled the working area. Built-in bookshelves lined the wall behind it.

Murphy came out of the bathroom holding a bag of toiletries and stood next to him. "Ray and I had our laptops set up on the desk, but Sheriff Huckabee took them away."

"You'll get yours back," James said. "Who else is staying on this floor?"

For the first time since she'd walked in the door, the old Murphy returned. A hard look crossed her face and she narrowed her eyes. "There are no other accommodations on this floor. Most of the space up here is used for storage. There's only one other suite and it's on the second floor. Valerie Norris has it."

"She played the eldest girl on the show? The blonde with the green eyes? Writes books based on *Hearth and Home*, doesn't she?"

"Contact lenses," Murphy hissed. "And they're crappy books. I had time to think while sitting in jail, James. Valerie Norris is my number-one suspect."

James's eyebrows rose. "What reason would she have for killing Edwards?" he asked.

Murphy snapped dresses and blouses from their hangers in the closet. She whirled around, her eyes glittering with anger. "To frame me! Professional jealousy, James. The silly stories she writes come out at the same time as my mystery novels. We both made the *New York Times* bestsellers list last year, only my book edged hers out for a higher spot. I hear that didn't go down well with her at all. She's lucky that TV show still has devoted fans or she wouldn't sell any books at all!"

"Come on, Murphy, do you really think that's enough motive—"

"Yes! We share a publishing house, an editor and publicist too. We're competing for not only their time but money, James. The publisher decides how much of an advance to pay us, how much marketing there will be for our books. And it's not all based strictly on previous sales. Valerie was their star before I came along. They love her and her wholesome, elegant image. Then my books come out and are very successful. I'm new, edgy. Valerie is jealous. With me out of the way, she regains the throne."

"We carry her books at the library," James mused. "When a new one comes out, there's always a waiting list. I don't know Valerie, but Kelly at Fountain Books over in Richmond told me that Valerie did a book signing at their store. Kelly said they had a good turnout and Valerie was very nice."

Murphy slammed the lid closed on her suitcase and swung the zipper around until the bag was secured. "Of course Valerie's nice in public! She won't do anything to damage her perfect image and her book sales. But she's been anything but nice to me and other authors I know. And now poor Ray is dead because of her jealousy."

"Assuming you're right, Murphy, how did Valerie get in the bedroom and kill Edwards?"

For someone who started out so woebegone, Murphy looked nothing short of triumphant. "I looked up all of Valerie's book titles and found one called *Josh Catches a Burglar*. I told my lawyer and he had his secretary download the book and skim through it. Sure enough, there's a scene where the burglar of the story describes how he picked the lock on the front door. Valerie had to have done research on lock picking in order to write that."

James directed his gaze to the bedroom door. *Was it possible?* James hated to think that anyone who could write a book could be so evil.

"I'm right, James. Valerie Norris picked that lock and killed Ray. I intend to prove it. Do you still want to help me? You and your friends?"

"Yes, Murphy. But I think we need to question all the TV cast members, not only Valerie." He held up a hand, seeing as how Murphy was about to object. "Not only can we get a better picture of who Valerie is as a person, but we can find out where everyone was last night, what they might have seen, if someone else had a motive."

"It was Valerie, I'm telling you," Murphy said stubbornly.

"Who else knew Ray?"

"Joel, of course." Murphy concentrated. "I don't know of anyone else."

"What were you and Edwards quarreling about last night?"

"How did you know we were arguing?"

"Murphy, everyone at the reception for the *Hearth and Home* cast saw the two of you exchanging harsh words. Then you flounced upstairs—"

"I did not flounce!" She looked away, then back at him. "Sheriff Huckabee asked me the same question."

"What did you tell him?"

"Nothing."

"Tell me instead."

Color came into Murphy's face. "Ray had bought the Hayes House and Tavern without telling me."

"And?"

"He wanted to level it. Put up houses like we planned for Buford Lydell's peach farm. I thought the tavern should be preserved. History and all."

James felt a grin spread across his face. Like the Grinch, Murphy did have a heart.

She raised her chin. "Tourism! The tavern is good for tourism. If people fall in love with Quincy's Gap, they'll like and buy my books and copies of my newspaper."

"If you say so. About Quincy's Gap, what happens to the development scheme now? Will you sell the land back to Buford Lydell?"

Murphy grabbed her suitcase. "I don't know."

"The majority of the townsfolk are against the development. Many are angry at you, Murphy. If you sell the land back to Lydell, it would be good publicity for you."

Murphy paused. "I'll consider it."

The bedroom door swung open. Donovan said, "Murphy, how long does it take for you to pack up a few clothes? You shouldn't even bother since the only thing you're gonna wear in the future is an orange jumpsuit."

"We'll see about that," Murphy replied.

Donovan replaced the crime scene tape across the door and added two more strips for good measure. He preceded them down the stairs. James carried Murphy's suitcase.

Halfway down, James whispered, "Murphy, where are you going to be tomorrow?"

She stopped. "I'm meeting with my lawyer in the morning. Besides working on my defense, we're trying to contact a woman named Kitty Walters in Louisville. She's listed as Ray's emergency contact. Guess she's his sister. Then I'll be at the *Hearth and Home* event asking questions."

James nodded. "I have questions too. I'll see you at the *Hearth and Home* reunion."

When they reached the bottom of the stairs, James handed Murphy her suitcase, and she went out into the night. Intending to talk to the cast members, James walked into the living room, only to find it empty. No one was in the dining room either. Not even Lucy had lingered to hear what Murphy had said.

James glanced at the time and saw it was past seven. Early for everyone to have dispersed. James thought the actors would be together eating dinner.

Unless the warmth he'd seen between them was fake. Maybe they didn't enjoy one another's company at all.

Chapter Ten

"I'm meteorologist Jim Topling and have I got bad news for the entire Shenandoah area."

Snickers barked once and then ran from the kitchen into the living room.

Jane flicked her eyes at James as the two stood watching the tiny television in their kitchen.

"Snow!" Eliot yelled from his place at the kitchen table.

Jane hushed him and turned the TV volume up.

"The conditions are ripe for an *epic* snowstorm, a history-making snowpocalypse set to dump up to twenty-six inches of snow on an unsuspecting populace! Unsuspecting, that is, unless you stay tuned to my updates here on WSHN. Be prepared, folks, if you can. I'm talking road closures and power outages lasting days. Drifts of snow piling up to three feet. When is it going to happen? Well, it's a devious storm system. Hard to predict exactly when the first flakes of doom will fall. It could be tonight, it could be tomorrow, it could be Sunday."

James walked over and turned the television off. "I can't take any more of this guy."

"When is it going to snow, Daddy?"

"Pop says when the hound next door to his house starts howling."

Jane said, "I think I'll believe the hound over that guy on TV."

James glanced at his watch. "Come on, son, if we hurry, we can feed the birds before we walk to the bus stop."

Eliot brought his plate, now empty of any trace of pancakes, to the sink, then raced upstairs.

Miss Pickles positioned herself in the window nearest the bird feeder. James privately thought the cat understood every word he said. She knew that, with food in the feeder, she'd soon get to give a piece of her mind to the birds that came by for an energy snack.

James pulled a brown bag containing his lunch out of the fridge. He turned and found Jane standing behind him, a playful look on her face. "Do I get a kiss before you go?"

"Don't you always?" James breathed before kissing his wife warmly on the lips. He pulled away and said, "Sure you won't come with me tonight to the first *Hearth and Home* event?"

"I'm sure. We might get all that snnooooowwwww," Jane said and laughed.

"Thank you for being so understanding about this, sweetheart. I won't be late."

"I'll hold you to that promise, James Henry."

James kissed her again.

"Dad!" Eliot stood behind Jane wearing his warmest coat with the hood tied and mittens.

James quickly put on his coat and scarf, handed Eliot his monkey-shaped lunch bag, grabbed the birdseed from the utility room, and opened the back door. A blast of February air hit him in the face along with the delicious scent of a wood fire burning nearby.

"All right, son. Have you got the scoop ready?"

"Hold the bag open wider. Okay, I'm ready. The birds will eat all this and be warm."

"Good boy." As he held Eliot up to the multilevel birdhouse that Gillian had given him one Christmas, James focused on his son and tried not to think about how much he disliked the dark days of winter. He dreamed of the two of them putting in a vegetable garden in the spring. Far enough away from the tree where Eliot's tree house was, but close enough so that when his son was playing in there, he could look out over the garden.

A short time later, James waved as the big yellow school bus carrying his son drove slowly down the road to the next neighborhood.

James started up the Bronco and let it idle for a few minutes, looking at his house and thinking how grateful he was to have his healthy family, soon to include one more, in the Shenandoah Valley, the most beautiful place on earth, in the community he loved with all his being.

His good mood shattered halfway to the library. The Bronco started shaking and shuddering. James managed to get the vehicle to the side of the road before it shut off completely. "No!" James shouted into the sudden silence. "Haven't I been good to you, Bronco? Premium gas the last two tanks means nothing to you?"

He tried the ignition. Silence. Mentally, he reviewed his options. He wouldn't call Jane to come and get him. He didn't want her out in twenty-five-degree weather in her condition, although he'd never admit that to her. Besides, what could she do? He needed a mechanic.

James thought about his bank account and groaned. Another expensive tow to Harrisonburg would put his balance dangerously low. Then he remembered the mobile mechanic Gillian had told him about. He pulled out his wallet and found the slip of paper with Ace's name and phone number on it. Without any further thought, James punched the digits into his phone.

The phone rang and rang. Just as James was about to give up, a sleepy male voice said, "Yeah?"

"This is James Henry. My friend Gillian O'Malley at the Yuppie Puppy gave me this number. Is this Ace?"

"Yeah."

Not exactly verbose, was he, James thought. "Gillian said you're a mobile mechanic. I'm on the side of the road and can't get my truck started."

"Where ya at?"

James gave his location.

Ace said, "Cash only."

"Well, if you get me on the road, you can follow me to the ATM."

"Be right there."

It was forty-five cold minutes later before a shivering James heard the rumble of a truck behind him. Looking in his side-view mirror, he saw a mostly faded red Chevy truck that had to be from the 1970s. The white trim on the bottom and on the roof showed large rust spots. A man opened the driver's door.

James climbed outside. "Hello, you must be Ace," he said in a friendly voice. "I'm James Henry."

The skinniest man James had ever seen in his life slouched his way toward him. Tall, he wore a T-shirt and jeans without a jacket and nodded at James without speaking. James stared at the man's mouth, puzzled. Ace's jaw worked and James could hear a rapid sucking sound. A minute stretched out before James heard a cracking noise. Ace swallowed, then said, "Hey."

James reached back into the Bronco and popped the hood. Leading the way to the front of the truck, he said, "Aren't you cold, Ace?"

"Don't feel the cold," Ace said. He slumped over the Bronco's engine, looking around and checking wires. Then he stood upright and rooted around in his pocket.

James saw a sunflower seed similar to the ones he and Eliot had put out for the birds before Ace popped it in his mouth and the sucking sound started again. James felt himself tense, waiting for the cracking sound. Seconds passed. Finally, Ace cracked the seed and swallowed. "Bad battery."

"What? I had it replaced last year."

"Lemme find my jumpers."

James watched helplessly as Ace rummaged through the cargo bed of the Chevy. Trying to establish some sort of rapport with the young man, James said, "Gillian told me you had a dog named Bacon."

"Yep."

"Where's she today?"

Ace shot him a look. "Too cold outside for a dog."

"True. I'm freezing."

Ace found the jumper cables. He got back in his Chevy and drove away.

James stood with his mouth open. Then he told himself to calm down. Ace had to turn the Chevy around on the two-lane road so it would be nose-to-nose with the Bronco.

Mrs. Kern drove up in her SUV. She was the mother of one of Eliot's classmates and a patron at the library. "You okay, Mr. Henry?"

"Yes, thank you. A little trouble with my Bronco. I'll be back on the road shortly."

"All right. See you up at the library, then." She rolled up her window and went on her way.

That's when it hit James. The twins! Scott and Francis would have been waiting outside in this weather for him to open the library for at least half an hour! He was the only one who had a key. Quickly, he punched in Scott's number on his cell phone.

"Professor! Are you all right? We've been trying to call you."

"My phone didn't ring. Scott, I'm sorry. The Bronco broke down, but I'm having it fixed right now. You and Francis go somewhere warm. I'll be there soon."

"Don't worry about us. We put a sign on the library door saying we'd be open soon. Francis and I are across the street inside the gas station drinking their awful coffee."

Guilt gripped him. "Please pass my apologies along to Francis. I'll be there as quickly as I can."

When he ended the call, James saw that Ace had the jumper cables in place. To his surprise, the Bronco started right away.

"You were right," James told Ace as the young man removed the cables. "Follow me to the ATM. How much do I owe you?"

Ace got another seed out of his pocket, put it in his mouth, and appeared to think about his answer. Once again, James waited anxiously for the cracking sound. He wondered if those seeds were the only thing Ace ate.

After Ace swallowed, he said, "Fifty dollars. Iffen you want, I'll git a new battery at the auto parts store. Put it in for no extra charge. You have to give me the money fer it first."

"Sounds like a deal. Follow me."

James kept the Bronco's motor running as he waited in line at the drive-through ATM. Once he had cash in hand, he drove to the library. In the parking lot, he gave the money to Ace, who nodded and drove off, the Chevy backfiring once.

James hastened to the library's front door, unlocked it, took Scott's sign down, and hurried to turn up the heat.

Scott and Francis were right behind him. "Professor," Francis said, "have you changed your mind now about getting new wheels?"

Scott deposited a box on the library counter. Then the three of them divested themselves of their outerwear.

James said, "No, but I'll tell you something I have changed my mind about. I'm having an extra key made to the library. The two of you can decide who is going to carry it."

"Yes!" the twins shrieked in unison and then high-fived one another.

"I feel like Frodo Baggins in *Lord of the Rings*," Francis pronounced. "Only the key is my ring. I'll rule all the libraries!"

"Wait a second, bro," Scott said. "The professor said we decide who's going to carry it. What will it be? A fight to the death like in *The Hunger Games*?"

James opened the box on the library counter as the twins

swapped ideas. They decided on an elaborate Excel spreadsheet indicating times, days of possession, and days of visitation for the proposed key.

"They're a little late, but here nonetheless," James said to himself. Inside the box was a plastic bag filled with Valentine conversation hearts. James had made up the messages on the candies himself. He went back to the break room, grabbed a large, clear cookie jar shaped like a thick book and poured the candy inside. He admired the job the company had done and read as the pastel-colored sweets poured into the jar. "Keep Reading. I Love My Library. Loves Books. Read Read Read. I Heart Books."

Proudly, James put the jar on the library counter and went about library business trying not to think about telling Jane about the latest trouble with the Bronco. Every once in a while, he peeked outside to see if Ace had returned and was installing the new battery. When he finally saw him, James breathed a sigh of relief.

After the young man left—James gave him a ten-dollar tip—James turned his mind to the problem of gathering the supper club members together. He needed to fill them in on everything that had happened in the murder case. In the end, he decided that he'd have to ask everyone to join him at the *Hearth and Home* event. There would be plenty of food available. They could have dinner there and discuss the case while observing the actors.

James left the twins munching on conversation hearts and discussing whether they should purchase a small treasure chest to house the key at home. He stepped back to the break room to call Gillian.

"What time does it start?" she asked.

"I looked it up online last night. It's from three until eight at the Cardinal's Rest Harvest Church fellowship hall. That's that nondenominational church outside of town."

"I went to a spiritual retreat there once. So *enlightening*. That hall is huge. Let's see, Lucy is working the events, so she'll already be there. Bennett tries to finish his route early on Fridays. He should be done around three. Although the kids leave earlier, Lindy stays at the school until five, but she might be able to leave early. I'll call her. Buddha knows I have no business at the Yuppie Puppy."

"Too cold for dogs to be out," James said, unconsciously parroting Ace's words.

"I make sure all the dogs I groom are dried thoroughly, but lots of folks don't want to drive their pups anywhere in below-freezing temperatures. Plus, we're supposed to get that big snowstorm any minute."

James scoffed. "I wouldn't hold your breath. It ain't over until the hound howls."

"What are you talking about, James?"

"Pop's neighbor has a hound that always predicts when it's going to snow."

Gillian laughed. "Probably more accurate than that Jim Topling meteorologist. I'll call you back."

Chapter Eleven

When James walked into the Cardinal's Rest Harvest Church fellowship hall at a little past four thirty, he had to agree with Gillian that the place was huge. Blue streamers were strung from brass ceiling lights high above the beige-and-gold checkered floor. Dozens of round tables for eight were set up across the hall, although James didn't think there were more than fifty people present. Delectable smells coming from his immediate right made him turn his head in that direction. A sign on a stand read *Serving Begins at 5pm Sharp!*

Long tables held an array of food warmers, shiny chafing dishes, and square bread baskets covered with cloths, as well as plates, napkins, and cutlery. He saw a kitchen behind the setup. Along with a professional catering staff, Dolly bustled about wearing her "Kiss My Okra" apron. She transferred her famous hot biscuits into one of the bread baskets. James's mouth watered as he thought about their flaky goodness.

At a single table perpendicular to the others, Milla stood taking a cake out of a carrier and adding it to the rest of the cakes and other desserts.

"James," she cried when he walked over. "I didn't know you were a fan of the *Hearth and Home* show."

"I watched it when I was young, but that's not why I'm here," he said, looking over the cakes. "You heard about the murder of Ray Edwards."

Milla nodded and lowered her voice. "Yes, dear. Your father and I hear that Murphy Alistair is the prime suspect. That can't be true, can it?"

"I'm afraid it is. I don't think she murdered him though. I want to question the actors. They're the only other people who were staying at the Red Bird besides Murphy and Edwards. They might have seen or heard something."

"Another of your investigations, dear! Murphy is lucky to have you on her side. Are your friends helping again?"

"Yes. They're supposed to meet me here so I can fill them in on what I know."

Milla tilted her head toward the merchandise table. "See that woman with the permed gray hair in the hot pink tracksuit?"

James glanced down the hall. "Yes. She was at the reception last night at the Red Bird."

"Give her a wide berth. Her name is Joy Carmichael. She's the president of the *Hearth and Home* fan club and the organizer of the event. When I got here, she told me that I'd have to find another table for my cakes. This one," she said, indicating a table a few feet away, "is, in her words, 'for the official dessert of the *Home and Hearth* reunion, banana bread.' You might remember that the mother on the show always served it when the family played Monopoly at the end of each episode."

"That's odd. I've never thought of banana bread as a dessert. It's a bread."

"She can call it whatever she wants, but it was her commanding, patronizing tone that I took exception to."

"I can't blame you. Who knows better about desserts than the owner of Quincy's Whimsies?"

Milla chuckled. "Aww, you are a dear boy and I love you so. Watch yourself when it comes to Joy Carmichael. She seems very protective of the cast. Almost like they belong to her. At least, that's been my observation."

"Thanks for the tip. I guess she won't make questioning them easy. Oh, look. I think I see Bennett and Gillian sitting next to that table marked *Reserved*. I need to go. But can you tell me what kind of cakes these are first? I'll be coming through the food line when it opens and want to know what to look forward to."

"Of course. Let's see, this is a caramel cream cake, over here is a chocolate red velvet cake with white icing, and that one is a lemon cheese layer cake."

Each cake was decorated with flowers of complementing colors. James hoped he wasn't drooling. "I'll see you soon."

Milla's sweet laughter followed him as James walked around the tables. He noted they were decorated in pale blue plastic tablecloths with cute white geese marching down the sides. James recognized the color and design as the one the Lewis family had on the *Home and Hearth* show.

Halfway down the left side of the hall, dividers had been set up with folding chairs facing a large-screen TV. Several people sat watching an episode of *Hearth and Home*. A wooden stage, empty at the moment, was farther along on the left wall. Midway up the walls were two wide screens projecting images of the cast. On one side, the actors appeared as they had on the show, on the other, their modern-day selves smiled out at the fans.

James saw that, at the far end of the room, in a roped-off area, a rectangular table had been set up in front of three large windows and two doors that led to the outside. Here, the cast members of *Hearth and Home* sat greeting their fans and signing autographs. A long banner above them had the show's tagline: *All Because Two People Fell in Love.* Lucy and Sullie stood guard at either end of the table. Sullie had positioned himself by Amber Ross. James frowned as he saw that the deputy couldn't take his eyes off the makeup guru. Lucy looked like she could spit nails.

He saw Joy Carmichael shaking her finger at an older couple. She pointed to a sign near the autograph tables that read *Tonight's Autograph Session for Friends of* Hearth and Home *Only!*

The older couple turned and walked away, disappointment clear on their faces.

"James!"

Bennett motioned him over. James pulled out a chair next to Bennett and sat down. "Hey, Bennett. Gillian, you were right; this place is huge."

Gillian wore a turquoise sweater with a turquoise and lavender swirled scarf that matched her skirt. Under the lights of the hall, James noticed that her eyelids sparkled with lavender eyeshadow. James had come to respect Gillian's artistic side, which carried over to the way she dressed and presented herself. He loved his friend's sense of style and her warm and caring heart.

"Makes the fact that the turnout isn't great all the more obvious," Gillian said.

"It's that Jim Topling and his scaremongering snow predictions," Bennett said. "That man has me wondering how my mail truck is gonna make it through three-foot snow drifts."

"Snow is Mother Earth's way of showing the land in a *pristine* condition," Gillian said.

"That's fine as long as I don't have to drive in it," Bennett said. "Quincy's Gap isn't prepared for those severe conditions. Not enough salt for the roads, not enough plows or crew to drive them."

James had to agree. "Maybe it won't be as bad as Topling makes out. His employment depends on ratings, doesn't it? Like Bennett said, Topling's trying to scare everyone so that they watch his updates. I did think there'd be more people here tonight."

"Tomorrow is Saturday. Maybe people are waiting until then. They'll have the day off work," Gillian suggested. "Listen, James, about the murder. Before you fill us in, I've thought of something. Oh, wait a minute, I see Lindy."

Lindy pulled the chair next to Gillian out and dropped into it, her shiny black hair flying. "Are they serving alcohol?"

Gillian put an arm around her. "I don't think so. What is it? When I talked to you on the phone, you said you wouldn't be able to be away from home during supper two nights in a row."

"Luis and I had a fight. A big one. I'm not cooking for him tonight. Let his mother do it."

James looked at his friend with concern. Lindy was the cheerleader of their group. She was the type of person who rarely lost her temper. "Is Alma going back to Mexico anytime soon?"

"Yes, she is, if Luis wants to stay married to me! Last night, I was late getting home," she said to Bennett and Gillian, "because I was at the library talking to James about a program to get my students reading."

Gillian nodded and rubbed Lindy's shoulder.

"Well! I come in the door and Alma is cooking a huge, traditional Mexican meal. Homemade tortillas, carne asada, rice, beans, she's making guacamole, everything Luis loves. Pots and pans are everywhere. Food all over the counters. And you know what she says to me?"

James, Gillian, and Bennett shook their heads.

"'A wife who doesn't cook for her husband soon finds he looks for food elsewhere,' that's what she said. And she did not mean Burger King! No, it was a warning."

Bennett said, "A man's stomach does have to be taken—ouch! Why'd you kick me, woman?"

"What happened then?" Gillian asked, ignoring her sweetheart.

"I found Luis in the den reading the newspaper. I told him that by the end of the day tomorrow, that is, today, he had better have a plane ticket for Alma and a plan to get her on board or else I was going to take a medical leave from school and go visit my parents in Washington. For an indefinite period of time."

"I take it Alma isn't seeing Luigi?" James asked, thinking of how the two had gotten along in the past.

Lindy shook her head. "No, he's busy with the pizza parlor. He told Luis he might even open another location, maybe over in Elkton."

James said, "What do you think Luis will do about his mom?"

Lindy flipped her hair back. "That is up to him. I must make my position in the house clear." Lindy's eyes filled with tears. "Alma doesn't like me, she never has. She wanted Luis to marry a girl in Mexico. The daughter of one of her friends."

"I remember," James said. "But Luis wisely chose you, Lindy."

Lindy seemed to deflate. "I don't want to hate her. She just makes it so hard for me to get along with her. Nothing I do is good enough."

"Did you tell Luis how you felt?" Gillian asked. "Communication is so important in a relationship."

"I did."

"Maybe Alma doesn't realize how she's behaving. Luis is her only son, living in another country," Gillian said. "She probably misses him when she's down in Mexico, but that's no excuse for treating you badly, Lindy."

"Speaking of ill treatment, who is that woman in pink with the gray curls over by the food line?" Lindy asked. "Why is she turning people away?"

Bennett stood. "I'll go find out. I'm hungry. She better not keep me from my food."

James looked toward the TV cast. "I hope I'll have a chance to talk to them."

"They're bound to take a break," Gillian said. "I picked this table deliberately. See the *Reserved* sign on the table next to us? That's for the actors. And I'm counting on Lucy joining us so that you can tell all of us what you've learned about Ray Edwards's murder."

Bennett returned and sat down. "Looks like all we'll be getting is scraps."

"Scraps?" James said.

"Yep. Tonight, the Friends of the *Hearth and Home* people get first dibs on the food. You have to show a membership card to get in the buffet line. After the members, that witch in pink said she'd sell tickets to the rest of us at ten dollars a head."

James thought that was a lot of money since a slice of one of Milla's cakes couldn't be guaranteed.

"I'm sure they have plenty of food for all of us," Gillian said. "While we're waiting, let me tell you about an idea I had about the Honeybee Heaven Farms Corporation. Murphy and Edwards were partners, right?"

Everyone nodded.

"But there has to be someone else who owns shares. A third person."

"Why do you say that?" James asked.

"Because a corporation like that is structured so that a third party owns a small amount of the company. This is so they have voting rights when the two principals of the company disagree on any financial matter. That way, there can't be a deadlock."

"Who is the third partner?" Lindy asked.

"Like I told you on the phone, James, I didn't have any business at the Yuppie Puppy because of the cold weather. So I went down to the courthouse and looked at the public records. It's Joel Foster."

"Joel Foster is the editor of *Southern Style* magazine," James said. "His being partner in Honeybee Heaven Farms, no matter how small his share, would explain how Murphy was able to convince him to name Quincy's Gap a best small town to live in."

"And use our photos," Bennett added.

"Exactly what I thought," Gillian said.

"He's down there at the autograph table," Lindy said. "We need to ask him some questions."

James quickly filled them in on his conversation with Murphy, how she didn't remember what happened the night before, how she'd locked the door to the suite and no one could get in, her suspicions about Valerie Norris, everything.

"I can't see Valerie Norris committing such a violent murder," Gillian said. "And Murphy's reasoning doesn't make sense. Jealousy over who was higher on a bestseller list?"

"Murphy says it's about money. I agree, though. It seems a stretch."

"But if Valerie Norris was the only one who could pick the lock . . ." Lindy said.

"I'm not sure that's true," James said. "I did a quick search on YouTube before I left the library. There were lots of videos showing how to pick a lock."

"Teachin' people how to be criminals," Bennett said and shook his head.

James then explained that Murphy wasn't the only person he'd questioned. He filled his friends in on his visit to the Lydells and also to Arthur Pritchard IV.

"Pritchard threatened your job," Bennett said. "Not cool, not cool at all. Hey, look, that woman is selling tickets for dinner. I'm starving."

Everyone got up and made their way over to the line.

Lindy put a hand on James's arm. "I don't know if this is important, but Edwina Lydell used to clean at the Red Bird for extra money before her arthritis got bad."

James had a sudden flash of Mrs. Lydell saying, *So we weren't the only ones who hated him,* when told of Edwards's murder. "It could be significant, Lindy. Good thinking."

Chapter Twelve

There was plenty of food available for the supper club members to fill their plates: sliced Virginia ham; pulled pork barbeque; collards; baked beans; green beans made with fatback; quinoa; butternut squash; a deep pot of Brunswick stew; Dolly's biscuits; and the show's trademark banana bread. However, James couldn't hide his disappointment when he saw that all of Milla's cakes were gone, as was the lady herself. Instead, his dessert was cherry Jell-O.

He and his friends sat at their table tucking into their supper and drinking iced tea. As James bit into one of Dolly's biscuits, made only with real butter, he felt guilty. "This is another meal I'm eating that's not exactly on the Mediterranean diet. My track record since we agreed to start the diet is dismal."

"My man," Bennett said, buttering a chunk of corn bread, "I look at it this way. We are supposed to have an extra layer of fat in cold weather. This"—he pointed to his middle—"is my winter layer of fat."

"I made a tuna garden pasta salad last night and took some for lunch," Lindy said. "I can pass the recipe on if anyone wants it."

"Sounds delicious, Lindy. You don't have to deprive yourself of food, Bennett," Gillian said. "The Mediterranean diet is a way of eating healthy, remember. Watch your portions and make sure you're not overeating."

Bennett leaned toward James. "I'll watch them as they go into my mouth. This corn bread must have been made with creamed corn in it. My mom makes it like that. The best kind there is."

James was about to agree when the noise in the hall lessened, then almost immediately the hum of chatter increased. A voice at his side said, "Hello, everyone."

About to bring a forkful of barbeque to his mouth, James paused and looked up. "Murphy. Why don't you get a plate of food and join us."

Murphy, dressed in black jeans and a tunic-length charcoal gray sweater, looked from James to Gillian to Bennett to Lindy. James thought she was searching for animosity, but she didn't find it among his friends.

"Thanks. I'm not hungry, but I'll sit for minute." She glanced around. "Heck, from the looks on some of these people's faces, I might be the meal."

Bennett speared a slice of ham. "They already grilled you down at the courthouse, didn't they?"

"Bennett!" Gillian remonstrated. "Murphy, don't pay attention to those folks. James has shared what you told him about the night Ray Edwards . . . passed away. We're all going to help you find the person who caused his death."

James noticed that the actors were making their way toward the reserved table next to them. Joy Carmichael fussed over them. On her pink tracksuit, she wore the large red button in the shape of a heart that read *"Home and Hearth* Always in Our Hearts." James heard her say, "Make yourselves comfortable. I'll be right back with your dinner," before she bustled to the kitchen.

"I appreciate it, Gillian, but didn't James tell you I already know who murdered Ray?" Murphy asked.

Lindy said, "Valerie Norris, the actress who writes the books?"

Murphy nodded. She turned her head to look at Valerie and glared. The actress and author pointedly ignored Murphy. Instead, in a carrying voice, she said, "There aren't enough of my fans here tonight. I don't know if these events are worth my time."

Doug Moore said, "It's all the fault of that weather forecaster and his snow predictions. My friend Mr. Sunshine is going to burn him to a crisp."

No one laughed at Doug's lame joke.

Brandon smoothed back his already perfectly styled dark hair and drawled, "Valerie, darling, don't you have enough money? You've been writing those books for over twenty years."

For the first time, Valerie turned Murphy's way, although she spoke to Brandon. "You couldn't be expected to know, Brandon, but one can never have enough money." She snapped her napkin in place on her lap and gave Murphy a cold smile.

Murphy, a glimmer in her eye, began to rise, but James reached out and put a restraining hand on hers. In a low voice he said, "I thought about what you said regarding lock picking. Last night, I searched YouTube and found hundreds of videos on how to pick a lock. I don't think Valerie's having written about a burglary is enough evidence to zero in on her as the murderer."

Gillian swallowed the last of her butternut squash, then said, "I have to agree with James, but that doesn't mean that we've ruled Valerie out."

"She's guilty. I feel it in my bones," Murphy said.

"Jealousy is a bone?" Bennett quipped.

Lindy shot him her schoolteacher look.

Gillian said, "By the way, Murphy, I know that Joel Foster is your partner in the Honeybee Heaven Farms Corporation."

Murphy raised her eyebrows. "How did you find out?"

"The courthouse public records," Gillian answered. "What do you and Joel plan to do with Buford Lydell's peach farm?"

"What's that got to do with Ray's murder?" Murphy asked.

Gillian shrugged. "I don't know. But I think there's one thing we've all learned in our investigations and that's to ask lots of questions."

"I haven't decided." Murphy turned to the table next to them. "Joel! Can you come over here for a minute?"

Joel Foster scraped his chair back and made his way to Murphy's side. "How are you? I haven't seen you since . . . well . . . since Ray died. Are you okay?"

"No, I'm not okay!" Murphy said in a high-pitched voice. "I've lost the man I love and the police think I killed him."

"I don't think you killed him," Joel said. He smiled, showing off his dimples.

Murphy introduced him around the table. He said, "I recognize all of you from the reception and, of course, the latest issue of *Southern Style*. I'm the editor, you know."

"We know all right," Bennett said.

"Never mind that right now," Murphy interjected. "I'm thinking about selling Lydell's peach farm back to him now that Ray is dead."

Joel frowned. "I don't see why you should. There's still plenty of potential for development. That's not changed. We need to find a new investor."

James pulled his bowl of Jell-O closer, then said, "The majority of Quincy's Gap is against expansion. Not only that, but Buford Lydell is heartsick over selling his land."

"Seller's remorse, Mr. Henry. Murphy, do you really want to sell the land back to Lydell?"

All eyes went to Murphy. James felt himself tense, hoping that Murphy would make the right decision.

"I think it's the best thing to do," Murphy said. "The town wants to stay small."

James nodded encouragement at Murphy.

"Edwards's death is a tragedy that could be connected with the development plans," Gillian put in. "All that negative energy can only be bad for investments."

"Joel!" Joy Cartwright called. "I have your steak. Medium well. You'd better eat it before it gets cold."

"Before you go, Joel," James said. "We're trying to find out who killed Edwards. Did you hear anything the night he was killed? Anyone coming up the stairs who shouldn't be? Did you see anyone who wasn't staying at the Red Bird?"

Joel put his hands on his knees and appeared to think. "No, no, I can't say that I heard or saw anything unusual." He rose. "Murphy, let's talk about the development later. Nice to meet everyone." He walked back to the actors' table.

The supper club members watched him go. Lindy said, "He's hiding something. I see that boyish guilt in my male students. Mark my words."

"Speaking of guilt," James said and nodded toward Sullie. The deputy had followed Amber Ross to the actors' table. He stood behind her chair in a protective stance. Every few minutes he leaned down to whisper something in her ear, which caused her to giggle. James could sense Lucy's anger and frustration.

He saw Lucy head for the food. Before she went, she looked pointedly at Murphy, then shot James a disapproving look. James thought that he needed to talk to Lucy, keep her in the loop of the investigation and comfort her over Sullie's behavior. He figured Amber Ross was merely indulging in a flirtation while she was in town. Sullie was a fool if he thought otherwise.

At the actors' table, Valerie could be heard asking, "After we've completed our obligations in this frozen tundra, where is everyone wintering? Palm Beach?"

"Are you kidding?" Brandon said. "Palm Beach is the world's biggest old folks' home."

Murphy muttered, "Valerie's baiting me. She knows I can't

leave town. She wants to cause a scene."

"Don't let her," Gillian advised. "It's the last thing you need right now, Murphy."

At that moment, a woman in her late forties approached the table. She wore a tight blue dress with short puffed sleeves and had a white faux-fur coat draped over one arm. Her platinum blonde hair, worn straight and halfway down her back, was set off by a deep suntan. In a gravelly voice that could only come from years of smoking, she said, "You're Murphy Alistair, aren't you?"

"Yes," Murphy answered warily. "And you are?"

"Kitty Walters. Your attorney got in touch with me about Ray."

Murphy stood and held out her hand. "It's nice to meet you, Kitty. Won't you join us? You must have driven from Louisville. Are you hungry?"

"No, I'm good." Kitty shook Murphy's hand and sat down.

Murphy made the introductions, but when she mentioned that Kitty was Ray Edwards's sister, the blonde said, "Ray's sister? Where did you get that idea?"

Murphy's face, which had been filled with concern, altered to one of suspicion. "You were listed as Ray's emergency contact. My attorney and I assumed you were his sister."

Kitty raised her left hand, which showed a sizeable diamond solitaire on her ring finger. "I'm not his sister. I'm his fiancée."

Murphy jumped to her feet. "That's not true. Ray asked *me* to marry him."

Kitty got up so fast her chair fell backward to the floor. People looked their way. "I doubt that. Ray and I have known each other for over a year. We live together and we've been engaged since last October."

Bennett leaned over and whispered to James, "Are they arguing over a dead guy?"

James and Gillian shushed him.

James saw Lucy, plate in hand, making her way toward their table at a brisk pace. She'd observed the scene playing out.

Murphy's eyes flashed pain. "I don't believe you. Last October? That's when I met Ray and we became business partners. He never mentioned a girlfriend, much less a fiancée."

"That's because Ray was a smart businessman. He knew you'd

be more likely to fork over your cash if he pretended to be single."

Murphy stood with her fists at her sides. "How dare you! Ray loved me. And he showed it in every possible way, if you get my drift."

"That's a lie!" Kitty howled. A tear ran down her cheek. She pulled a lace handkerchief out of her purse and wiped it away. "You may have tried to seduce him, but Ray wouldn't cheat on his baby cakes!"

"Baby cakes?" Murphy growled. "That's what Ray called me when we were in bed." She reached across the table and grabbed James's bowl of Jell-O.

James vaulted to his feet and grabbed Murphy's arm before she could throw the wiggly concoction in Kitty's face.

Lucy reached them and put her plate on the table. "What's going on here?"

Kitty screamed, "It's true! You killed Ray! Murderer! Now I know why you did it. You found out about me! You're a jealous old hag!"

Murphy burst out of James's grasp. She lunged for Kitty and slapped her across the face, sending her blonde hair flying. Kitty drew in a sharp breath and put a hand to her cheek. Her fingers came away with speckles of blood. Murphy had not only left an angry red handprint but a small, slanted cut courtesy of the oversized blue topaz ring she wore.

Lucy steamrolled her way around James. She grabbed both of Murphy's wrists and handcuffed her. "Murphy Alistair, I'm arresting you for assault."

"I didn't mean to s-slap her that hard," Murphy stuttered.

Joy Carmichael stood between James's table and the actors' table, her arms spread out wide like a mother hen protecting her chicks.

James watched as Lucy led a protesting Murphy from the hall.

People stood on chairs filming the incident on their cell phones.

Kitty Walters, holding her hand to her cheek, stormed out the doors behind the autograph table.

From the actors' table, James could hear Valerie Norris say, "Murphy's editor won't want to hear about this." Then she chortled with glee as she pulled out her cell phone and tapped in a number.

"Murphy didn't even let her jail cell grow cold before she's back there again," Bennett said.

James pushed his plate away. "And we're back to square one."

"Negative square one," Lindy said. "Murphy looks guiltier than ever."

Chapter Thirteen

James stood on the bathroom scale and viewed the results with a disbelieving eye. "I've gained three pounds," he moaned to himself. "I've got to get serious about my diet."

He showered, then walked with a towel around his waist to the closet. Selecting gray slacks and a white button-down shirt from what he called the "fat" section of his clothing, he dressed. He picked a thick black cable-knit sweater from the dresser and pulled it on, then studied himself in the mirror, turning for a side view. "This sweater adds a couple of inches to my waistline, but I'd rather be warm." He turned off the light and left the room.

On impulse, he peeked into the room that had been his office and was now a soft pink nursery waiting for the birth of his daughter. A white crib, rocker with pink cushions, and a small white dresser had been the only furniture he and Jane could fit in the tiny room. A copy of *Pat the Bunny* sat on top of the dresser next to a stuffed bunny, a tan bear wearing a pink ribbon around his neck, and a fluffy white lamb. Over the dresser, a framed Charles Dickens quote that read, "Chapter One: I Am Born" hung on the wall. Above the crib, Lindy had painted butterflies in white and a darker shade of pink than the wall.

James closed the door behind him, wondering again what name he and Jane would give to their little girl. After some discussion where they'd tossed names back and forth, Jane had said she'd like to wait until they could see their daughter before naming her. James wanted to name her Jane after his wife, but she had said the name was too ordinary. James had his own ideas about that, but they could wait until after the birth.

Downstairs in the living room, Eliot sat on the floor playing with the Lincoln Logs set Jane had found at the church yard sale the previous year. Snickers sat nearby watching him. Jane was curled up on the sofa in her warm floral robe, a mug of hot chocolate in one hand, the TV remote in the other. The TV volume had been muted. James was amused to see Jim Topling, the overexcited meteorologist, pointing and waving his arms in front of a graphic of the Quincy's Gap area. James noticed that the snowfall totals printed in large, bold numerals had increased from

Topling's previous prediction of twenty-six inches to thirty inches.

James dropped a kiss on the top of his wife's head and smelled her eucalyptus shampoo. "Not that guy again."

"Daddy! I'm building a house!" Eliot hollered.

James bent and kissed his son. "I see that, and you're doing a great job. Have you had breakfast?"

Eliot nodded. "Mommy made blueberry pancakes."

James's stomach growled.

Jane made as if to rise. "Eliot and I ate all that I made, but I can whip up another batch. There are more blueberries."

James placed a hand on her shoulder. "Sit right where you are, honey. The bathroom scale's headline was worse than Topling's. I'm going to grab a yogurt and make some whole-grain toast with avocado."

"Mmm, avocado toast sounds good."

"I'll make you a piece too," James said, pleased that she had a good appetite and hadn't been sick to her stomach.

"Are you going down to Cardinal's Rest for the Saturday reunion events today?" she asked.

James lowered his voice. "After Murphy was arrested again last night, I think I need to. I'm hoping Lucy will be there so that I can talk to her. There's also the reunion organizer, Joy. I figure she knows everything about the actors. She's a superfan, if you know the type. Devotes her life to the show and its fans."

"I can imagine."

"She's protective, though. I don't know how to question her."

"Flatter her. Offer to help her. Do they have merchandise out that you could fold? Programs that need straightening?"

"Those are great suggestions. It certainly comes in handy having an intelligent, beautiful wife," James said.

"A lazy wife. I've got all the ingredients to make pumpkin bread, but I don't know if I can get up off this sofa."

"Then don't. Eliot, you help Mommy out today, okay. I have business to attend to."

"Okay," his son responded, his attention on building construction.

James and Jane smiled at one another. James went into the kitchen and made enough avocado toast for him and Jane to share.

91

After breakfast, he packed himself some apples and peanut butter for a snack, then returned to the living room. "Eliot, do you want to get dressed and help me feed the birds?"

"I'll help tomorrow, if that's okay," Eliot said, carefully positioning a crosswise log.

"All right. But remember that the birds need our help more than ever in winter. They need the energy that food provides to keep warm."

James went to the hall closet to get his coat.

Jane said, "Before you go, James Henry, tell me how the Bronco is doing."

James came back into the room, feeling like he had a guilty sign painted on his forehead. He didn't want to leave Jane on a bad note. "I had a little trouble yesterday, but it was just the battery."

"The battery, huh? Didn't we replace that last year?"

"Must have gotten a lemon."

"I see. James, I've been meaning to tell you. You know my friend Denise in Lamaze class found out she's having twins."

"Oh?"

"They already have four children, so this will make six. She and her husband have decided to sell their Ford Explorer and upgrade to a larger Chevy Suburban. Denise said she'd give us a good deal on the Explorer. It's a 2010 and only has sixty-four thousand miles on it."

James raised his eyebrows. "That's well below the average miles for an eight-year-old vehicle."

"It is. So what do you think?"

James wrapped his scarf around his neck. How he wished he didn't have to answer the question. "Well, if we decide to get another vehicle . . . I mean, in the future if the Bronco . . ."

Jane turned the volume back up on the TV.

"I love you," James said, raising his voice to be heard.

"Love you, too," Jane responded without taking her eyes from the TV.

James saw that Miss Pickles watched him, tail swishing back and forth in a gesture he knew indicated displeasure.

James stepped outside into the frigid air, which seemed to cut through to his very bones. He got in the Bronco. "She's got your replacement lined up," he told the truck. "You'd better start or else." He turned the key in the ignition. The Bronco roared to life.

By the time he got to the fellowship hall in Cardinal's Rest, James had decided that Jane was jumping the gun. They didn't need to junk the Bronco. It had done fine. Sure, it needed repairs now and again, but that was cheaper than replacing it.

He entered the hall and immediately noticed that the turnout today far exceeded that of the day before. The actors were back at the autograph table, each with long lines of people waiting to meet them. Valerie Norris had a pile of her books on her table. A young man took money for the purchases, then passed the books to Valerie to sign. Up on the big projectors, one side showed the cast members from an episode of the show playing Monopoly. The other showed a photo of the actors as they were today playing the game. The photo was from the shoot James had witnessed at the Red Bird.

James saw Gillian and Bennett sitting together at the same table as yesterday, the one next to the table reserved for the actors. He reached them and said, "Where's Lindy?"

"She's at my house," Gillian said.

"Statistics show that between forty and fifty percent of marriages end in divorce," Bennett said.

"Bennett! Lindy and Luis haven't even been married two months. They aren't getting divorced! This is their first major fight and it's a doozy. They have to learn how to handle disagreements. Lindy needs a quiet space away from Luis to meditate about her expectations in regards to Luis and his mother."

"I take it Luis didn't send Alma back to Mexico yesterday," James said. He thought about Lindy's hot temper and imagined that the argument must have been intense.

"No, he didn't," Gillian replied. "As I told Lindy, it was unrealistic to expect him to send her off with one day's notice. Still, they did have another fight about it, and Lindy felt the need to leave for a while. I think it's a positive sign that she couldn't bring herself to go to her parents in DC and is remaining in Quincy's Gap. This way, she can continue teaching and seeing Luis every day without the stress of living under the same roof as his mother until the situation is resolved."

"What can I do?" James asked. "Should I talk to Lindy?"

"Between all the special teas Gillian's been brewing, the essential oils burning, the healthy food, and the sappy movies those two watched on TV last night, I'd say Lindy is doing pretty good," Bennett opined. "It's Luis I'm worried about. I'm going over there later today to check on him."

"Let me know if you want me to go with you," James offered, then remembered his ongoing disagreement with Jane over the Bronco. "Not that I'm an expert. Today, I want to talk to Lucy. With everything that happened after Kitty Walters showed up yesterday, I never got a chance to fill her in on our investigation. Maybe she can talk to me while she's on duty."

"Should be okay," Bennett said. "That Joy person would throw herself between anyone bothering any of the actors. But let me warn you before you go over there: Lucy's been watching Amber Ross's YouTube videos."

"Bennett, there's nothing wrong with Lucy trying to improve her appearance," Gillian said.

Bennett snorted. "Square eyebrows and brown stripes across her face aren't helping her look better. Sullie snickered when he saw her."

"They're not brown stripes, or at least, that's not what they're supposed to be. It's called contouring and the technique is supposed to shape the face. I've never tried it myself."

"You'd better not, woman. I won't be seen with you if you start doing yourself up that way."

Gillian sighed. "You'll hardly be seen with me regardless, won't hold my hand in public, won't kiss me outside of the house."

"Let's not start that," Bennett said with an edge to his voice.

"I'll be back soon," James said, thinking it an excellent moment to leave.

As he made his way to Lucy, he saw that *Hearth and Home* was once again playing on a large TV set up in front of folding chairs. At least two dozen people sat watching it.

"Instead of signing autographs, why not reenact a scene from one of the shows?" a woman in the row nearest James said.

"I think that would be wonderful," replied her friend.

"So many memories," stated another woman. "Precious

moments throughout the show. Such a great family. And they're still all together except for little Tammy."

"She's hit the big time. This reunion is small potatoes for her," the first woman responded.

Joy Carmichael's voice boomed from behind James. "Miss Bell, the actress who played Tammy, is shooting her new action-adventure movie. She's sent her regrets and has filmed an apology to fans, which we'll show during tonight's activities."

The women looked chagrined and went back to watching the show without further comment.

James seized the opportunity to speak to Joy, who today wore a vivid blue tracksuit with her *"Hearth and Home* Always in Our Hearts" button. Remembering Jane's advice, he spoke in a tone of polite formality he reserved for strangers. "Ms. Carmichael, may I say that you have amazing organizational skills? As Quincy's Gap's head librarian, I can appreciate how much time and effort went into putting these events together so flawlessly."

She smiled. "What a nice thing to say! And you are?"

"James Henry. I'm here with friends. We plan on staying all day, so if there's anything we can help you with during the break, please allow us to be of assistance." *There,* James thought, *that sounded nonthreatening and ingratiating.*

Joy looked toward the merchandise table. James noticed there were boxes behind it. "I might take you up on that. In the meantime, you should watch the next episode of *Hearth and Home.* It's special."

"Oh? I think I saw all the episodes when I was younger," James said.

"You'll want to rewatch this one. While the exteriors of the house were filmed at what's now the Red Bird B and B, everything else was shot on a soundstage in Hollywood with the exception of this episode." Joy's voice grew animated with excitement. "It's called 'We Don't Speak French Here' and is set at the beginning of autumn. Joshie—that's Brandon Jensen—takes a sleeping bag and hides out in the woods because he and his father have fallen out."

James felt a glimmer of a memory.

"Although Joshie helps out on the family peanut farm, he wants to go with a group of fellow high school students, including his best friend, who are taking a two-week trip to France. When his father tells him that they can't afford it and that it would be a waste of time anyway, they argue. It's a brilliant display of Joshie's—I mean Brandon's—acting abilities as he lives in the woods on a supply of granola bars. He was only twenty-two playing seventeen when they filmed it. Of course, he had a crew with him."

"That's, um, quite an accomplishment," James said. "I'll try to catch it. Well, I won't keep you." James resisted the urge to bow.

He turned his steps in the direction of where Lucy stood. As he got closer he silently groaned at his friend's appearance. Bennett was right. Lucy had used some makeup product to shape her eyebrows into a square with a tail. The brown streaks on her cheeks had a bright, shiny white cream or powder smeared above them. The same white cream ran down her nose, ending at the tip, which gleamed under the hall's fluorescent lights. Her lips had been outlined above her lip line with a dark color, then filled in with a lighter color lipstick. The over-lining made her lips look unnaturally big. Even with all that, James thought the worst was her eyelashes, or rather, her false eyelashes. Extraordinarily long and spiky, Lucy had glued them above her natural lashes, but left a gap where her eyelid showed. The lashes must have been uncomfortable because Lucy kept blinking rapidly.

James's heart went out to her. Darn Sullie for behaving like a fool over Amber Ross! James didn't say anything about Lucy's makeup, though. Instead, he touched her on the arm. "Can you talk to me while you're watching them?" he asked, motioning toward the actors' table.

Lucy crossed her arms. "Sure, James, but even you can't deny that Murphy is guilty of assaulting Kitty Walters. You saw her."

James nodded. "I did. Murphy's not herself. She's grieving over Ray Edwards, and to find out that he had another woman must have thrown her over the edge. But I'm not trying to make excuses for her."

"Good. She's being held in jail until she can go before a judge on Monday morning."

Which meant she wasn't out trying to find Ray Edwards's killer. The supper club needed to step up its efforts. "Lucy, I want to fill you in on what I've found out."

James proceeded to tell Lucy everything Murphy had told him about the night Edwards was murdered, his own observations of the actors staying at the Red Bird, his conversation with the Lydells and with Arthur Pritchard IV.

Lucy frowned while he spoke. James couldn't help noticing that the false eyelashes on her left eye started peeling off toward the inner corner of her eye. Lucy must have felt it, because she smashed her fingers down on the lash. "So you're telling me that Murphy thinks Valerie Norris, having learned how to pick locks while doing research for a book, picked the lock on the door, entered the suite, and killed Ray Edwards all so that Murphy would be pushed down the ladder of the publishing business. Really, James?"

"I don't think it's enough of a motive either. But maybe someone else picked the lock. There are hundreds of videos on YouTube that show how to do it."

Lucy shook her head. "We examined the lock. There are no scratches, no marks, no signs that someone tried to force it. And you won't convince me that either of the Lydells would commit murder. I've known them all my life."

"What about Arthur Pritchard? You saw him arguing with Edwards that night we were all at Mamma Mia's."

"You shouldn't have gone out to his farm without me, James. Pritchard or Lydell."

"I didn't think to ask you. I thought you were convinced Murphy is the killer."

Lucy tapped her foot. "I am. Come on, James. Pritchard wouldn't get his hands dirty. He's wealthy and wouldn't risk his freedom."

"But his racehorses—"

"At most, Pritchard would build a stable on the opposite side of his land for them. Maybe even buy another property and move them. No, James, as I told you before, this comes down to a matter of opportunity. Only Murphy had the opportunity because she was the sole person in a locked room on the third floor with Edwards. I admit that her sentiments about saving the Hayes House and Tavern are admirable, but you told me that Murphy and Edwards argued about it. Who knows what other business decisions they disagreed on. Plus, now that we know Edwards lied to Murphy about being in love with her and wanting to marry her, it makes her motive even stronger."

"Murphy didn't know about Kitty Walters until she walked in here yesterday," James argued.

"So Murphy says."

"When it comes down to it, we only have a ring and Kitty Walters's word that Edwards was engaged to her," James pointed out. "She could have bought that ring herself. Maybe it's not even a diamond. I hear they make convincing fakes nowadays."

Lucy bit her lip and looked toward the actors, behaving as if she were considering their safety. When her gaze reached Brandon, she smiled. "Brandon's still a heartthrob. Very masculine, and the way his dark hair has that deep wave is sexy. Not to mention his dreamy eyes."

"All right, Lucy. Enough stalling. What did you find out about Kitty Walters?"

"I shouldn't be telling you."

"Lucy! How can you say that? We're a team, the five of us. Or has your dislike of Murphy made you forget?"

Lucy's cornflower blue gaze swung back to him. "She had my doppelganger in her book become disfigured. She said she was using our photos for a feature in the *Star*, which was a lie. She used us to promote her book and her land development scheme. Why should I care what happens to her?"

"You don't mean that. I know that you want to see justice served as much if not more than I do, given your profession."

Lucy expelled a breath. The false eyelash on her left eye threatened to come off again. Lucy reached up, ripped both false eyelashes off, tucked them in her pants pocket, and said, "Kitty Walters told me that Ray Edwards left everything to her. She claims to have a handwritten will that he wrote."

"Does that mean Kitty owns Edwards's share of the corporation? If so, maybe she killed Edwards when she found out he was sleeping with Murphy. That way, she'd own his shares and make a ton of money. Have you thought of that?"

"That's not the way it works. Sheriff Huckabee told me that Edwards's shares would revert to the corporation. Murphy would get the lion's share, with Joel Foster getting only a token few shares. It's standard procedure for a corporation like that to have big life insurance policies on its principals. If anything, Kitty would get the insurance money, unless Edwards named another beneficiary. That's all assuming the will is legal. Sheriff Huckabee says an attorney for Edwards's estate will make that determination."

"Are you saying that Murphy now owns almost all of the Honeybee Heaven Farms Corporation?"

"Yes, James, she does. Murphy gained the most from Edwards's death."

James thought about Murphy's tears, her grief, the pain in her eyes when Kitty Walters told her she was Ray Edwards's fiancée. "Not if she loved him, Lucy. And I think she did."

Chapter Fourteen

James was walking back to the supper club's table when his attention was caught by the large TV showing the *Hearth and Home* episode Joy had spoken about. Brandon, looking very young, sat on a sleeping blanket in a clearing in the woods, a small fire burning in front of him. James watched for a couple of minutes then joined his friends.

Gillian and Bennett had plates of food in front of them. Gillian had a bowl of salad, but Bennett's plate contained a heaping serving of chicken fried steak, corn pudding, and shrimp and grits. Off to one side, a smaller plate contained a slice of pecan pie. James thought about his apples and peanut butter out in the truck, probably frozen solid. *Oh, well,* he thought, *it wouldn't kill me to miss a meal.*

Gillian tapped her fingers on the table. "Bennett, I thought you didn't want to get full-blown diabetes."

"I'm hungry," he replied. "I had some of that multigrain cereal you bought me for breakfast at the crack of dawn this morning. I haven't had anything else since I finished my route."

Gillian slid the pie away. "At least don't bombard your body with all that sugar."

Bennett looked woefully after his dessert. "They had peach cobbler. Can I have that? It's fruit."

"You're too late," James commented. "They've taken up the buffet. Joy is shepherding people out of the hall. The break's about to start. Here's the plan: when Joy comes back, we're going to volunteer to help her straighten the merchandise. Look over at that table."

Gillian and Bennett dutifully looked where James indicated.

"The T-shirts and sweatshirts need to be folded, the *Hearth and Home* buttons lined up, and probably those boxes behind the table need to be unpacked. Lending a hand will keep us in the hall, able to question the actors."

"And Joy," Gillian said. "Good idea, James."

"Actually, it was Jane's idea. I can't take credit."

Lucy appeared and rested her hands on the back of a chair. "How's Jane feeling?"

"Better, thank you, Lucy," James said.

Lucy had her eye on Sullie, who personally escorted Amber Ross to the reserved table, talking to her and making her laugh. He stole a glance at Lucy and then he and Amber tittered.

James wanted to punch him, but since one person had already been arrested for assault, he thought better of it. "Sullie's not thinking clearly by flirting with the actress-turned-makeup-guru. He'll realize it soon enough."

Lucy tossed her hair. "I don't care. Brandon is way hotter. He reminds me of that English actor Clive Owen. I'll be the one to question him."

Gillian put her fork down. "Lucy, I'm going to powder my nose. Will you come with me?"

Lucy nodded and the two made their way out of the hall with the remainder of the reunion attendees.

Bennett finished the last of his food and gazed longingly at the slice of pecan pie. "Man, I get tired of Gillian telling me what I should and shouldn't eat. Guess I'd better get rid of the pie."

James held the plate and brought it to his nose. He could smell the nutty sweetness of the confection and wanted to pick up the pie with his bare hands and shove a bite in his mouth. "She loves you and doesn't want you to have to take pills or inject yourself with insulin."

"Go ahead and eat that, James. I know you want to."

"Thanks. I haven't had lunch."

"Hurry before Gillian sees you."

James consumed the pie in four bites. He bolted over to where the dirty dishes were stacked and added the pie plate. Then he contemplated who he was really deceiving by cheating on his diet.

He looked around for Joy but didn't see her, so he returned to the table. The actors sat around their table. Amber listened while Sullie told what was probably a wildly embellished story, if his hand gestures were anything to go by. Amber looked bored.

Valerie Norris spoke to the young man who'd been helping her with her book sales. Her eyes gleamed as she counted the money he'd collected in a leather sleeve. When she was done, she handed the young man a twenty-dollar bill and dismissed him with a curt, "You may go."

Brandon said, "Where's Joel?"

"Gone to meet the pretty Kitty," Doug said.

"I believe you mean Kitty Walters," Brandon said. "Where's she staying?"

"A motel in Mayberryburg."

James pursed his lips. "Excuse me. Do you mean Harrisonburg?"

"One of these bump-in-the-road towns," Doug said. "Where's Joy with our sushi, Brandon?"

"Here I come," Joy said in a singsong voice. She balanced a paper bag and five covered trays, which she handed out. "Where's Joel?" she asked in a panicked voice. "He shouldn't have left the hall without telling me where he was going."

"He'll be here soon," Brandon soothed. "Don't worry. Thanks for getting these for us. Got any chopsticks?"

"For you, darling boy, anything," Joy cooed. She pulled chopsticks out of the bag, as well as soy sauce. "Don't forget that I have a masseuse coming in. She'll be setting up in the basement. Remember to take one of the deputies with you for protection against overeager fans. I don't want any of you stressed, so be sure to take advantage of this service. We've sold a lot of tickets for tonight's special discussion panel and the silent auction. You need to be at your best so that we don't let the fans down."

"Yeah, we wouldn't want that," Doug said. He fumbled with his chopsticks, dropping them on the table twice, and cursed.

James had the fleeting thought that Doug might have been drinking. And not the water Joy had placed at their signing table. His demeanor was markedly different from the night the cast members played Monopoly.

Bennett said, "Ms. Carmichael, I'm Bennett. Can I help you over there by the merchandise table? Looks like you've got some heavy boxes to unpack."

She smiled. "Yes, you may. Go on over and begin straightening the merchandise on the table. Make sure you stack the same sizes of the sweatshirts and T-shirts together. Wait for me to supervise you before you open any boxes."

Bennett shot James a look that said that if he could sort mail, he could handle a few dozen clothing items, but did as Joy instructed.

Gillian and Lucy returned from the ladies' room. James broke out in a wide smile when he saw Lucy. Somehow Gillian had convinced their friend that she was better off without all the heavy cosmetics. Lucy's face had been scrubbed clean. She wore a pretty pink lipstick and, James knew from watching Jane do her eyes, had applied a coat of black mascara that contrasted nicely with her blue eyes.

Lucy smiled back at him. She pulled out the chair next to Brandon and said, "May I sit here?"

Brandon gave her a blinding smile that showed off his super-white teeth. "Sure. You're Lucy, right?"

The two started chatting. James was pleased to see Sullie's annoyed expression.

Joy said, "Lucy, now that you're here to guard our stars, I can supervise Ben at the merchandise table."

"His name is Bennett," Gillian said politely.

"It hardly matters," Joy said and marched away.

James placed his hand over Gillian's, knowing that otherwise she would launch into the *importance* of one's name and how *disrespectful* it was to mispronounce or mangle it.

At that moment, Joel entered the hall with Kitty Walters in tow. Kitty wore another tight dress, this one in a leopard print. She carried the same white fur coat. When they reached the table, James saw that Kitty's face where Murphy had slapped her was faintly bruised but not swollen. A butterfly bandage covered the small cut Murphy's ring had inflicted. Kitty immediately noticed Lucy flirting with Brandon. James could have sworn that, for the briefest moment, her eyes narrowed in anger.

Gillian said, "I think I'll go help Bennett."

When she left, James turned his chair toward the other table.

"Everyone," Lucy said, "this is my friend James Henry. He's the head librarian in Quincy's Gap."

"A librarian?" Doug said and rose to his feet. "Think I'll check out the masseuse."

Lucy said, "Sullie, would you go with Doug?" The tone she used implied an order rather than a request. He nodded and the two walked away.

"Ms. Walters," James said, "I'm sorry for your loss."

"Call me Kitty," she said, bringing out her lace handkerchief and touching a dry eye.

"Kitty, where are you from?"

"I live in Louisville with Ray. That's how I know Joel. He runs *Southern Style* magazine out of Louisville."

James had been asking where Kitty was born, not where she lived now, as Kitty didn't have even a ghost of a Southern accent, but her answer got the wheels turning in his head.

Brandon said, "Doug told us you were staying in Harrisonburg, Kitty. I spoke to Mrs. Anderson, the innkeeper at the Red Bird where we're all staying. She said the police have released the suite on the third floor where Ray and Murphy were staying. If you want, you can take my room. I'll stay up there."

Kitty glowed at Brandon's attention. "That's kind of you, Brandon. There's no need for you to change rooms, though. I'll stay in the suite."

"How morbid," Valerie said.

"Not at all," Kitty declared. "I'll feel closer to my Ray staying where he spent his last moments. By the way, I don't believe we've been introduced."

Valerie looked at Kitty as if she were an insect crawling on the buffet table. "I'm Valerie Norris, the author."

"Oh. I wouldn't know that since I don't read books."

James cringed. *How could anyone not read books!* He had a mad urge to take Kitty back to his library and show her all of his beloved books.

Amber Ross got out her phone and began mindlessly tapping away.

"Kitty, are you an actress?" James asked, knowing she wasn't but wondering how he could ask her what she did for a living without sounding pushy. Her response surprised him.

"Maybe once upon a time," Kitty said, observing Brandon, who kept his attention on Lucy. "I'm a Realtor."

"A Realtor friend in Quincy's Gap, Joan Beechnut, told me that Ray Edwards was going to bring in a Realtor to sell the houses in his planned community," James prompted.

"That would be me," Kitty chirped. "With the money I'll get from Ray's estate, I'm thinking of investing in Joel's corporation in addition to selling the new houses built later this summer. What's it called again, Joel? Bees Heaven?"

Brandon cut his eyes in Kitty's direction. A muscle twitched in his jaw. An emotion passed between them. Not a pleasant emotion, James thought. Then James felt he should be remembering something else, but he couldn't think what.

"Honeybee Heaven Farms," Joel said. "You did bring Ray's handwritten will with you, right?"

"Yes. It's here in my purse. I keep it close to me always. Another way to still have Ray with me."

"I may lose my lunch," Valerie muttered.

Kitty heard her. "You must never have been in love, Valerie."

"Such a silly emotion. I won't share my royalties, I mean, loyalties with any man," Valerie declared.

"As we've told Joel, Kitty," James said in a friendly tone, "none of the townsfolk in Quincy's Gap want to see a big explosion in population that the development would bring. Our school structure couldn't handle the extra pupils, more people mean more crime, and our town would lose its personality. Murphy agrees that, with the passing of Ray Edwards, the development shouldn't go forward." The second the last words were out of his mouth, James realized he'd made a mistake.

Kitty stiffened. "Oh, well, if Murphy doesn't think we should go ahead then, Joel, I think you and I should proceed. Besides, with Murphy in prison for Ray's murder, she won't be able to profit from the corporation, will she?"

"If Murphy's convicted, which I don't think she will be," Joel rushed to say, "her shares would revert to the corporation."

Kitty smiled. "Then you and I could own it all, Joel. Of course, we'd have to let someone buy a few shares so they'd have voting rights but no real control. Maybe you could do that, Brandon."

Brandon snapped his chopsticks in half. "You're getting ahead of yourself, Kitty. First, an attorney has to verify that the handwritten will is authentic."

"That's a nasty thing to say," Kitty retorted, her face wrinkling with annoyance. "Do you think I'd forge it?"

"I didn't say that," Brandon said in a bored tone. He turned his attention back to Lucy, picking up a strand of her hair and winding it around his index finger. Lucy had the same expression as when faced with a new can of frosting.

Kitty fumed.

James stood. "If you'll all excuse me, I need to get some work done at the library."

Mumbled goodbyes followed this announcement.

Amber Ross never took her eyes from her phone.

James had his hand on the door to the hall when Bennett caught up with him. "You're leaving?"

"I'm going back to the library so that I can get on the Internet. I want to check on someone."

"It's not Doug Moore, is it? Because I can tell you about him."

James gave Bennett his full attention. "What did you find out?"

"Joy plays favorites with her 'darlings' and Doug is at the bottom of her list. She's not above a little gossip when it comes to the show she's obsessed with. Especially if one of the cast isn't living up to the morals of the show. Seriously, man, I bet you the walls of her house are covered with pictures of these actors. Anyway, seems Mr. Doug Moore likes his liquor. Joy told me that she wrote in the *Home and Hearth* newsletter—yes, there is such a thing as well as a fan club Joy runs—that Doug was off on a 'spiritual trip' to India when he was actually drying out at a rehab in Cleveland."

"Cleveland? I would have thought some fancy place in California since he lives in Los Angeles."

"Cheaper to get sober in Cleveland, I guess. Doug probably lives in a studio apartment in LA. Drank all his money away, according to Joy. Then, listen to this. He put an ad online that, for a hefty price, he would read screenplays and give feedback. A moneymaking thing, but Joy says he took it a step further."

"How's that?"

"Doug stole one of the screenplays, changed a few names and locations, and passed it off as his own. Sold it to a Hollywood producer for a big chunk of change. Only luck wasn't on Doug's side. The screenplay had been making the rounds. An assistant in the producer's office recognized it. Doug had to give the money back and pay off the screenplay writer so the guy wouldn't sue him."

"Wow," James breathed. "A man who would do that—"

"Might kill," Bennett finished for him. "But why? How would he benefit from Edwards's death? I don't think Doug even knew Edwards unless he met him at the Red Bird."

James heaved out a sigh. "I don't see a motive either. Look, tell Gillian I'll see you two back here tomorrow afternoon. When I'm done at the library, I'm going to the Sweet Tooth to pick up some of their cheddar and herb cheese straws. Jane loves them."

"Not in the doghouse, are you?"

James thought of Jane's chilly goodbye. "No, but I'm in the yard nearby and don't want to get closer. See you tomorrow."

Lucy came up to them. "James, I see you're trying to leave, but I wanted to tell you that I asked Brandon if he'd seen anyone at the Red Bird who shouldn't be there. He said no. I also asked if he'd heard anything unusual. Again, his answer was no."

"All right," James said. "When Doug Moore comes back from his massage, can you ask him the same questions?"

Lucy shrugged. "Sure, but I'm telling you, Murphy killed Edwards."

"Can't you try to have an open mind, please, Lucy?"

Lucy leaned in to him and enunciated each word. "Not while Murphy was the only one inside a locked room with the murder victim." With a last glance, Lucy turned and walked back to the actors' table.

• • •

When James arrived at the library, the Fitzgerald twins were busy helping patrons. James smiled when he saw the library had a healthy number of people browsing the stacks and others at the checkout counter with books in hand. With the threat of being snowed in, people were stocking up on reading material. He should help out, but first he had to look something up on the computer.

James went back to his office, took off his outerwear, and booted up his computer. When he Googled "Kitty Walters," hundreds of thousands of results popped up. He scrolled through the first three pages, then gave up. None of them were the Kitty Walters he sought.

He tried "Kitty Walters Realtor" and was equally daunted by the number of search results. James huffed out a breath and sat with his arms crossed. His mind drifted to the vending machine and the snack-size bags of cheese puffs there. He restrained himself with an effort.

Then his fingers flew over the keyboard as he typed in "Kitty Walters actress." The first result took him to a sparse Wikipedia page that listed acting credits, including "waitress," "girlfriend," "girl in video store." All of Kitty's acting jobs were bit parts in well-known TV shows. Which meant, James thought, that she lived in Los Angeles during the time *Hearth and Home* was filmed. Was it possible that Kitty knew some of the cast members from that time?

Then James scrolled back to the top of Kitty's Wikipedia page. The very first sentence struck him. *Kitty Walters, born Kathleen Alison Richardson in Washington, DC, to lawyer Rowan Richardson and socialite Faye Carlisle Richardson.*

After reading about the expensive girls' school Kitty/Kathleen had attended, followed by a term at George Mason University, James grew impatient. He clicked the link to Rowan Richardson's Wikipedia page. Near the bottom of the page, after an extensive account of Richardson's education, rise to prominent attorney specializing in corporate law, and list of cases he'd been involved with, James read, *"Among Richardson's many real estate holdings was Fairbridge in Cardinal's Rest, Virginia, which the family used as a summer house. Built in 1888, the Victorian house served as the exterior for the television show* Hearth and Home. *It is now a bed and breakfast known as the Red Bird."*

Chapter Fifteen

James sat with Jane, Eliot, Milla, and his father at the nine thirty church service Sunday morning. Eliot wiggled between James and Jane. Jane spoke to him in a soft voice.

Last night, when James had brought home his cheese straws peace offering, Jane had smiled. "James Henry, you are the sweetest man."

James had grinned ruefully. "That's probably accurate since I consumed a slice of pecan pie at the reunion events and then, when I was at the Sweet Tooth, Megan offered me a couple of 'sample' chocolate chip cookies to eat while I waited. I'm full of sugar."

Jane had chuckled. "How's the investigation coming along?"

They'd talked about the case after Eliot went to bed. Jane had suggested that James speak with Mrs. Lydell after the church service to see what she remembered about the Richardsons, since she used to clean for them.

Now, people filed out to where tables were set up with coffee and glazed doughnuts. Everyone seemed to be talking at once, but James clearly heard his father say to Milla, "I'll have a doughnut if I want. I'm tired of this diet you have me on."

"Dear, part of your stroke prevention plan is a healthy diet. Sugar is limited—"

"One dang doughnut ain't gonna kill me," Jackson interrupted and stomped over to stand in the line of people waiting for the treat.

James spotted Mr. and Mrs. Lydell about to walk out the double doors. "Jane, I see the Lydells."

"Go ahead. I know you need to speak with Mrs. Lydell. I'll take Eliot to the little boys' room and we'll meet you back here."

"Mom," Eliot protested, "I don't have to go. I want a doughnut."

James heard Jane tell him how it might spoil the dinner Milla had planned before the two headed off toward the restrooms.

"Mrs. Lydell!" James called as he made his way through the thick crowd.

The farmer and his wife turned at the sound of his voice. Mrs. Lydell smiled at him. "Hello, James."

Mr. Lydell said, "Henry, any news about my land? Is Murphy Alistair going to sell it back to me? We heard you and your friends have been investigating Edwards's death."

"Let's go somewhere private," James said. He led the older couple to a small meeting room and closed the door after them. "Mr. Lydell, I don't have any definite word on what Murphy will do. I'd hate to get your hopes up, but it's my belief that she wants to do the right thing. The problem is that there's another person involved. In fact, that's who I wanted to ask you about."

"Who is it?" Mr. Lydell asked.

James turned to Mrs. Lydell. "Actually, I had hoped you might know her. Kathleen Richardson. She's the daughter of the Richardsons who owned the Red Bird when it was still called Fairbridge."

Mrs. Lydell nodded, her soft brown eyes looking off into the distance. "Of course I remember them. I first started cleaning the house when the Richardsons owned it. Rich folks. They just summered at Fairbridge. The rest of the time Fairbridge was shut up. Buford and I drove out there once a week to make sure the place was okay; rake the leaves, plant flowers, that sort of thing. Mrs. Richardson would let me know when the family planned to arrive. I'd go over there ahead of time and give everything a good scrub, then stock the pantry with whatever groceries she wanted."

"Didn't get paid much for our work," Buford Lydell put in. "But when you're a farmer, every bit helps, especially during the winter."

James nodded. "Was this before or after the time the TV show was filmed there?"

"Oh, afterward," Mrs. Lydell said. "I never met Kathy Richardson, but I heard stories."

"Yes, ma'am. I know you don't want to gossip, but any information you could share might help with the investigation and possibly getting your land back," James said.

Buford Lydell tugged on his short white beard. "Tell the man, Estella."

"I don't know much, James. When I cleaned the house, I didn't see the Richardson children often. There were four of them, three boys and the girl, Kathy. Like I said, she was gone before I started working there. But I heard that she had a wild streak and tended to get on the bad side of her father. He was protective since she was his only daughter. Story goes that when Kathy was nineteen and in, let's see, it would have been the first semester of her second year at George Mason, she got involved with a young man who her parents disapproved of."

Buford Lydell said, "Young guy thought he was a poet. Worked in a restaurant near campus. Mr. Richardson wasn't having it. He had plans for his daughter to marry up, you know what I mean?"

"Yes, sir, I do," James said.

"Kathy refused to stop seeing the young man," Mrs. Lydell claimed. "As punishment, her father pulled her out of school in the middle of October. He sent her out to Fairbridge with an old nanny to look after her. Kathy was told that she had two weeks to decide to give up the poet or her father would stop paying her tuition at George Mason."

"There was talk that he threatened to disinherit her too," Mr. Lydell said.

"I never heard that," Mrs. Lydell said, "but I wouldn't be surprised if he did."

"What happened?" James asked.

"Kathy stayed out at Fairbridge for almost the whole two weeks, then she ran off to Los Angeles!" Mrs. Lydell said. "Imagine. A nineteen-year-old taking off across the country like that. 'Course, no one found out for weeks afterward that's where she'd gone. She was an adult in the eyes of the police, so they wouldn't look for her. The Richardsons only learned where Kathy was when she sent them a postcard telling them not to come after her, that she had decided to become an actress."

"Mr. Richardson thought she'd run off with the poet, but he was still in DC and claimed to have his heart broken," Mr. Lydell said. "You can bet money Mr. Richardson kept an eye on the boy to make sure he was telling the truth."

Mrs. Lydell nodded. "And he was. Kathy started acting, but as far as I know, she never came back to Virginia. Changed her name, I think."

"Kitty Walters," James said.

"That's right. One of her brothers called her Kitty," Mrs. Lydell agreed. "As for the 'Walters,' it must have been a show business name. We never heard of Kathy ever getting married. And that's all we know. The Richardsons sold Fairbridge to the Andersons, who turned it into the Red Bird. I never saw the family again. I cleaned for Mrs. Anderson the first year they owned the house until my arthritis got so bad I couldn't do it anymore. Mrs. Anderson does the cleaning herself now, so I haven't been out there in, oh, Lord, I guess it's been eight years."

Mr. Lydell had been there, threatening Ray Edwards, but James didn't think it prudent to mention that.

James thanked the couple and assured them that he'd let them know of any news regarding the peach farm.

• • •

On the way over to Jackson and Milla's for Sunday dinner, James told Jane what the Lydells had said while Eliot looked out the window with a pair of kids' binoculars Milla had given him for Christmas.

"Hard to believe that a nineteen-year-old girl, probably sheltered, would take off to the opposite end of the country all alone," Jane mused. "I'll bet she had someone with her, or someone waiting for her."

"Anything's possible," James said.

When they got to Jackson and Milla's, Eliot ran ahead to the door. Finding it locked, he turned to his parents. "Hurry up. I want to go inside."

Puzzled, James knocked on the door, which Jackson usually left off the latch.

Milla answered, wiping her eyes on her apron. She'd clearly been crying. "Don't mind me. I'll have dinner on the table shortly."

James and Jane exchanged looks as they took off their coats and helped Eliot out of his.

Jackson sat scowling at the kitchen table. "Is it too much to ask that a man have a decent Sunday dinner?"

Milla walked to the stove. In a quiet voice she said, "James, we're having bucatini with pesto sauce and sweet potatoes. It's vegetarian for Eliot. I also have filet of flounder in the oven."

"Sounds delicious," James said.

Jackson pounded his fist on the table. "It's not delicious! It's some jumped-up spaghetti with potatoes. That's no Sunday dinner. Sunday dinner is roast beef. I'm tired of you feeding me this pap, Milla!"

Jane led a wide-eyed Eliot through to the den.

James looked at his father and said, "Pop, how can you talk to Milla that way? I'm sure she's worked hard on this meal."

"Oh, yeah. She works hard on everything: telling me how long I can sleep, how long I can sit at my easel before I have to get up and walk around whether I want to or not, how many vitamin pills I have to swallow every morning. I can only have a tiny glass of Cutty Sark every other day. That's no way to live!"

Milla turned from the stove, spoon in hand. "That's the *only* way to live, Jackson. You had a stroke and now you have to change a few things if you want to prevent another one."

"You won't even let me salt my food," Jackson grumbled.

"Pop, it must be hard, but what Milla is saying makes sense. It sounds like you just need to have a little self-discipline."

Jackson scoffed. "Look who's talking about self-discipline. The man who can't stay on a diet for more than a few weeks. Always complaining about being overweight, but still packing in the food."

James felt as if his father had slapped him. To his horror, he felt the sting of tears behind his eyes. He took a deep breath even though he felt his chin tremble.

Milla rushed forward and wrapped him in a hug. "Don't listen to him, James. You're trying and that's what matters."

Jackson scraped his chair back. "I'm going out to my shed. And I don't want to be bothered!"

So saying, he took his jacket off the coat rack and slammed the door on his way out.

Jane came into the room. "What happened? Where's Jackson?"

Milla moved back to the stove.

Forcing himself to present a composure he didn't feel so that Jane wouldn't be upset, James said, "He's gone to paint. He didn't feel like eating."

Although the meal was excellent, as was all of Milla's cooking,

James found himself taking small portions. He felt ashamed every time he put a bite of food into his mouth. His father was right; he hadn't been self-disciplined enough. Well, that would change. He'd have the support of the other supper club members, his friends. Jane would support him too. He knew that he'd slip sometimes, but promised himself he'd get up every time he fell.

In the Bronco on the way home, Eliot fell asleep in the backseat. Jane yawned. "I think I'll sleep the rest of the afternoon away, James," she said. "I'm awfully tired."

"It's the last afternoon of the reunion. I'd like to go down there even though I'm sick of that hall, to tell the truth. Bennett texted me that he and Gillian will be there. Lucy is still working the event. I hope Lindy will come. Do you need me to bring anything home for dinner later tonight?"

"Just yourself. I'll put a pot of vegetable soup on before my nap. Now tell me what your father said that upset you."

James squirmed in his seat at Jane's shrewdness. She didn't miss anything when it came to him, good or bad. "He basically said I didn't have any self-discipline when it came to food. That I can't stay on a diet."

"That's not true, James. You've had success in the past. You will again. Besides, aren't you only about twenty-five pounds overweight?"

"More like thirty-five pounds."

"Okay, so how about setting a small goal. Say, fifteen pounds over the next six months. That would be good for your health. Your growing family needs you around for a long time."

Lose fifteen pounds over six months? Surely he could do that, James thought. "When you put it that way, I feel more motivated. Confident."

"Of course. Who wouldn't be discouraged thinking about taking off thirty-five pounds in a short period of time? Not to mention that it's not healthy to lose weight fast. You'd be more likely to put it right back on."

James felt that stinging behind his eyes again at Jane's understanding. He didn't dare try to speak.

"Your father is set in his ways. He's stubborn and probably mad at his own body for betraying him by having that stroke. Seems to me like he's taking out his anger on those who love him. That's no excuse, but it's an explanation."

James swallowed. "I love you, Jane."

"And I love you, James Henry. No matter if your belly jiggles or if you have sculpted abs like Daniel Craig."

James darted a look his wife's way. "James Bond? The guy who plays James Bond?"

Jane started laughing.

"You think he's hot, huh?"

Jane laughed harder.

"Don't ask me to take you to the next James Bond movie."

Jane gasped for breath. "I won't. I'll have more fun if I go with Denise from Lamaze class. Oh!"

"What is it? Are you all right? Is it the baby?"

Jane placed a hand on her stomach. "Only a twinge. Don't worry. I had them at this stage when I was pregnant with Eliot. You shouldn't have made me laugh so much," she said playfully.

James exhaled. "Okay. You scared me there for a second."

"We have a little over two and a half weeks to go. I'll know when it's time."

Even with her assurances, James stayed at home for the next hour to make sure Jane was okay. He let Snickers out. The dog made a lightning-quick pit stop and ran back into the warm house. James put Eliot down for a nap after reading from *The Lion, the Witch, and the Wardrobe*. He helped chop carrots, potatoes, and onions while Jane diced celery and got out cans of diced tomatoes and packages of frozen corn, green beans, and peas.

Once the soup was simmering and Jane was tucked up in bed with her cell phone in reach, Miss Pickles asleep at the end of the bed, James drove to Cardinal's Rest. He glanced at his watch when he got there and noted that only an hour of the reunion remained.

Hurrying into the hall, he saw the cast members up on stage. The round tables were gone. In their place, folding chairs had been set up fanning out from the stage. In the aisle, a microphone stood on a stand. A woman spoke into it. "This question is for Brandon. I want to know how you are still so handsome after all these years." She giggled then made her way back to her seat. A ripple of giggles and chuckles sounded through the hall.

Valerie Norris passed him the microphone. Brandon said, "Years? What years? It was only yesterday, wasn't it?" He smiled in that way that women found so attractive.

The audience laughed and clapped.

James saw Gillian and Bennett in the back row. Lucy stood behind them. There was no sign of Lindy.

James started walking toward his friends, when Joy Carmichael intercepted him. "Mr. Henry, isn't it?"

"Yes, Ms. Carmichael. How are you?"

"My volunteers all seem to be sitting in the audience instead of volunteering. I can't understand their lack of dedication to our sweet Lewis family children. It was a delicate operation that I undertook, working closely to make sure this event fit into their busy lives and didn't interrupt the dears. These volunteers should be grateful that they're able to rub shoulders with such talent. Besides," she continued, looking around furtively in case someone was listening, "there's going to be a very, very special announcement made in a few minutes."

"Oh, what's that?"

"I am sworn to secrecy," Joy said. "All my dears have known for months. They trusted me enough to tell me their wonderful news when I arranged this reunion."

"That's nice. So what can I help you with?" James asked.

"I need someone to help me lift the cake off the counter in the kitchen and place it on that table."

James looked in the direction she pointed. Near the merchandise table, a long rectangular table had been set up with paper plates and plastic forks. "I'll help you. Let me take off my coat."

As James walked to the empty chair next to his friends, he removed his coat and scarf and draped them over the back.

Onstage, Doug Moore sang "I Will Always Love You" off-key.

Bennett looked at James and rolled his eyes.

"I'll be right back," James said. He turned to Lucy. "You're going to be around, aren't you? I have some new information."

She nodded, keeping her eyes on the crowd. "I have news too. Actually, it's the same old news. I questioned Doug Moore regarding the night of the murder. He didn't see anyone or hear anything out of the ordinary. Sullie questioned Amber Ross. Same answer."

That left Valerie Norris, Murphy's prime suspect, as the only one who hadn't been questioned. "Okay, thanks for asking. I'm going to help Joy Carmichael."

"Where's Lindy?" he whispered in Gillian's ear.

"Luis took her out to eat," Gillian replied.

"It was my idea," Bennett said. "I told him he needed to romance Lindy back to the house. He's miserable without her."

"I hope it works," James said before he walked away.

James noticed that many fans wore the same red heart-shaped button that Joy wore. The one reading *"Hearth and Home* Always in Our Hearts."

In the kitchen, Joy flipped open the top of the large white box that held the cake. Nestled inside was an eighteen-by-twenty-four sheet cake with white icing and "Happy Anniversary, *Hearth and Home!"* written in blue letters.

James said, "Let's take the entire box to the table, then take the cake out."

"Good idea," Joy agreed.

Once they had the cake set up on the table, James helped Joy put out cups. "Are you happy with the way the reunion events went?" he asked.

Joy's face radiated happiness. "Yes, I am. Anytime I can see my kids, my dears—that's what I call the cast members—I'm in heaven."

James noticed that Joy didn't wear a wedding ring. Married to *Hearth and Home.* He supposed there was no harm in her devoting herself to a TV show. There were better things Joy could spend her time on, but it wasn't his place to judge.

When they finished arranging the table, Joy thanked him and said she would bring out the punch by herself.

James got to his seat in time to see a man he didn't recognize take the stage.

"Folks, I'm Lenny Matthews from the television network that brought you *Hearth and Home.* I wanted to take this opportunity, while the *Hearth and Home* family are all together, to announce that there will be a reboot of the *Hearth and Home* television show."

Audible gasps and a burst of loud applause followed this announcement. A photographer stood near the stage. The flash of his camera went off several times.

Mr. Matthews waited until the audience was quiet, then said, "All the original cast members have signed on. The new show will follow their grown-up lives as they incorporate their values into adulthood. We'll start filming in three weeks."

So this was the big secret. James noticed that Brandon broke into a huge grin. Doug got up and did a little dance of joy. Valerie Norris looked bored. Joel Foster smiled and nodded at the fans. Amber Ross flipped her long hair and sat up straighter.

Joy got up onstage, a bright, sunny smile on her face, and took the microphone. "Folks, isn't that the best possible news we could get?"

Hoots and hollers greeted her words.

When everyone had calmed down, Joy continued, "We still have merchandise for sale at the back of the room, so feel free to pick up a *Hearth and Home* button, T-shirt or sweatshirt. And, in a few minutes, we'll have punch and a special cake to share. Show your ticket to our volunteers." She stared at a group of four women in the front row, who scrambled from their seats and headed for the cake table. They quickly put slices of cake on plates and began spacing them around the table. "Now, let's all give a big round of applause to thank our dear cast members, who continue to bless us with their love and talent."

The actors stood and bowed. The crowd gave them a standing ovation then began a stampede toward the cake.

At that moment, James noticed Sheriff Huckabee enter the hall. He made his way to the side of the stage, where Joy diverted him.

"What's happening?" James asked Lucy.

Lucy crouched down in front of the other supper club members. "The sheriff is going to tell Brandon, Joel, Doug, Valerie, and Amber that they can't leave town yet because they're potential witnesses in an ongoing murder investigation. Sshhh, don't tell anyone. I have to go back him up." She walked down the aisle briskly.

Bennett whistled. "That news won't go down well with those actors."

"I bet they were all planning on getting on a plane out of here tonight," Gillian said.

"Maybe this means Sheriff Huckabee isn't convinced Murphy is the killer," Bennett said.

Gillian rested her head on his shoulder. "I hope so."

Bennett scraped his chair away so fast that Gillian fell sideways before she jerked herself upright.

"Woman, what are you thinking?" Bennett's gaze darted around, as if making sure no one had seen Gillian's affectionate act.

Gillian gaped at him. "What do you mean?"

"You can't drape yourself over me like that in public. Are you crazy?"

Gillian's cheeks turned bright pink. "You have to get over this irrational fear that people won't approve of our relationship because we're an interracial couple. Times have changed."

"Not that much."

"Bennett, are you going to refuse to hold my hand when we walk down the street even after we're married?"

Bennett's eyes popped out like a cartoon character's. "Married?" he squeaked. "We're never getting married! Everything is fine as it is. You have your house. That's fine! I have my house. That's fine! We're not changing anything because everything is fine!"

Gillian's face fell. She stared at Bennett for what felt like minutes. Then, with a clinking of her silver bracelets, she picked up her purple cape and swung it around her shoulders. Holding her head high, she left without saying another word.

Obviously, everything was not fine.

Bennett stood looking after her as if paralyzed. "She doesn't understand," he muttered. "She doesn't know."

"What doesn't she know, Bennett?" James asked.

"I can't marry her. I can't."

"Why not? Have you two discussed marriage?"

"No! Never!"

"Maybe Gillian sees marriage as a natural progression of your relationship. She was married once before, a long time ago. Her husband was killed. Remember when she told us about it? Someone ran him down while he was riding his bicycle."

Bennett tugged hard on his mustache, a sure sign that he was distressed. "I know."

"You love her, don't you?"

"'Course I do. Said so when I was on *Jeopardy!* That's national television! Why isn't that good enough for her?"

"Maybe she wants to make a home with you."

"That would be a mistake," Bennett said. "A huge mistake."

James didn't want to press his friend further when he was so upset. Instead he said, "I've been wondering, why does Gillian want you to shave off your mustache?"

Bennett trembled. "Says it scratches her. I'm not shaving it off. I'm not marrying her. I want some cake."

James said, "Sit down, friend. I'll get you a piece."

Chapter Sixteen

While James ate his yogurt Monday morning, Jim Topling the meteorologist cheerfully told him that the temperature outside was fifteen degrees. "Our devious snowstorm is playing shy, but she'll show her vengeance any time now," Topling proclaimed gleefully from the kitchen television.

Jane zipped Eliot's lunch bag. "Why is Topling calling the storm a 'she'?"

"Because he's a dumbass," Eliot said. Then he paled under the stern gazes of both his parents. "That's what you said, Daddy."

Jane shot James a severe look, ruined by the fact that her shoulders shook with suppressed laughter. Still, she composed herself and joined James in a short but potent discussion with Eliot about bad words. This included an apology from James. "I shouldn't have used that word, Eliot, and neither should you."

"Okay," Eliot said. "Can I get my coat now? Do we have time to feed the birds? They must be extra cold and hungry."

"Yes," Jane said. "I'll help you get your coat and hat on."

Miss Pickles took up her post at the window, where she could safely boss the birds and squirrels around, chattering and twitching her tail.

After kissing Jane goodbye and apologizing again for soiling their son's ears, James led Eliot through the biting cold to the multilevel birdhouse. James held his son up so that the boy could pour out the birdseed.

"Daddy, am I in trouble? Will you still read *The Lion, the Witch, and the Wardrobe* to me before bed?"

James eased his son down until his feet touched the frozen grass. He spread some of the birdseed on the ground, hoping the squirrels would eat that instead of hogging the feeder. "You're not in any trouble, son. We talked about the bad word and now it's over. We'll read tonight."

"I'm glad. I was thinking, Daddy. See my tree house?"

"Yes," James said patiently, even though he felt like his eyelids would freeze any second.

"It needs a secret closet so I can pretend to go to Narnia."

"Wardrobe," James corrected as he used a clothespin to secure the bag of birdseed. "We'll see about constructing something when the weather gets warm. Now, I think it's time to get going."

James saw Eliot to the bus and, as usual, waved until he was out of sight. He got in the Bronco, hoping it would start when he turned the key. He smiled when it did and sat for a few minutes while the truck warmed up.

Then James realized something. He struck his forehead. "Of course! I'm so stupid for not thinking of it before!"

Excited, he drove through the streets of Quincy's Gap in a hurry to get to the library. He did notice that there were far fewer people around. The folks in town for the reunion had left, and with the fate of the development up in the air, potential residents had gone too. His little town was back to normal.

James remembered to grab the books out of the outside book return drop, then he unlocked the library door, flicked on the lights, turned up the heat, and went into the break room. He stored his lunch in the fridge. Was eight forty too early to call Mrs. Lydell? He decided it was and struggled to contain his impatience.

The Fitzgerald twins arrived, cheeks ruddy from the cold. "Hey, Professor," Scott said. "I hope that snow we're supposed to get comes on our day off. Francis and I want to go snowboarding."

"We've never been. Can you believe it?" Francis asked, taking off his coat.

James stood behind the counter, checking in the books from the book return drop. "That depends. Have either of you ever broken an arm or a leg?"

The twins laughed, then must have realized James was serious. "No, Professor," Scott said.

"Please keep it that way. I want you to have fun, but I need the two of you here sans crutches or casts. I'm sure you've found a professional to give you some lessons before you hit the slopes."

The twins looked at one another. "Dude," Francis said. "We need to get online and do some research."

James held up a hand. "One other thing. Wednesday is Valentine's Day."

"Like we could forget with the Valentine tree and the conversation hearts," Scott said.

"What do the two of you have planned for Fern and Willow?"

James asked. "I'm not trying to be nosy; I thought I could offer some advice."

Scott and Francis beamed in unison. Francis said, "We've got it covered. Wait until you hear this."

"Let me tell him," Scott said. "Professor, you're gonna be astounded at our brilliance."

"Good," James said. "Those are two nice young ladies and they deserve your brilliance."

Scott said, "We've got the new Nintendo Switch complete with the Mario and Rabbids Kingdom Battle video game! We're having Fern and Willow over to play the game and eat pizza. What could be better?"

James hid his dismay. "Oh, I didn't know Fern and Willow liked video games."

The twins' smiles vanished. Scott said, "Everyone likes video games, right?"

"Sure they do," Francis said in a weak voice.

James thought quickly. "The evening you've got planned sounds great. Maybe you could add one thing to it."

"What?" the twins asked at once.

"Allow me to help. I'll talk to Milla about putting together extra-special boxes of candy from Quincy's Whimsies for Fern and Willow. I know Willow works there, but Milla can keep a secret. How about that? You know how women are about Valentine's Day and chocolate."

"Right, right," Scott agreed. "Do you think she has any Super Mario–shaped chocolates?"

"Um, I can check," James said.

"That would be awesome, Professor. We like chocolate too," Francis said. "We'll pay Mrs. Henry whatever it costs, don't worry."

"Sounds like a plan. Let me call her right now. Why don't you two start shelving these books?"

James waited until the twins were busy in the stacks before he picked up the phone and dialed his father's number. Milla answered on the first ring.

"Hello, James, how are you?" she asked.

From the downtrodden tone of her voice, James knew that his

father had not apologized for his behavior the previous day. Maybe preparing boxes of chocolate for Fern and Willow would take her mind off things. At least he hoped so. "Milla, I have a special chocolate mission for you to undertake, if you're willing to accept it."

"What is it, dear?"

"Are you going in to work at Quincy's Whimsies?"

"Oh, yes. We're awfully busy with Valentine's Day this Wednesday. Jackson told me he's going to paint today. I'm fixing him a lunch to leave in the refrigerator."

James explained the situation, ending with, "Do you think you'll have time to make up the boxes? What about Willow? Do you think you can keep what you're doing from her?"

Milla chuckled. "That young lady is very intelligent. I'll wait until she's on lunch break. Failing that, I can always tell her that I'm going in the back to make up something for Jane."

"Jane," James said in a faint voice.

"James, don't tell me you haven't gotten a Valentine's present for Jane."

"Okay, I won't tell you," James said, feeling short of breath.

"All right, now calm down. I can hear you gasping for breath. I'll make up a box for Jane too. I'll let you know when everything is ready. I'll bring everything to the house. You can pick it up there."

"You're an angel on Earth, Milla. I can't believe I didn't think of something for Jane. I'm a terrible husband."

"No, dear, you're human. You've been doing a lot at home, I imagine, you have a full-time job, and you've got a lot going on with this murder investigation, don't you?"

"Yes, but that doesn't excuse my thoughtlessness. I probably wouldn't have remembered until the day itself."

"Stop now," Milla said. "You're going to have a lovely box of chocolates for Jane. It's all handled."

James thanked Milla again and hung up the phone. First Eliot had picked up a bad word from him, then he'd forgotten his wife's —his pregnant wife's—Valentine's gift. *Really batting a thousand, aren't you,* he asked himself. He felt especially ashamed as, when they'd been married before, James had been lax about buying Jane gifts. He vowed not to make the same mistake twice.

A rush of patrons kept him busy for the next hour. Instead of the planned development, everyone speculated on the impending snow. How would Quincy's Gap cope with record-breaking snow totals? How long would they be without power? How much bread and milk should they buy?

Finally, at almost eleven, James had a chance to call Mrs. Lydell. When he put his question to her she said, "Why, I haven't thought of that in years, but yes, there is, and exactly where you guessed."

They spoke for a few more minutes. When James hung up, his mind raced, but he couldn't devote himself to conjecture because the patrons continued to pour into the library.

At noon, there was a lull. James sent the twins to the break room to eat lunch. He called Lucy and got her voice mail. He left a message asking her to come to the library as soon as she could. He had information that would change the entire investigation.

He was looking over a catalogue of newly released books about thirty minutes later when Bennett burst through the door. His eyes were huge. His uniform looked like it had been dragged through a hedge. He had powdered sugar around his mouth, on his sleeve, and on his hands. He dropped the library mail on the counter. "She won't take my calls. I've been trying since last night. I've left eleven voice mails. I texted her, too. I need to use the computer here. I can send her an email."

"Slow down." James kept his tone calm. "We're talking about Gillian, right?"

"Of course we are!"

Library patrons looked their way, their disapproval of Bennett's loud voice clear.

"Bennett, you need to lower your voice. We're in the library."

"Sorry, man. I'm kinda freaking out. I went by the Yuppie Puppy, but there was a sign on the door that read *Closed for Snow.* There is no snow, James! That man on TV keeps yelling about it, but there's no snow!"

James held out both his hands and pushed them down in rapid movements, indicating Bennett needed to stop being so noisy.

"Sorry. I know she's okay because I delivered her mail and I could see her moving around the house. I went up to the door and knocked, and she pulled the blinds in the living room closed and didn't come to the door. She's broken up with me, James. It's over. I'm history. What am I gonna do?"

"Give her a day. Gillian likes her space sometimes. It's more likely she's blending special healing oils. Have you gotten her a Valentine's present?"

Bennett put a shaking hand to his forehead, leaving a trail of powdered sugar there. "I totally forgot."

"Don't feel bad. I had to call Milla a little while ago and ask her to make up something for Jane. I'd forgotten too."

"I keep picturing Gillian and Lindy in that house feeling free because they've gotten rid of their men."

"I don't believe for a minute that's what Gillian and Lindy are doing. For one thing, Lindy is at school now. Gillian is probably drinking a special tea and sitting in an impossible yoga position, meditating."

Bennett smiled half-heartedly, then swiped a hand over his eyes. "Sounds about right. I love that woman, James."

"She loves you too. That hasn't changed overnight. Remember what Gillian said about Lindy and Luis's fight? How important communication is?"

"Yeah, but I've been telling you how she won't communicate with me."

"She may be more receptive tomorrow. Don't send her an email. You've left her all those messages. She knows you love her and want to talk with her. The message she's sending *you* is that she's not ready to talk yet. Wait until tomorrow and try again."

Bennett nodded. "Thanks, James. I better finish my route."

"Okay. Hey, Bennett," he called to his friend's retreating back. "How about coming over to my house tonight and having dinner with us? We have a huge pot of vegetable soup to get through."

"I appreciate the invite. Can I let you know later? I may go home and crash. I didn't sleep much at all last night."

"Sure."

When Bennett left, James gave Jane a quick call and told her what had happened and that Bennett might be joining them for dinner. "I told him it would be vegetable soup."

Jane said, "I'd love to see him. Poor thing. Sounds like he's hurting."

"He is. Listen, Lucy's coming in. I have to go. Love you, honey."

"Love you too, James."

Lucy, dressed in her uniform and a heavy brown sheriff's department coat, walked over to James. "What's going on with Bennett? I saw him outside. He had the most hangdog expression on his face and told me he was too busy to talk."

"He and Gillian are on the outs. It's all about Gillian wanting to show her affection in public and Bennett feeling that, since he's African-American, folks wouldn't approve."

Lucy thought a moment. "Everyone in Quincy's Gap knows they're a couple. I can't picture people being anything but happy for them. I'm not saying it's impossible some idiot would shoot them a dirty look."

"I feel like there's more to it," James mused. "Bennett seemed genuinely afraid when Gillian rested her head on his shoulder."

Lucy raised an eyebrow. "We need to get him alone and see if we can pry into that statistic-filled mind of his. Find out what he's thinking. You wanted to see me? Information that might change the case?"

"Yes," James said eagerly.

Lucy held up a hand. "You'd better hear the news first. And, James, I know you won't like it."

Chapter Seventeen

James braced himself for bad news. "Go ahead."

"Before Murphy could go before the judge on the assault charges, Charlottesville sent us the results on the prints on the cardinal statue," Lucy said. "The killer wore gloves, but there was a smudged print and half of a perfect one. They compared the half-print to Murphy's. It was a match."

"Surely half a fingerprint won't be enough for the judge—"

"The judge charged Murphy with the assault of Kitty Walters and the murder of Ray Edwards."

"N-no, I can't believe it," James faltered. "Where is she?"

"Her lawyer, Cyril Morton, argued for bail. The judge said she was a flight risk because of her financial resources. He did release her on a hundred thousand dollars bail once Morton delivered Murphy's passport to the court. I don't think Murphy wasted any time getting out of there."

"Let me tell you what I've discovered," James said. "Remember how you've said all along that Ray Edwards could only have been murdered by Murphy because she was the only one with the opportunity? You've thrown that word 'opportunity' out over and over."

Lucy's eyes glimmered with anger. "Yes, James. The room was locked. No one else could have gotten inside."

"That's where you're wrong," James said.

Scott and Francis came out of the break room, greeted Lucy, then went to tidy the children's section.

James continued, "Lucy, it was actually something Eliot said that put me onto this information. Jane and I are reading him *The Lion, the Witch, and the Wardrobe*. This morning, Eliot asked me if I could build him a secret closet in his tree house."

Lucy tapped her foot. "What has a child's desire for a trip to Narnia have to do with an opportunity for murder?"

"The secret closet gave me the idea that there might be a secret passageway in the Red Bird. I called Mrs. Lydell this morning—remember Lindy said Mrs. Lydell used to clean there—and she confirmed it. In the back of the clothes closet in the third-floor suite, the suite that Edwards and Murphy were staying in, there's a panel that opens to a passage that goes all the way down to the kitchen. Keep in mind, the house was built in 1888."

"You've got to be kidding me," Lucy said.

"No. This means that someone could have come up from the kitchen, entered the suite from the closet, killed Edwards while Murphy was passed out, then exited the room the same way he or she came. Blows your theory that only Murphy had the *opportunity* to kill Edwards right out of the water."

"It's not just my theory. The whole sheriff's department believes it." Lucy pulled her hair back into a ponytail and secured it. "Who knew about this secret passage, if it even exists?"

"The Lydells, but we've ruled them out as suspects. There's someone else. Kitty Walters."

"She wasn't even in town when Edwards was murdered," Lucy said.

"Do we know that for sure? She could have been staying at a different motel. Maybe she found out about Edwards's relationship with Murphy and killed him in a rage."

"How would she know about the secret passage?"

"Her parents, the Richardsons, owned the Red Bird when it was a private home called Fairbridge. Her real name is Kathy Richardson."

Lucy drew in a sharp breath. "What? How did you find that out?"

"I did a search for 'Kitty Walters actress,' that's how. She had made an off-the-cuff remark to me that she might have been an actress 'once upon a time,' that's why I Googled her that way. Her name brought up hundreds of thousands of results. Anyway, her Wikipedia page gave the name of her parents, the Richardsons from DC, and the fact that they owned Fairbridge."

"Did they own it while the *Hearth and Home* show was on the air?"

"Yes. It was used for the exterior shots. Anyway, Mr. and Mrs. Lydell were sort of caretakers at the house when the Richardsons owned it. The Richardsons live in DC and only used the house as a summer place. I questioned the Lydells after church yesterday and they told me about Kathy."

James filled Lucy in on Kathy's wild past and her move to Los

Angeles. "Walters appears to have been a show business name. Eventually, Kathy—or Kitty, as she was known by then—made her way to Louisville and got engaged to Edwards."

"Kitty is staying at the Red Bird, isn't she? Brandon Jensen offered her his room, but she said she'd take the suite on the third floor. The murder suite. You might be on to something, James."

"Does this mean you're willing to consider that Murphy might not have killed Edwards?"

"It means I want to talk to Kitty Walters. Now."

"I'm going with you. We need to check out the secret passage."

Lucy hesitated a moment, then said, "All right, but you can't interfere in my talk with Kitty. Sheriff Huckabee might not like me letting you tag along on official business."

"Deal," James said. "I just want to check out that passage."

"I've got the patrol car. We'll take it. I hear you've been having trouble with your Bronco."

"It's fine," James said defensively. "But I'll go with you."

James asked the twins to hold down the fort, bundled up against the weather, and got in the car with Lucy. Like her Jeep, the patrol car contained empty fast-food wrappers.

She gave him a rueful look. "I haven't been doing the greatest job on my diet."

Sullie, James thought. *She's upset about Sullie flirting with Amber Ross and is stress eating.* He pushed a wrapper out of the way and sat down. "Don't feel bad. I haven't been good either."

She got them on the road and said, "I wonder if Kitty met any of the actors from *Hearth and Home* while she was in Los Angeles."

"I had that thought."

"What made her choose Louisville as a place to settle when she's from DC? Could it be that she knew Joel Foster? He's based there."

"And he's a partner in the Honeybee Heaven Farms Corporation. Kitty's a Realtor. She said she was going to sell the new houses in the planned development."

"Right. It would make sense that Joel Foster would have introduced her to Ray Edwards."

"Do you believe that Kitty and Edwards were engaged?"

"Pretty much. That handwritten will she has needs to be

examined for authenticity, though. If they were engaged, Edwards was rotten to Murphy. He played her. Which brings us back around to Murphy and motive."

James wanted to keep the conversation on other possible suspects, so he said, "How did the actors react when Sheriff Huckabee told them they'd have to stay in the area?"

"About like you'd expect. They didn't like it one bit. Valerie Norris threatened to sue the department, saying she had to return to her home in Los Angeles and finish writing her latest book."

They crested a rise and the Red Bird came into view. As they pulled into the driveway, James saw Murphy's car. Lucy must have seen it too. She swung the patrol car into a parking spot. "Let's go, James. I don't like the idea that Murphy is here."

Before they could knock, Carol Anderson swung open the door, her husband behind her. "You got here fast, thank goodness, Deputy Hanover."

Lucy and James entered the hall. James saw the actors, minus Valerie Norris, standing around the living room. Joel's face was ashen. Brandon stared off into space. Doug and Amber were looking at their cell phones.

From upstairs, James heard two women arguing. Murphy and someone else. Valerie?

"What do you mean, Mrs. Anderson?" Lucy asked. "Why did you call us?"

The older woman pulled the sides of her cardigan together and crossed her arms. "I told the 911 operator. I went upstairs with fresh towels. In the third-floor suite, I found Kitty Walters dead!" She burst into tears. Her husband put his arms around her.

Lucy and James took the stairs two at a time. On the second-floor landing, Murphy stood with her hands on her hips, anger vibrating off her as she looked at Valerie Norris. Valerie leaned against the wall in a posture that showed a lack of concern.

"What's going on?" Lucy demanded. "What's this about Kitty Walters being dead?"

Valerie said, "Mrs. Anderson came flying down the stairs saying that Kitty was lying against the fireplace hearth—it's brick, you know—with blood running down the side of her head. She felt for a pulse, but couldn't find one."

"You killed her! You killed Kitty like you did Ray. You wanted to frame me," Murphy snarled. "You're jealous of me and have been since my books topped yours on the bestseller lists."

"Murphy, don't say anything else," James warned.

Valerie's lip curled. "Don't flatter yourself, mystery novel writer. I've been in the publishing game a lot longer than you have. I have more fans than you could even dream of. I don't need to kill anyone on paper or in real life."

"You're greedy. Never enough money or fame for you, is there, Valerie?" Murphy demanded.

Valerie tilted her head. "As your favorite author, Agatha Christie, once said, 'A murderer is seldom content with one crime.' I suppose you can't help emulating your idol's words."

Murphy made a sound deep in her throat that James could only label a growl. Lucy stepped between the women. "One at a time, without interruptions, I want to hear what happened."

The sound of footsteps rapidly climbing up the steps caught their attention. Sheriff Huckabee and Deputy Keith Donovan arrived with a forensic team. The latter continued on to the third floor.

Sheriff Huckabee took in the situation and addressed his remarks to Lucy. "What's the state of affairs?"

"I just arrived, sir. I haven't had a chance to view the crime scene."

"We got a dead body and you're chitchatting with the women," Donovan said. "I'll go, sir."

"Who found the body?" Sheriff Huckabee asked. He slid a look at Murphy but didn't say anything more.

Valerie said, "Mrs. Anderson, the innkeeper, did."

"And where were you, Ms. Norris?" the sheriff wanted to know.

"I came out of my room" — she pointed to a door nearby — "and saw Murphy."

Donovan raced back down the stairs. "The Walters woman's been murdered, all right. Looks like someone shoved her, hard, into the brick hearth. There are marks on her neck, too, like whoever did it tried to choke her first."

"Why did you come out here to the Red Bird, Murphy?" the sheriff asked.

"I wanted to confront Valerie and clear my name," Murphy

answered. "She's trying to frame me, like I've been telling you all along."

"Ms. Norris, you were saying that you saw Murphy when you exited your room," the sheriff said.

Valerie patted her blonde hair and slid a glance at Murphy. "Yes, I did see her."

James did not like the way this was going.

"Where was Murphy Alistair coming from when you saw her? Upstairs or downstairs? Think carefully, Ms. Norris."

"Downstairs!" Murphy blurted. "I stopped to talk to Joel about our corporation before I came upstairs."

Sheriff Huckabee ignored her. "Ms. Norris?"

Valerie's brow furrowed. "I'm sorry, Sheriff, but I can't be sure. She was on the landing when I opened my door. She could very well have come from upstairs after she killed poor Kitty Walters like she did Ray Edwards."

"Liar!" Murphy howled. "She's lying, Sheriff. I swear. I met her on this landing. Valerie could just as easily have come from the third floor."

Valerie gave a short laugh. "What reason could I have to kill Kitty Walters? We've been introduced, but I've had little contact with her. Whereas Kitty was Ray Edwards's fiancée. Murphy's been played for a fool. And she knows it."

James tried to put his arm around Murphy, but Donovan edged him away.

Sheriff Huckabee nodded at Donovan. "Place Ms. Alistair in cuffs until I can view the crime scene and interview the people here. Make sure no one leaves."

Donovan slapped the cuffs on Murphy. Silent tears ran down her cheeks.

The sheriff started walking upstairs. Lucy followed. James grabbed her arm. "Don't forget about the secret passageway. Find it and tell the sheriff."

Lucy nodded.

James was left with Donovan and Murphy. Valerie returned to her room.

"Murphy," James began, "I think I've found an explanation for how—"

"Shut it, Henry," Donovan said.

"Why?" James challenged. "Murphy hasn't been charged with anything. I mean, not with Kitty Walters's murder."

Donovan sneered. "She will be. And this time, there won't be any bail for Murderess Murphy."

Murphy opened her mouth, but James held a finger to his lips. "Not now. You'll only make things worse. Donovan, you could at least take Murphy down to the foyer and let her sit down. She looks like she's about to fall down. You don't want a lawsuit on your hands, do you?"

The three of them walked downstairs.

James saw Deputy Truett taking statements from the actors in the living room. He stayed with Murphy until Sheriff Huckabee returned.

"Let's go, Murphy. I'm not arresting you, but I want to question you down at the courthouse."

Murphy started crying again. Her forlorn, wretched expression, so different from the confident Murphy he knew, alarmed James.

Before the sheriff took her away, James pressed her shoulder. "The supper club members and I haven't given up, Murphy, and won't. I promise we'll find out who killed Edwards and Kitty Walters."

"Thanks for saying so," Murphy mumbled. "I'm starting to think I'm beyond any help you and your friends can offer."

Chapter Eighteen

James slid past Deputy Truett and into the kitchen. He called Gillian and explained that Kitty Walters had been murdered and that Murphy was in custody again. He told her about the secret passage and how he felt the supper club members needed an emergency meeting.

"We can meet at my house, James," Gillian had said. "Lindy will be here after school. Come around six."

"May I bring Bennett? I don't want to make you uncomfortable, Gillian, but neither do I want to exclude him." James had crossed his fingers while Gillian took a moment to think about it.

"Yes, he's part of our club no matter what happens between the two of us personally. Please ask him to come. Lindy and I will fix supper for everyone. Let Lucy know."

"Thank you, Gillian," James said and hung up. He called Bennett, who sounded half asleep when he answered. James said, "There's been another murder. We're meeting at Gillian's. She said it was okay for you to come."

Those words served as a shot of espresso to Bennett. "Who's dead? Gillian invited me? Oh, man, I have to shower and put on something spiffy."

"Kitty Walters. Now, play it cool with Gillian. She included you because this is an emergency and we're a team. Don't push it."

"I can be the epitome of cool. Watch me."

While he waited for Lucy, James sat at the kitchen table. He called Jane and filled her in on Kitty Walters's murder and the secret passage. "Honey, I feel bad about leaving you, but I should be home by eight or eight thirty."

"There's no reason to feel bad, James. I'm perfectly capable of heating up some vegetable soup for Eliot and myself. Just think, our son unwittingly gave you a clue that might help your investigation."

James smiled. "Smart little guy."

"He's excited at the moment. We went outside to the mailbox together earlier. He saw that the copy of *Mary Poppins* I ordered came. He hasn't let the DVD out of his sight since then. I'm afraid that, before I knew you wouldn't be here, I promised him we'd watch it tonight."

James groaned. "I wanted to see it with him. Any chance he'll wait until tomorrow night?"

Jane chuckled. "You wanted to watch it yourself, James Henry. Admit it."

"Guilty as charged. I loved *Mary Poppins* when I was a kid. I was looking forward to seeing it again."

"Don't worry. Eliot will want to watch it over and over. You'll get another chance."

James had just ended the call when the pantry door swung open, startling him. Lucy, Sheriff Huckabee, and Keith Donovan entered the kitchen and closed the pantry door behind them. The secret passage! It must lead from the third-floor suite to the kitchen via the pantry.

James stood and looked at Lucy expectantly. She gave him a tiny shake of her head.

Sheriff Huckabee tugged on his walrus mustache. "Henry, Lucy tells me you gave her the idea of a secret passage."

"Yes, sir."

"Well, I appreciate it, but I need you to keep the information to yourself for now."

"Yes, sir," James answered, thinking that his promise did not apply to his wife or the members of the supper club.

Lucy drove him back to the library, tight-lipped. As she waited for him to exit the patrol car, she said, "I have to go to the courthouse. If I'm not going to make it to Gillian's, I'll call."

• • •

James finished his day at the library and drove to Gillian's. He parked the Bronco and crossed the street to Gillian's pink house. From the corner of his eye he saw a man in a dark, pin-striped three-piece suit carrying a bunch of flowers wrapped in plastic walking toward him.

"Bennett! I almost didn't recognize you."

"I've been waiting for an opportunity to wear this suit. Picked it up on sale after Christmas. Fits good, doesn't it? I only had to have the pants hemmed."

"It's handsome. You look great," James said. He didn't have the heart to ask Bennett if he didn't think he was a mite overdressed. Was this his friend's idea of the "epitome of cool"?

"You think these flowers will be okay?" Bennett asked, studying the bouquet critically. "They're the kind you get at Winn-Dixie. Half the men in Quincy's Gap were at the regular flower shop placing last-minute Valentine's orders. I couldn't wait."

"Gillian will love them. You know how she is about all things to do with nature. Let's go inside before we freeze."

They walked up the steps to the wraparound porch. A voice behind them said, "Who died, Bennett?"

Bennett scowled at Lucy. "Can't a man look his best without being accused of going to a funeral? Besides, you already know who died. That's why we're meeting tonight."

Gillian opened the door. She wore a cream-colored tunic with embroidered yellow and red flowers over leggings. Her eyes darted over Bennett's suit, but she didn't comment. "Come in, friends. Lindy and I have dinner almost ready."

They went inside and James inhaled the enticing smells coming from the kitchen.

"These are for you, Gillian," Bennett said, holding out the bouquet. "I know you like flowers. I mean, look at the top you're wearing. A flower lady. That's what you are. Flowers are your thing."

James nudged him.

"Thank you, Bennett. I'll go put them in water," Gillian said politely.

They walked through to the periwinkle kitchen.

"Hey, Dalai Lama," Bennett said to Gillian's tabby cat where he sprawled on the hutch.

The cat hissed at him.

Lindy turned from the stove. "Hi, everyone. Food's ready."

The supper club members sat around the table while Lindy passed plates of Florentine ravioli around. At each place setting, there was a bowl containing a salad of beets and kale. Bennett shot James a panicked look, but said, "That salad is colorful."

Beets were right there with rhubarb and green peppers on James's short but firm "no eat" list, but he said nothing.

While they ate, James filled Lindy, Gillian, and Bennett in on his theory of a secret passage. When he finished, Lucy confirmed that the passage was there.

"But that means anyone staying at the Red Bird could have killed Ray Edwards," Lindy said.

"Anyone who knew about the passage," James said, sprinkling a little extra parmesan cheese on his ravioli. "I figure the only people who knew were the Lydells and Kitty Walters." He then explained how he came to find out that Kitty Walters was actually Kathy Richardson.

Lucy told them that she and James had their suspicions about Kitty's motives because of Murphy's romantic relationship with Ray Edwards, but when they arrived at the Red Bird to question her, they found she'd been murdered.

"How was she killed?" Gillian asked.

"Blow to the head. Someone first tried to choke her, then shoved her hard against the brick fireplace hearth," Lucy said. "Sheriff Huckabee had Murphy in a holding cell when I left. You know, when Edwards was killed, I was certain Murphy had done it. I guess the tricks she's pulled on us, the unflattering way she writes about us in her novels . . . especially the way she disfigured my character . . . I let that cloud my judgment. I refused to even consider another suspect until James told me about the secret passage. But a little while ago, at the courthouse, I talked to Murphy. It's like she's accepted that she'll be wrongfully imprisoned for these murders."

"That doesn't sound like her," Bennett said.

Lucy said, "She's been through a lot in a short period of time, and maybe I'm gullible, but I think it's changed her. One of the things she says she regrets is not being able to preserve the Hayes House and Tavern. She said that she'd imagined that school-children would take field trips there one day to learn more about Quincy's Gap history."

"Murphy Alistair didn't suddenly become a killing machine," Gillian said. "She's a lot of things, as we've all agreed, but murderer is not one of them."

Lucy took the bottle of white wine in the center of the table and poured herself a glass. "Don't anyone faint, but now I agree with Gillian. Murphy also told me that she's consulting with her lawyer as soon as she can about selling Buford Lydell's land back to him."

Lindy said, "Because I didn't like her either, I thought Murphy could have killed Edwards in a drunken fit of passion. But I can't picture her coldly walking up the stairs of the Red Bird, knocking on Kitty Walters's door, trying to strangle her, and then shoving her into the brick hearth. No."

"Who would want to kill both Edwards and Walters?" Bennett asked. "And that someone had to know about the secret passage."

"There has to be a connection between Edwards and Kitty. I mean besides their alleged engagement, which I need to confirm," Lucy said. "As far as the secret passage goes, Mrs. Anderson and her husband claim that they didn't even know about it. So other than the Lydells, it's anyone's guess as to who was aware of it."

"If we assume that Kitty discovered it when she was a child and remembered it, can we also assume that she told someone of its existence?" James asked. "If she was engaged to Edwards and knew he would be staying there, could she have told him?"

"And then he unwittingly told the person who killed him?" Lucy mused, adding pepper to her ravioli. "That's possible. I think the killer is one of those actors."

"Murphy thinks Valerie Norris killed Edwards," James said.

"Valerie strikes me as a *cold* woman," Gillian said. "Both of these murders were committed with *passion*. I don't think Valerie's capable of strong feelings. Remember when the subject of love came up at the reunion, Valerie scoffed at the idea of love's very existence."

"She did," Bennett agreed.

"If we rule out Valerie, then who's left?" Lindy asked. "Amber Ross can't stop looking at herself in the mirror long enough to care about anyone else. Certainly not enough to drive her to murder."

James looked at Lucy. "Lindy's right. Lucy, I told you that Amber doesn't care two pennies about Sullie."

"Whatever," Lucy said. "That Brandon is dreamy. He asked me for my phone number."

"What does Brandon do for a living now, Lucy, did he say?" Gillian asked. "I wonder if, like Doug Moore, he needs money. His face practically glowed with happiness when that TV executive announced the reboot of *Hearth and Home*."

"That could be ego," James said. "Being on television again. Being adored by women across the country."

Lucy put her wineglass down. "You know, Brandon didn't say he had any kind of job. From the description he gave me of the house he lives in—complete with in-ground pool—I assumed that he's independently wealthy."

James had that feeling that he should remember something. He thought hard.

"Where does Brandon live, Lucy?" Lindy asked. "Out in Los Angeles?"

"No, he's in Louisville. That's why I gave him my number. It's possible we could get together for dates since he's not across the country."

"Louisville! That's it!" James said. "I remember!"

"Remember what?" Lucy asked.

"When I went out to Arthur Pritchard's horse farm, he kept me waiting in his study a long time before he would see me. He had a copy of the Louisville *Courier-Journal* on his desk. I read almost the whole issue."

"And," Bennett prompted.

"I saw an ad, a large ad, maybe a quarter of a page, for Walters and Jensen Realty. How much you want to bet that's Kitty Walters and Brandon Jensen?"

Lucy whipped out her cell phone and began tapping on the keyboard. "He never said anything about being a Realtor, much less being in business with Kitty."

"But he *did* seem to know her," Gillian said. "He went so far as to offer her his room at the Red Bird so that she wouldn't have to stay in the suite where Edwards was murdered."

Lucy turned the screen of her phone so that the other supper club members could see it. "Here it is. Walters and Jensen Realty. There's a photo of Kitty, but none of Brandon. The only phone numbers listed are under her name. You'd think they'd put up Brandon's photo to draw in clients."

"Kitty suggested that Brandon might buy into the Honeybee Heaven Farms Corporation. I wonder why he didn't do so before," James said. "If Brandon lives in Louisville and knows Kitty, he's bound to be in touch with his former cast-mate, Joel Foster. It stands to reason he knew Ray Edwards too."

"They're all connected to real estate," Lindy said. "But what would Brandon's motive be for killing Edwards. Or Kitty, for that matter?"

"I need to question him," Lucy said. "First I'll find out what he told Truett in his formal statement about Kitty Walters's murder, then I'll talk to him."

"Guess dating him is off the table then," James said.

"Don't be silly," Lucy said with a toss of her hair. "I might get more out of him over a candlelit dinner."

Gillian had finished eating and held a crystal in her hand. "I feel it has to do with the Honeybee Heaven Farms Corporation. Money is one of the top reasons why people murder. We can't rule out Joel Foster."

"What about Doug Moore?" Bennett asked. "He's a drunk, a thief, we know he needs money."

"What's his motive?" Lucy asked. "If he's broke, he can't buy into the corporation. Still, he bears investigating. So we're down to Joel Foster, Doug Moore, and Brandon Jensen? Do we all agree that we can rule Valerie and Amber out?"

Everyone nodded.

"Lucy, can you get the handwritten will Kitty claimed Edwards had written?" James asked. "We need to know if he actually wrote it, if Kitty was really the beneficiary of a large life insurance policy and all of Edwards's holdings. If we find out the answer to that, maybe it will help narrow down the suspects."

"That's true. I'll check and see who Ray Edwards's lawyer was," Lucy said. "Murphy will know. Sheriff Huckabee would have the information, but I'd rather ask Murphy."

"Is that because the sheriff thinks Murphy's guilty?" James asked.

"I can't comment, James," Lucy said. "Go with it."

"We still don't know who had knowledge of the secret passage," James said to his friends. "Lucy has said all along that someone had to have the opportunity to kill Edwards. Which one of those actors knew about the passage?"

No one had an answer.

"We may not have the answer to that question, but can we

agree that the same person who killed Edwards killed Kitty Walters?" Gillian asked.

Everyone nodded again. Then Gillian got up to clear plates. Bennett jumped to his feet to help.

Lindy said, "Okay, everybody, I've made dessert. It's not on our diet, but I thought since the rest of the meal was, we could have a treat."

"Yes!" Lucy exclaimed.

Lindy brought out a large plate with a golden, custard-type mold. "This is Mexican flan with caramel sauce."

James's mouth watered.

"Oh, Lindy," Lucy breathed. "That looks incredible. You made it yourself?"

Lindy cut slices of the confection and put them on plates. As she passed the plates around, she said, "I did. Alma taught me how to make it."

James forked a piece of the smooth, creamy dessert into his mouth and let it melt on his tongue, savoring the texture and caramel flavor. He was determined to make the delicacy last. After he swallowed, he said, "I'll say one thing for Alma: she knows some tasty recipes."

"Thank you for making this, Lindy," Lucy said. "I've never had anything like it."

"You know," Bennett said, pointing his fork at Lindy. "When I went to Winn-Dixie tonight to get flowers for my wom—for Gillian," he said and then cleared his throat. "I saw that the French restaurant in the shopping center has finally closed."

"I'm not surprised," James said. "Who could afford to eat there unless it was a special occasion?"

"True," Bennett said. "But, Lindy, what if Luis arranged for Alma to open a Mexican restaurant in that location? Luis could get tips on running a restaurant from Luigi. He's done well with his pizza place. And what about this: There's no Mexican restaurant in Quincy's Gap now. The closest one is in Harrisonburg. Could be profitable. And I happen to know from delivering the mail that there's an apartment above the restaurant."

Everyone had stopped eating and looked at Bennett.

"Did I say something wrong?" he asked.

Lindy jumped up and ran around the table and hugged Bennett. "No, you didn't say anything wrong! Luis has wanted to invest in a business. This could be the very thing. Plus, it would give Alma somewhere to live and something to do other than interfere with my marriage! I love you, Bennett!"

For the first time that night, Gillian looked at Bennett and smiled.

Everyone started talking about how popular Mexican food was. They reminisced about meeting Milla when she offered classes on Mexican cooking and the scrumptious enchiladas they'd made.

Bennett sat in his chair staring at Gillian. But she didn't smile at him again, James noted. In fact, she looked sad and kept her eyes downcast. She made tiny folds in the bright yellow tablecloth and adjusted the dolphin figurine.

Gradually, as the supper club members noticed the tension between Bennett and Gillian, their chatter ceased. An uncomfortable silence grew.

"Gillian," Bennett said, "I want to talk with you."

"Not now, Bennett," she said.

"Yes, woman, now. I want to explain why I can't hold your hand or show you any affection in public like you want. I need the strength and support of my friends around me while I do it." This last part came out as a croak, as if Bennett's mouth had gone dry.

Chapter Nineteen

James spotted Bennett's empty glass and said, "Let me get you some more water before you start."

Gillian got to her feet. "I have a diet Dr. Pepper in the fridge." She got it and, when she handed Bennett's favorite to him, James saw that their fingers touched.

Bennett took a deep drink, then said, "I've told you before that I'm the eldest of eight kids. We grew up in Maddox Heights, which is a tiny town, smaller than Quincy's Gap, down near Lynchburg. Back in the late seventies, black folks lived on one side of town, white folks the other. Mama and Daddy worked on the farms. I eventually helped out with money, but that came much later. What I'm gonna tell you about happened when I was a couple of years older than Eliot is now," Bennett said, nodding at James and taking another drink of his Dr. Pepper.

"I don't like the sound of this," Lucy murmured.

"My family lived in a trailer at the end of a dirt road. There were three of us kids then, my parents, and my father's brother, Uncle Abe, who worked in a machine shop in Lynchburg. Wasn't a big trailer, either," Bennett said, his eyes brightening with the memory. "But my mama made sure it was full of love and good home cooking. A typical day for me was to get my two little sisters—Trinity and Grace—up and give them cereal. Then Mama got them dressed and herself ready for work. Then I'd go to school. While I was at school, one of Mama's cousins, Aunt Mimi, would watch my sisters. Aunt Mimi was a nurse and worked nights, so she was real tired by the time she got to our house in the morning, but I never heard her complain. Then, when I got home from school, Aunt Mimi would leave, and I'd take care of my sisters, getting them snacks and toys, until Mama and Daddy or Uncle Abe got home."

"So even as a little boy, you had to be a parent," Lindy said. "There are kids like that in my class."

"I think that's why, as an adult, I've never wanted children of my own," Bennett said. "But I ain't complaining, no, sir. I had a good childhood. Uncle Abe was a big part of it. He was twenty-nine then, the proverbial guy who'd give you the shirt off his back. Liked to cook and grill and would fight Mama for the stove sometimes. Uncle Abe ran the local Cub Scout den. That's how I got involved with scouts."

"You told us once that you made it to Eagle Scout," James said.

Bennett nodded. "Yeah, and it's all because of Uncle Abe. He got me in his troop in the spring of the time I'm telling you about. Man, Uncle Abe's troop was the best. With next to no money, he'd set up scavenger hunts, take us out on nature trails, organize baseball games — or, Uncle Abe's version of baseball, which was a lot like stickball. We used broom handles and a tennis ball because families in our troop couldn't afford baseball bats and gloves. Plus, we saved our money for the big event, camping out. Everybody brought hot dogs to cook over the fire Uncle Abe would build. We'd roast marshmallows and make s'mores." Bennett laughed. "Uncle Abe could tell the best ghost stories too. He'd save the scariest for last so that we'd all run to our tents and hide afterward, eventually falling asleep for the night."

Bennett turned the Dr. Pepper can around in his hands. "One Saturday morning in July, I woke up extra early because I was so excited. I got dressed and packed some clothes in a grocery bag. Uncle Abe was taking our troop on an overnight camping trip. He'd promised to have us back in time for church Sunday morning, but a whole night of camping! I couldn't wait. I set the table with bowls, took out the cereal box, and turned on the old black-and-white TV real low so I could watch cartoons until it was time to go. I was eating Cheerios and watching Bugs Bunny, trying not to laugh too loud at Elmer Fudd chasing him and wake my parents when, all of a sudden, there was a crash behind me. I stood up so fast, I dropped my bowl on the floor, milk going everywhere on Mama's rug."

Bennett blinked a few times, and then said, "My Daddy came through the front door carrying Uncle Abe like he was a child. I knew something bad had happened. There was blood all down the front of Uncle Abe's shirt and his face . . ." Bennett grew quiet for a moment, his eyes misty.

None of the supper club members said a word.

"I ain't never told this story before," Bennett said, his voice breaking. He cleared his throat, and then said, "Daddy yelled for Mama. They laid Uncle Abe on his bed. Mama called Aunt Mimi, and then started cleaning some of the blood off of Uncle Abe's face. His lip was all busted up. Split. They didn't notice me, but I stayed by Uncle Abe's door, watching while Aunt Mimi ministered to him. Daddy told Aunt Mimi that when Uncle Abe hadn't come home the night before, he'd gone out looking for him. He found him unconscious in a ditch down the dirt road, his truck off in the grass. I heard Aunt Mimi say the word 'concussion,' but I didn't know what it meant. I was so scared Uncle Abe was gonna die that I didn't even think to wonder at first what had happened to him."

"Someone had beaten him," Gillian whispered.

"That's right," Bennett said. "The Delford brothers. Three no-account teenage white boys whose parents owned the farm next to the one Mama and Daddy worked at. They took exception to something Uncle Abe was doing. Uncle Abe had a girlfriend that he'd met in Lynchburg. She'd graduated from the private college there, and then worked her way up to an administrative position at a big-name insurance company. I'd never seen her but I knew about her from listening to Mama and Daddy talk when I shouldn't, like I did when Daddy brought Uncle Abe home that morning. Uncle Abe had taken Linda—that was her name, Linda Lloyd—to the movies. They didn't go into the theater together because, as you've probably guessed, Linda was white."

James felt his stomach knot.

Gillian, who rarely consumed alcohol, poured herself the last of the wine.

Bennett struggled out of his suit jacket and hung it on the back of his chair. "Uncle Abe was in love with Linda, and his feelings were returned. The plan was that the two of them would elope up in DC, where interracial couples were more common. Linda's parents didn't know anything about it, even though she was living with them. She hid the tiny diamond ring Uncle Abe had given her whenever they were around. But somehow the Delford brothers found out Uncle Abe and Linda were dating. Lord knows what might have happened that night if they knew the two planned to run away together. As it was, one of the boys saw them at the movies and called his brothers, who called two of their friends. When Uncle Abe and Linda parted ways after the movie, Linda went to get in her car. Way I heard it, two men were waiting for her inside."

"Oh, God," Lucy breathed.

"They didn't hurt her in the way you're thinking, Lucy. Instead, they roughed her up, left her with a black eye, and told her if she didn't stop seeing Uncle Abe, there'd be much worse to come. They also made sure that Linda's parents knew she was dating a black man. As for Uncle Abe, the three Delford brothers waylaid him when he was almost back at the trailer, ran him off the road, and beat him. Three against one. He recovered physically, but Linda had to be sent away to an older relative up north in Pennsylvania, she was so traumatized. I guess her parents wanted her far away, too. In any case, she never came back. Uncle Abe wanted to follow her but didn't have any money. When he'd saved up enough, he found out her relatives had set her up with a white man up there, and she'd married him. Whenever I think about it, I can still hear Uncle Abe sobbing his heart out when he heard."

Bennett sat silent.

"Where is Abe now, Bennett?" James asked.

"He's dead. He never did date anyone else. He took to drinking, the Cub Scout troop disbanded, and one November night on Highway 29, he hit a deer and was killed instantly. Linda's picture was in his wallet when they recovered his body. He was only thirty-three years old."

James blinked back tears. Lucy and Lindy's cheeks were wet. Lindy handed Lucy a tissue and they both blew their noses.

Gillian reached across the table and touched Bennett's hand. He turned his palm over and held her hand tightly. He said, "I've never talked about this before, Gillian. But, do you see now why I can't be affectionate with you in public? Why I can't marry you? Maybe if we were in a bigger area, say, DC, like Uncle Abe planned on with Linda, but we both love Quincy's Gap. We have homes and good friends here. I can handle myself if there's trouble. It's you I worry about. I don't want you threatened. Or worse. I'm scared to death of something happening to you because of me."

"Bennett, it's terrible, to say the least, what happened to your uncle," Gillian said, her face filled with concern. *"Unforgiveable.* And no little boy should have to see hate in action like that. But it's not the seventies anymore." She held up the hand not holding Bennett's. "I'm not trying to minimize the issue, but I believe that people are more tolerant now. I choose to believe they're also more understanding and accepting."

"That's true to a certain extent. I know it's not the seventies. But what about the justice in Louisiana who refused to marry an interracial couple. That was in 2009," Bennett said. "How about those rallies in Charlottesville last year?"

"The organizers of those rallies came in from out of town," Lucy put in.

"No one's saying that racism isn't a huge problem," James said. "But everyone in Quincy's Gap has known that you and Gillian are a couple since you announced that you loved her on *Jeopardy!* That was well over a year ago. Has anything hateful happened?"

"I delivered a certified letter to Mr. Laxman last November. He thanked me, but then asked if I didn't think I was punching above my weight by dating Gillian."

Lucy snorted. "That old fool."

"He may have meant my beauty and perfect figure," Gillian said, adopting a teasing tone. "Not the color of my skin."

If she'd meant to lighten the mood, she succeeded. Even Bennett smiled.

Then Gillian said, "I have never been worried about my safety because of my relationship with you, Bennett. I choose not to live my life in fear. We all know that when you give in to fear, fear is in control."

"True," Lucy said. "I know it's not the same, but think of the hate often directed at law enforcement. I've had the word 'pig' written with shaving cream on my patrol car. Of course, the person who did it could have seen me eating directly out of a can of frosting."

This brought smiles to the group.

Lindy said, "I can't go into my classroom every morning thinking of the tragic school shootings that have occurred in our country. I've been trained, and I am prepared for an incident, but I can't dwell on it."

Gillian looked at Bennett. "I do understand your point of view now that you've told me what happened. It hurts me to think of the pain you carry around inside you from what happened to Uncle Abe and then of losing him. I hurt for Abe, even though I never got to meet him."

Bennett's shoulders relaxed. "Really?"

"Yes," Gillian affirmed. "I love you, Bennett. That's what matters most. I'd rather live my life with you in it even though it means no marriage and separate houses, than have you stressed and worried all the time. Stress causes all kinds of damage to your body that could result in early death."

Bennett expelled a breath. "I love you, Gillian."

Gillian smiled. "How about another slice of that flan? Lindy, there's some left, isn't there?"

The supper club members indulged in another round of the creamy treat, and then everyone got ready to face the cold weather.

Lindy said, "I'm going home, Gillian. I want to tell Luis about the restaurant idea for Alma. I miss my husband so much. I shouldn't have left the house in the first place. We can work things out."

Gillian gave her a big hug. "I know you can."

Lucy said, "Tomorrow morning, James, let's get together and visit the Red Bird. I need to question Brandon Jensen, Doug Moore, and Joel Foster."

"Do you think you'll know about the authenticity of the handwritten will by then?"

"Can't promise that. I'll be going to the courthouse first, though." She frowned. "I wonder if they're still holding Murphy." She punched in a few numbers on her cell phone, spoke with someone, then disconnected. "She's still there."

James sighed. "All right. Why don't you swing by the library and pick me up when you're ready?"

"See you then."

James waited while Gillian gave Bennett a warm kiss. Then the two men walked outside.

"Look at the stars, James," Bennett said. "No snow tonight."

"Nope," James said. He stayed next to his friend in the freezing cold, sensing that Bennett had something to say.

"Telling that story, man, it was like reliving it all over again."

"It was brave of you, Bennett, and showed how much you care about Gillian."

"You're wrong. I haven't been brave," Bennett said solemnly. "That's what I learned tonight. I've been acting like a coward."

"Don't say that."

"No, it's true. If Gillian was black, I would have married her already. I *want* to marry her, James. I don't want fear to control the rest of my life."

"But would the Dalai Lama accept you?" James quipped.

Bennett burst out laughing. James joined in. They stood next to each other, almost frozen, laughing their heads off.

"Have a good night," James said when they got control of themselves. He turned his steps to the Bronco.

"James," Bennett called and then caught up with him. "I don't know the first thing about engagement rings. Would you go with me to the jewelry store tomorrow afternoon when I'm done with my route?"

James grinned. "I'd be honored."

Chapter Twenty

At the library Tuesday morning, James surveyed his kingdom of books. He had to admit that he was distracted. He'd not slept well, thinking not only about the investigation but of the awful fate of Bennett's uncle.

After the second time that he'd woken Jane—and Miss Pickles— with his tossing and turning, he'd slipped downstairs and set himself up on the sofa with blanket and pillows. All set to sleep, he gave in to a confused Snickers's whining and let the dog out and waited until he came back inside. Near dawn, James had finally fallen asleep, only to be roused by Eliot shaking his shoulders and asking for breakfast what seemed like minutes later.

James saw his son off to school and then came back in the house for his packed lunch. Jane had told him that one of the members of their Lamaze class had called and said that Denise had given birth to her twins during the night. Both mom and baby boys were doing well. James avoided Jane's hint about Denise's Ford Explorer.

Now, as he filled the copier and printers with fresh supplies of paper, tidied the bookmark displays, and greeted patrons, James realized he was waiting for Lucy to call. He'd had an idea and hoped she'd go along with it.

The Fitzgerald twins dawdled in the Romance section, where Fern, along with Willow, added red construction paper hearts to the Valentine tree on the wall. Wandering over, James saw that Fern and Willow had blue markers in their hands. They wrote the names of literary couples on the hearts before adding them to the tree. James saw Romeo and Juliet, Elizabeth Bennett and Mr. Darcy, Jane Eyre and Mr. Rochester, and Rhett Butler and Scarlett O'Hara, among others.

Scott said, "Hey, Professor, do you think Jay Gatsby and Daisy Buchanan should have a heart?"

Francis laughed. "Dude, did you hear what you just said? Gatsby had a heart. I'm not sure about Daisy."

Willow smiled.

Fern said, "Their story didn't end well, but a happy ending is not the criteria for selecting couples."

"The love between them is what matters," Willow explained.

"I agree," James said. "Willow, it's good to see you, but I'm surprised Milla let you have time off. The day before Valentine's Day must be one of your busiest."

"Mrs. Henry gave me an hour for lunch," Willow answered. She glanced at her watch. "I'd better start back. See you later, Francis."

"I'll walk you to the door," Francis said. "Don't forget about our super-special plans for tomorrow night."

James saw Willow smile at Francis and silently thanked Milla for the chocolate boxes she promised to put together for Fern and Willow. He suspected Milla let Willow have a full lunch hour today so that she could put the boxes together.

With Fern busy with the Valentine tree, James called Scott and Francis over. "Here you are," he said, holding out a brass key with the words "Do Not Replicate" on it. "Your own key to the library."

The twins gasped. Each one held out his hand to take the key, then they looked at one another. With a nod, they performed some complicated version of rock, scissors, paper, and a grinning Francis plucked the key from James's hand.

James had to smile as he watched them handle the key with reverence. He shook his head and chuckled when he saw them produce a mini treasure chest, no bigger than the size of Scott's hand, and place the key inside.

Turning away, James decided to update his section of the "Staff Picks" rack, when his phone rang. He saw "Lucy" on the phone's screen and couldn't answer fast enough. "What have you found out? Anything on Edwards's will?"

"Good morning to you, too. I spoke to Pat Hearne, Edwards's attorney. She's sent the handwritten will out to a handwriting expert. She promised to get back to me as soon as she hears anything."

"Excellent."

"About the statements Deputy Truett took from the actors regarding the time Kitty Walters was murdered," Lucy said. James could hear her shuffling papers. "Valerie, you already know, was in her room. Amber, Brandon, Joel, and Doug were all downstairs by the fire in the living room on their phones, probably playing games or checking social media. Truett told me that he thought Doug had been drinking. On a hunch, he went by the White Horse bar; you know, that dive a few miles south of Cardinal's Rest?"

"No, but go ahead."

"The woman behind the bar told Truett she's sold bottles of bourbon to Doug three times since he's been in town. She also told him to check with the night manager. Truett did and said the man told him Doug was in one night last week, possibly Thursday. He couldn't be sure."

"The night of the murder?"

"That's right. If it was, then Doug lied to us when they were all questioned the next morning. He claimed to be asleep."

"We need to ask him about it. Here's something else. I thought of a way we could find out if Edwards and Kitty really were engaged. Or, at least, if that diamond she flashed around is real."

"How?"

"I'm going to a jewelry store in Harrisonburg to buy Jane a Valentine's present later today," James said, unwilling to reveal that Bennett was buying an engagement ring for Gillian.

"Nothing like waiting until the last minute."

"Milla is making up a special box of chocolates too. I thought if you could sneak Kitty's ring out of the evidence room, I could take it with me and ask the jeweler if it's a real diamond."

"Whoa. I could get in a lot of trouble if Sheriff Huckabee finds out."

"You can bend the rules one time. How's Murphy this morning?" James asked.

Lucy sighed. "Bad. Not the same woman we know. Depressed and hopeless. All right, I'll get the ring."

"The sheriff hasn't charged her with Kitty's murder, has he?"

"No. He'll have to do something today, though, because Murphy's lawyer will be in here demanding her release. James, Murphy told me that since she's now the major shareholder in the Honeybee Heaven Farms Corporation, she can decide whether to sell Buford Lydell his land back. She only asked Joel if he wanted to sell as a courtesy. Joel has no real say. Murphy also said that as far as she knows, she is the beneficiary of Edwards's life insurance policy, not Kitty."

"Why didn't she say so before?"

"Think, James. The policy is for one million dollars. Some people would kill for that amount of money. She'd only look more guilty."

James whistled. "Murphy didn't want to give Sheriff Huckabee more ammunition against her."

"No, but it's all going to come out. You be ready to leave in about fifteen minutes, okay? I'm on my way."

"Don't forget the ring."

"It's in my pocket. I snatched it while we were talking."

• • •

When Lucy pulled up in her patrol car, James walked down the library steps and got in.

Lucy stretched and reached into her pants pocket. She handed him a small, clear plastic ziplock bag containing Kitty's ring. "Don't lose it, James," Lucy cautioned.

"I won't."

"What are you getting Jane at the jewelry store?" Lucy asked as they got on the road to Cardinal's Rest.

"I'm waiting until I get there to be inspired."

"What about Jane's push present?"

"Her what?" James asked, turning in his seat to stare at Lucy.

"A lot of women ask for a specific present to mark giving birth. That's why it's called a 'push' present. You can give her the present before or after the baby's born, or even in the delivery room. It's usually diamonds. Hasn't Jane asked for something?"

James sat with his mouth open. Then he said, "You have got to be kidding me. Diamonds? We don't have the money for that. Jane hasn't said a word about a special gift. When did this 'push' present custom start?"

"Been a while now, years. Mariah Carey allegedly got a diamond and sapphire necklace from Nick Cannon when she gave birth to their twins. If Jane hasn't asked for anything, then maybe she feels the baby is present enough. Almost half of women feel that way."

"And probably a large portion of the men! This sounds like an idea the jewelry companies cooked up to increase business."

"Probably. You've got a couple of weeks left to ask Jane about it.

Here we are at the Red Bird. Let me zip up my parka. I'm tired of this freezing cold weather, I can tell you that."

But James's head was reeling from the whole "push present" idea and it took the blast of cold air for him to concentrate on the investigation.

When they walked inside the inn, Mrs. Anderson had her foot on the first step to the bedrooms while holding a basket of what looked like clean laundry. "They're in the dining room. That woman, Joy Carmichael, brought food. My cooking isn't good enough today."

James and Lucy exchanged looks, then followed the voices coming from the dining room. Brandon, Joel, Doug, and Valerie sat at the table, the remains of another lunch of sushi in front of them. The actors glanced their way, but only Joel nodded a greeting. James thought the mood in the room could only be described as sullen.

Joy gave them a sour look. "I suppose you'll want to bother these good people with your questions, Deputy Hanover. You too, Mr. Henry. There's nothing I can do about it, but you'll have to wait a few minutes. Sit down," she commanded.

James and Lucy did as they were told.

Joy bustled around like a mother chick, a clipboard and pen in her hands. She wore a gray tracksuit today with her *"Home and Hearth* Always in Our Hearts" button prominently displayed over her heart. "Now, don't worry, dears. I know you all want to go home so you can rest up before filming starts, but while you're being made to stay here, I'm going to take care of all your needs. Brandon, your Egyptian cotton sheets will be here via Fed Ex tomorrow."

"Thanks, sweetheart," Brandon said and gave Joy one of his blinding smiles.

Joy tittered. "I'm expecting another delivery today, and then I can make up baskets for each of you. I have Asian pears, fresh strawberries, crates of baby pineapples, coconuts, satsuma tangerines, all your favorites on the way."

"Organic, of course," Brandon said.

"Naturally! Only the best for all of you. The Kobe beef should be here today for your dinner. Where is Amber? I have the dragon fruit she likes in her morning smoothie ordered."

"She's in her room trying out a new eyeshadow palette for her YouTube subscribers," Joel said.

"Always working so hard! Valerie, your cashmere blanket won't be here until tomorrow morning. I gave the woman a piece of my mind, but she insisted that, because this place is so isolated, they can't get it here any sooner. I'm sorry. I won't use that vendor again."

Valerie flicked a piece of rice across the table. "I'll die in this dreadful cold weather. To think, I could be on the beach in Malibu working on my tan and writing my next book. I have to finish it before we begin filming." She rose. "Unless I'm needed, Deputy Hanover, I'm going to see about obtaining extra blankets from that innkeeper woman."

Lucy shot Valerie a fake smile. "Please go right ahead. We don't want any deaths from hypothermia. The paperwork is unreal."

Valerie arched a brow, but swept from the room.

"I do think she's upset!" Joy cried, looking after Valerie. She glared at Lucy, then said, "How could you be so catty to such a wonderful woman? I'd better go help her unless anyone can think of something else they'd like?"

"I'd like to get out of here," Doug said. "I want to meet with Lenny Matthews from the TV network. I've thought of some important points the writers need to include in my new storyline."

"I'll make sure there's gas in the rental car," Joy said, making notes on her clipboard and then going after Valerie.

Lucy sat forward, opened her tablet, then looked Doug in the eye. "Mr. Moore, with two people dead, I'm not in the mood to play games. I have it on good authority that you left this inn on the night Ray Edwards was murdered. You were seen at the White Horse bar. Now, I'd like you to tell me the truth about exactly where you were that night."

Go, Lucy! James thought.

"The trouble with women," Doug said to the room in general, "is that they can't keep their mouths shut. I suppose that little groupie told you that we met at the bar and she took me home with her."

"Her name?" Lucy asked.

Doug snorted. "Who knows? Cute little redhead. Drove me back here in a truck, though. Not sexy."

"What time did you return to the Red Bird?" Lucy asked through gritted teeth.

"Maybe an hour before that Murphy Alistair started shrieking about her man being dead. I'd just gotten to sleep."

"What time did you leave the night before?"

"I don't know. I was bored at the reception. Only beer to drink. I cut out before it was over."

Lucy said, "I'll have a statement prepared for you to sign. Maybe you won't be charged with giving false information to a law enforcement officer. You can go."

Doug's eyes bulged. He wasted no time getting out of the room.

Brandon smiled at Lucy. "You are a naughty girl, tricking Doug like that."

Color came into Lucy's cheeks. "He needed to tell me the truth, Brandon. And so do you."

"I didn't go anywhere," Brandon said, still smiling at Lucy. "I was watching you."

"You didn't tell us that you're a Realtor in partnership with Kitty Walters either," James said. "Did you know that her real name is Kathy Richardson?"

Brandon's smile faded. "No, I didn't know that. To be honest, I haven't done much with that Realtor business. I agreed to help Kitty out, so I told her she could use my name."

"Are you saying that you're not a licensed Realtor in the state of Kentucky?" James persisted.

"Well, sure I am. It would be wrong of me to present myself to the public as a Realtor if I didn't have a license. I have my reputation to protect."

"How did you know Kitty?" James asked.

Joel said, "Louisville is much bigger than Quincy's Gap, of course, but within the world of real estate and property development, we all know one another."

"That's right, Joel," James said. "You were the one who introduced Murphy to Ray Edwards, weren't you?"

"Sure. Ray had a great business model, Murphy had money to invest. Why not? As a thank-you, they gave me a few shares once the corporation was formed. You'll find it's all aboveboard."

Lucy tapped notes into her tablet. "What about Kitty's relationship with Edwards. Was he engaged to her while he was here in Quincy's Gap romancing Murphy?"

Joel held up his hands. "I don't know anything about that and don't want to get involved."

"Two people have been murdered," James reminded him. "I think you should tell us what you know."

"Okay, okay, Edwards was a bit of a dog. He might have been seeing them both, but I don't know that for a fact," Joel stressed, ever the peacemaker.

"I wouldn't put it past him," Brandon said.

"Why do you say that, Brandon?" Lucy asked.

"Just a feeling. I didn't know the guy except for the few times I saw him at real estate functions. He flirted with every woman he met," Brandon said.

"If you were all in real estate, Brandon, why didn't Edwards cut you in on the development corporation?" James asked.

"I couldn't be bothered," Brandon told them. "And I don't need the money. I'm only doing the show again because I like to act."

Lucy glanced at James with an "I told you so" expression.

James changed tactics. "Murphy plans to sell Buford Lydell back his land. How do you feel about that, Joel?"

"She's the majority shareholder and can do what she likes."

"As long as she's not convicted of murder," Lucy said. "Then you'd get all the shares, wouldn't you, Joel? Didn't you and Kitty plan to run the corporation if Murphy was out of the picture?"

"As I've told you, I only have a few shares. Kitty might have thought that Edwards left her everything and had hopes based on that, but I've never believed Murphy would be tried, much less convicted, of murder," Joel said with a placating expression on his little-boy features. "Actually, it's not just Doug who will be meeting with Lenny Matthews. I have some ideas for the new *Hearth and Home* show that I want to go over with him. With my years as a writer and editor for *Southern Style*, I think he'll listen to a creative person. I'm an actor and writer first, a businessman second."

Frustration threatened to overcome James. Both men were too smooth, too polished, he thought. He didn't believe Joel wasn't interested in grabbing as much as he could of the Honeybee Heaven Farms Corporation. The magazine editor had an excellent motive for murder.

As for Brandon, James didn't think a word out of the man's

mouth was the truth. "Brandon, getting back to Kitty, was her real estate business a success?"

"Yes, it was. Kitty didn't want for anything," he said.

"Did you know she'd been an actress at one time?" James asked.

Brandon tilted his head. "She was? Really?"

Joy came into the room then, a large parcel in her arms. "Are you two still here wearing out my dear ones?" she asked, banging the box on the table.

James looked at Lucy. She said, "We're leaving, for the time being."

• • •

In the patrol car, on the drive back to Quincy's Gap, James said, "I was waiting for you to ask about the secret passage."

Lucy snorted. "What good would it have done? Brandon and Joel were both lying. If only I knew about what. I feel as though I'm missing something. I should be doing better."

"Look at it this way: we're down to two suspects, Brandon and Joel. That's further ahead than we were last night. I wish I'd been able to see the secret passage. I wonder if Mrs. Anderson told the actors about it."

"The sheriff instructed her not to tell anyone while we're investigating. And the passage is a set of stairs, nothing exciting."

"Let me find out about Kitty's diamond ring. Maybe you'll hear about the handwritten will today. Does the sheriff have any forensic evidence in Kitty's murder?"

"No. She had faint bruising around her neck, but nobody would be able to get fingerprints from that. The killer shoved her into the brick fireplace. The medical examiner said that blow to her head is what killed her."

Lucy pulled into the library parking lot. "Call me later and we'll exchange notes."

"And I need to give you back Kitty's diamond."

"If it is a diamond," Lucy said.

Chapter Twenty-one

No sooner had Lucy driven away than Bennett walked out the door of the library and greeted him. "You ready to go, man?"

"Yes, let's take the Bronco."

"Uh, I don't think so. I need to get to the jewelry store today," Bennett said. "We'll go in my car."

James didn't want to argue about the Bronco's abilities, so he got into Bennett's car. It wasn't long before they pulled up in front of Noble's Jewelers. When they got to the door, Bennett said, "I think I'm having a panic attack."

"You haven't changed you mind about marrying Gillian, have you?" James asked.

"No. But look how fancy this place is. I wonder if I can afford anything in here."

"One way to find out," James said and opened the door.

The store's walls had been painted a light gray. The plush carpet was steel-toned, and a large crystal chandelier overhead threw prismed light across the room. Other, more discreet lighting showed the cases full of sparkling rings, necklaces, and earrings to their best advantage.

A tall middle-aged woman in a black pantsuit and royal blue blouse approached them. Diamonds shone from her earlobes under her close-cropped dark hair, from her wrists, and from her fingers. She looked down her nose and said, "Good afternoon, gentlemen. Welcome to Noble's. I'm Priscilla Mortmaigne. How can I assist you?"

James looked at Bennett expectantly. "Go ahead."

Bennett cleared his throat and said nervously, "Engagement ring."

"For the two of you?" Ms. Mortmaigne asked.

Bennett gaped at the woman.

"No!" James blurted and held up his left hand, which sported a gold wedding band. "My friend is getting engaged. I'm here for moral support and maybe a Valentine's gift for my wife."

A crocodile smile spread across the woman's face. "Step this way." She led them over to a case of dazzling diamond rings. "And your name is?"

"Bennett."

"Bennett, what type of ring do you think your lady would like? A traditional solitaire? Something new, but vintage-inspired? Or would you prefer to have a ring made especially for her?"

"Uh, she's not traditional, right, James?"

"Definitely not."

"I wanted to give her the ring tomorrow, on Valentine's Day, so there's no time to have something made."

"Would you appreciate seeing our sale items first?" she asked.

Bennett furrowed his brows. "All right, but I want something Gillian will love and want to wear for the rest of her life."

Priscilla Mortmaigne selected a wedding set from the case. "This is a one-and-a-half-carat princess-cut stone set in fourteen-karat white gold and surrounded by diamonds. As you can see, the matching wedding band is comprised of diamonds, bringing the total carat weight to three. It's regularly seventeen thousand dollars but it's on sale for only thirteen thousand. I'm sure Gillian would love it."

"And I'm sure the only way that Gillian would end up with that ring on her finger is if I robbed a bank!" Bennett said, his eyes wide.

Ms. Mortmaigne placed the rings back in the case. She straightened and said, "Perhaps you'd like to share with me what your budget is for the most important piece of jewelry you'll ever give Gillian."

"Nowhere near the prices you quoted me," Bennett said.

"Very well." She looked at the rings in the case and selected another wedding set. "This is on sale for sixty-six hundred dollars and—"

"Look, Prisc, I'm a working man. I don't have that kind of money in my piggy bank, know what I mean?"

Ms. Mortmaigne stiffened. "We have budget-friendly payments, if that's what you require."

James saw that Bennett was about to lose his temper. He said, "Why don't you let us look around. If we need help, we'll find you."

"Fine," she said. She returned the ring to the case and locked it. "Did you want me to show you something for your wife's Valentine's gift, er, James, is it?"

"Yes. I'm not really sure what I want," James said, thinking of the two hundred dollars he'd had hidden in his sock drawer.

Jackson had always taught him that a man should have a few dollars cash in the house. "She's pregnant and her hands are a little swollen, so not a ring of any kind."

Ms. Mortmaigne brightened. "You'll want a push present in addition to a Valentine's present then. Does your wife prefer emeralds, rubies, sapphires, or diamonds?"

Bennett had walked away to the opposite end of the store. James said, "I better join my friend. Thanks for your help."

James moved to stand next to Bennett, who gazed into a case. "Look at that, James. I wonder if that ring could be considered an engagement ring. I bet Gillian would love it."

"Which one?"

Bennett pointed. "Third row, second from the left. The dolphins."

James looked at the white gold or silver, he didn't know which, ring comprised of two dolphins with their noses pointing toward one another, a diamond held between them. "I don't know if it's an engagement ring or not, but you're right—this is right up Gillian's street, or ocean, as the case may be. She loves dolphins."

"That's what I thought. Got that dolphin statue on the kitchen table in her house and I've seen her wear silver dolphin earrings."

Just then, a young woman with long dark blonde hair walked over. She wore a black pantsuit too, but her blouse was white and was dotted with red hearts. "How are y'all doing today? I'm Shelly. Did you want to see something from the case?"

"I don't know," Bennett said. "That double dolphin ring. Do people give those as engagement rings?"

"Sure," Shelly said. "While lots of couples still like a traditional engagement ring, plenty of women like an alternative to a diamond solitaire. I think the fact that there are two dolphins makes it romantic. Do you want me to get it out?"

Bennett held up a hand. "Before you do that, I'm on a budget."

"Aren't we all," Shelly said and smiled. She used a key to open the case. Picking up the ring, she brought it around and read something on a tag attached to it.

"The rings over in the case up front didn't have those tags," Bennett observed.

"Those are all a set price. Now, this is white gold, which is good for a ring your lady will wear every day. Silver would tarnish and be harder to keep up. The diamond is right at a half carat. Here, see what you think." She handed the ring to Bennett. "I take it she likes dolphins."

"Yes," Bennett said, accepting the ring. He examined it closely. "They have blue stones for eyes. Reminds me of the color of Gillian's eyes."

"Those are one-point each. They're aquamarines."

James silently prayed that the ring would be within Bennett's budget. He knew Gillian would love those dolphins.

"Go ahead and give me the bad news," Bennett said.

Shelly chuckled. "I hope it won't be bad news, but keep in mind I can put it on payments for you, no problem. The retail price is twenty-two hundred, but we have a Valentine's Day sale going on. You can have it for seventeen twenty-five."

"Sold!" Bennett exclaimed.

James laughed. "Gillian will be ecstatic."

"I'm so pleased," Shelly said. "It always makes me happy when a ring meets the right person. Come on down to the end of the counter and I'll write it up. Now, don't worry about the size. There's plenty of gold on this ring. If we need to size it . . ."

James smiled after his friend. While Bennett finalized the deal, James wandered around looking at jewelry possibilities for Jane. He didn't know if he could get anything at all with his two hundred dollars. Last year, he'd bought Jane a sterling silver apple blossom necklace at a fair. She wore it often, but James wanted something more meaningful.

He was at a loss when Bennett returned, a bag in his hand, with Shelly, who said, "Don't hesitate to bring it back if Gillian doesn't like it, okay? We'll find her something else."

Bennett grinned from ear to ear. "I don't even know if I can wait until tomorrow to give it to her. I may pop the question tonight."

"Shelly," James said, "I want to get my wife a special present, but my budget is only two hundred dollars. Should I go over to the mall? Do you have any ideas?"

"What about an infinity necklace?" She walked the men over to another jewelry case and pointed. "See, there are a half dozen of them there."

James peered at the necklaces. "They look like sideways eights. The mathematical symbol for infinity."

Shelly smiled. "That's right. Let me see." She walked around the counter and unlocked it. She picked up each necklace, read the tag, then pulled two out. "This plain gold one is on the small side, but it's regularly two hundred and fifty dollars, on sale for a hundred and thirty-nine. Ten-karat gold."

"That's a good deal, James," Bennett said.

James held the pendant in his hands. Delicate, it did look small.

"Does your wife wear a yellow gold wedding ring like you?" Shelly asked. "If so, that would match it."

"She does. What's that other one you picked?"

"I'll tell you right up front that it's a six-hundred-dollar necklace, but it's been reduced once and now it's on sale too. But I can't sell it for less than two hundred and fifty-five dollars."

"Are those diamonds?" James asked.

"Yes, set in ten-karat yellow gold." She held it up to her neck so he could see what it looked like. James liked the way the tiny diamonds sparkled in the light. And it looked much more substantial than the small plain gold necklace.

Bennett said, "If you get Jane the diamond one, maybe she won't want that push present."

"Oh, is your wife pregnant?" Shelly asked.

"Yes," James said curtly.

"Congratulations," Shelly said with a smile. "I have a little boy myself. He's almost three. I told my husband I'd skin him alive if he went out and bought me some expensive present for having the baby. A healthy baby is all the gift I need. We need the money for other things. My husband did get me a nice gift basket of lotions and spa items so I could pamper myself. They have them over at the mall, if you want to take a look."

James grinned. "I think that's what Jane would say about a push present. If she doesn't, I'll be sure to bring her in here to see you, Shelly, and you can help her pick something out. Right now, I'll take the infinity necklace with the diamonds. I'll have to pay you cash for part of it and put the rest on my credit card." He handed the necklace back to Shelly.

"Come on over to the register and we'll ring it up. Then I'll gift-wrap the necklace. Do you know if you're having a little boy or a little girl?"

"A little girl. Shelly, before we go to the register, may I ask you for a favor?"

"Sure."

James pulled Kitty's diamond engagement ring from his pocket. "I'm doing this for a friend. I need to know if this is a real diamond or a fake."

Shelly hesitated.

"It's not going to break up a marriage or anything if it's fake. It's a confidential situation or I'd explain," James assured her.

Shelly took the ring. "Wait just a moment."

She left Bennett and James at the cash register and went in the back. She returned almost immediately. "I'm sorry, James, but this is a cubic zirconia, not a diamond. It's probably worth about forty dollars, maybe even less. The setting is silver-plated and the cubic zirconia itself isn't even high-quality."

"Thank you. I appreciate the help."

• • •

By the time Bennett and James got back to Quincy's Gap, both had praised Shelly's customer-service skills to the sky. They patted themselves on the back for getting gifts their ladies would love. James felt a lump in his throat when he thought of Jane wearing the diamond infinity necklace.

They were back in Quincy's Gap when Bennett said, "So Lucy let you borrow Kitty's diamond, or cubic zirconia, I should say. Either Edwards took her for a fool or Kitty was lying about being engaged."

"Shelly said it wasn't even a good cubic zirconia. Something tells me Kitty would have known Edwards hadn't given her a diamond. My money's on Kitty lying about being engaged."

When Bennett pulled into the library parking lot, it was after four. James said, "If you ask Gillian tonight, good luck," James said, opening the passenger door and bracing himself for the cold.

"I'm gonna do it right, man. Get down on one knee and everything."

"Don't hurt yourself," James joked. He got out of the car while Bennett was still laughing. When Bennett drove off, James headed toward the library steps. He called Milla to see if the Valentine's boxes of candy for Jane, Willow, and Fern were ready.

"Oh, James, I thought you were Jackson," Milla said.

James could detect her concern over the phone. He stopped walking. "What do you mean? Isn't Pop home?"

"No. He left this morning in his truck. He didn't want to say where he was going. I'm worried. It'll be dark in an hour."

James felt a shiver of pure fear. "Did Pop get crankier or did anything else happen Sunday after Jane and I left?"

"Jackson spent about two hours out in his shed painting. When he came inside, I know he was on the phone a few times, but he didn't tell me who he was talking to."

"I'll be right there. We'll figure out what to do."

James stuck his head inside the library to tell the twins to wait for him. The library closed at six during the winter.

Then he sprinted to the Bronco. While it warmed up, he called Jane on his cell phone and told her he had errands to run and might be late for supper.

"That's fine. I've been eating all day and won't be hungry again until later. I made a skillet pot pie. It's in the fridge. We can warm it up when you come home. How's everything with the investigation going?"

"That's one of my errands. I'll explain when I get home. Is Eliot okay?"

"He's still trying to convince me to get a magic bag like Mary Poppins has."

James chuckled. "I have to go, honey. I love you. I'll be home as soon as I can."

Jane yawned. "Oh, excuse me. I'm feeling extra tired today. Love you too."

The moment he disconnected, James put the Bronco in gear and took off toward his childhood home.

Chapter Twenty-two

James drove as quickly as he dared. Where could his father be? He hadn't had another stroke, had he? James pictured his father lying in a hospital bed somewhere, the doctors and nurses unable to reach Milla because Jackson didn't have any identification on him. Worse, what if he'd gotten confused and wandered off somewhere? No, Milla had said he'd taken the truck. He wasn't on foot in the elements. Maybe he should call Lucy.

By the time James pulled into the driveway and parked next to Milla's Quincy's Whimsies van, he'd worked himself into a state of panic. Telling himself it wouldn't do Milla any good to see him like this, he relaxed his expression and knocked on the door.

Milla answered him almost instantly. "I heard your truck. Come in out of the cold. I've got all of your boxes of Valentine's chocolate on the kitchen table."

"Thank you," he said, wrapping her in a warm hug. "Now, where do you think Pop took himself?"

"James, I'm so worried. This isn't like Jackson. I don't know what to do. Should we call someone?"

"Let's think. Is it possible he went out for more art supplies?"

"I checked the shed. He has plenty. And he's been gone all afternoon. He left after grumbling about how I wouldn't fix him French fries with his hamburger. I made some nice sweet potato wedges, but he wasn't too happy with those. Then I had to go to Quincy's Whimsies for a couple of hours. When I came home, he still wasn't back."

"Did you check for a note? Does he usually leave you a note if he's going somewhere?"

"He does, but there's none. I can look again, though. Maybe I'm overreacting."

At that moment, the kitchen door opened. Jackson's back was to them. He seemed to be trying to haul something into the house. "Come on, now, it's okay. You'll love it here."

"Pop! What's going on? Where've you been?" James said.

Jackson bent down and picked up whatever it was he was trying to get into the house. When he turned around, James and Milla saw that, cuddled tightly in Jackson's arms, was a full-grown reddish-colored corgi. The dog looked around with frightened eyes.

Milla gasped and put her hands to her cheeks. "Jackson! Who is this?"

Jackson grinned. "You'd better learn how to curtsy because this here is Queen Elizabeth. And she's all yours."

Milla slowly stepped forward, her face a picture of delight. "Hello, Your Majesty. May I call you Elizabeth? Or would you prefer Queen?"

The dog whined and Milla let her sniff her hand. Then she petted her and the dog's short tailed wiggled back and forth. Milla said, "Dear, where did you get her?"

"That friend of James's, the one with the red hair and all the bracelets. Gillian, that's her name. Runs that dog grooming place." Jackson gently put the dog on the floor while Milla rushed to get a bowl and fill it with water. "I know you miss Prince Charles, Milla, and I know I've been a bear lately. I wanted to do something for you."

"I can't think of a better gift." Milla coaxed Queen Elizabeth to the water bowl. The dog gave it a good sniff before drinking thirstily. "How old is she?"

"The lady at the rescue center over in Charlottesville, that's where Gillian sent me, says she's only two years old. They said she belonged to breeders who wanted her to have pups. When she couldn't, the breeders took her to the pound. A woman there called the corgi rescue lady and they picked her up. They've been calling her Queen Elizabeth, so you might have to stick to that."

"Poor little dear! I'm already in love with her. Thank you, Jackson," Milla said and started to cry. She sat down on the floor and called softly to the dog, who came to her shyly. Milla spoke to her in a quiet tone while stroking her fur.

James got a tissue from the box on the kitchen counter and handed it to Milla. He turned to his father. "You done good, Pop."

Jackson squeezed his shoulder. "So have you, son. I'm proud of the way you're taking care of your family. Can't wait for the new little one to come. You're a good father. That's what counts. Not being forty pounds overweight."

"Thirty-five," James said, feeling the sting of tears behind his eyes. Only rarely did his father show him any sort of physical affection, such as squeezing his shoulder. And for him to praise his parenting abilities! James felt as if he could fly. He cleared his throat and managed to say, "Thanks, Pop."

"I need to get Queen Elizabeth some food," Milla said.

"Don't worry. The rescue lady gave me a bag. It's out in the truck," Jackson said. "I'll get it while you show the Queen around."

Milla kept an eye on the dog while she washed her hands. Then she handed James three heart-shaped boxes. Each one was red satin. The top one had beautiful gold hand-lettering that read "To Jane, Love, James." James put it down and looked at the other two. One simply said, "Fern" and the other "Willow." "Milla, these are more than I expected. I'm sure they'll be well-received. Thank you."

"No trouble, dear," Milla said, watching the Queen.

James smiled. "I'd better go help Pop."

"Thank you for coming over," Milla said as she trailed after the corgi into the den.

James walked outside. "You need help with that dog food bag, Pop?" James asked, loading the boxes of chocolates into the Bronco.

"I've got it. Jane doing all right?"

"Yes."

"Don't forget now, anytime day or night, when the little one is ready to come, you bring Eliot over. If it's at night, we can come to your house." He lifted the bag of dog food.

"Thanks, Pop. We've got another two weeks."

James waited to be sure his father made it into the house, then he climbed into the Bronco. As he was about to close the driver's door, he heard the hound next door let loose a long, loud howl. James looked at the sky. Clear as a bell. "Probably howling because he knows his new neighbor is royalty," James said to himself and chuckled.

He drove back to the library and gave the Fitzgerald twins the Valentine's boxes.

"Personalized and everything," Scott said. "Fern likes monogrammed stuff."

Francis lifted the lid of one box. "Wow, these chocolates smell delicious."

"Don't start on them without Willow," James warned.

With both the twins pleased with the gifts for their Valentines, they locked up the library and headed home.

James called Lucy before he started out. "Are you at home? If so, I'll come by for a minute and drop off Kitty's ring."

"Come on over. I'll put the dogs out back," Lucy said.

James felt relieved. Lucy had three German shepherds. Being a fan of eighties music, she had named them Benatar, Bono, and Bon Jovi. Whatever their musical connections, James tried to steer clear of the big animals and their sharp teeth.

A few minutes later, he pulled into the driveway of Lucy's clapboard house, noting Lucy's patrol car, not her Jeep, was parked out front. As he walked up the brick walkway, he heard the dogs barking wildly and reminded himself there was a chain-link fence between him and them.

Lucy still had her deputy's uniform on. "I came home about fifteen minutes ago to take care of the dogs and grab a bite to eat. I'm on call. Come in."

"I can't stay too long," James said, standing in the foyer. "I've got to get home to Jane." He pulled the plastic bag containing Kitty's ring from his pocket.

"Let me guess," Lucy said. "It's not a diamond."

James handed it to her. "Cubic zirconia. How did you know?"

"Pat Hearne, Ray Edwards's attorney, called me right at five o'clock. She'd received a call from the handwriting expert. The will Kitty had wasn't written by Edwards. Pat said it wasn't even a good fake. I'll return the ring to the evidence room tonight."

"So Kitty tried to con everyone. Did she really think she could get away with it?"

Lucy rolled her eyes. "Criminals always think they can get away with their crimes, James, otherwise they wouldn't commit them. Brandon said that Kitty didn't want for anything, remember? So I guess this was greed, pure and simple."

"You told me Murphy said Edwards made her the beneficiary of the corporate life insurance policy, not Kitty. Between that and the ring being fake, I wonder what Kitty's relationship with Edwards actually was."

"They were living together in Edwards's house, according to Pat."

James raised his eyebrows. "Well, then they were lovers, at least."

"Possibly. The thing is that Pat told me she never could detect any warmth between them. She said they acted like roommates. Maybe Edwards did love Murphy."

"But if Kitty was successful, why would she need a roommate?"

Lucy bit her lip. "Good question. I wonder if Kitty owned any property of her own."

"You'd think she would, being a Realtor."

"I can find out. Glenn Truett was at the courthouse when I left. He can log into our data information system and find out. He might have already done it," Lucy mused. "Can you wait a few minutes?"

James nodded.

They walked through to Lucy's blue and white kitchen. The microwave dinged. Lucy took a frozen lasagna dinner out and placed it on a trivet shaped like a rooster. She looked at James ruefully. "Closest I could get to the Mediterranean diet in a hurry."

"I had a microwaveable frozen angel hair pasta primavera for lunch. No judgment from me on your lasagna."

Lucy made the call to her fellow deputy. James watched as she wrote down information on the back of an envelope. "Thanks, Glenn. Yeah, go on home and forward calls to me."

She disconnected and then picked up her tablet from the kitchen counter. James could hear the dogs at the back door. Lucy said, "I've got to let them in before they get cold. But listen to this, James. Truett had pulled Kitty's property records. Under the name Kathy Richardson, five years ago she bought a million-dollar home in Spring Farm, one of the wealthiest neighborhoods in Louisville, if not the wealthiest."

"But she doesn't live there?"

"Nope. And Truett says she doesn't rent it out either. Here it is on Google Maps," Lucy said, turning the tablet screen so James could see.

James saw an impressive brick home meticulously landscaped with rich green grass, azalea bushes, boxwood hedges, and a small stone fountain in the middle of the long walkway from the street to the double front doors. He squinted at the screen. "That red car in the driveway. It's a BMW, don't you think?"

Lucy turned the tablet toward her. "I'd say so. Let me see the satellite image. Wow, there's an in-ground pool in the back. Can't tell for sure about the car. But it's not the one Kitty brought to Cardinal's Rest. She drove a Lexus."

James saw the time on Lucy's oven. "I've got to go. We should talk more about this tomorrow. Do you have any objection to me sending out an email to the rest of the supper club members letting them know what we've learned?"

Lucy walked him to the door. "No, go ahead."

His hand on the doorknob, James said, "I assume Sheriff Huckabee let Murphy go."

Lucy shook her head. "Still holding her."

"Really? I thought by now he would have had to release her."

"Not on a possible murder charge, especially since this would be the second one. Her lawyer's throwing fits, but the sheriff's arranged for Murphy to go before a judge tomorrow afternoon. It's likely he'll rescind bail since she's a suspect in Kitty Walters's murder too."

On the drive home, James tried not to think about Murphy in her jail cell. "Focus, you've got to focus," James told himself. *Brandon or Joel? Who had the most to gain from both Edwards's death and Kitty's?*

It had to be Joel. The baby-faced magazine editor must have had a falling-out with Edwards regarding the Honeybee Heaven Farms Corporation. Once Joel saw how big the development plans were and their potential effect on Quincy's Gap, not to mention the national attention the scheme had brought, maybe he decided he needed a bigger share. He could have found Edwards, argued with him, then later killed him, knowing that Murphy would be blamed. But how had he gotten into the room? Did he know about the secret passage?

Then there was the handsome heartthrob, Brandon. Seemingly part of the idle rich, or at least well-off enough not to have to worry about money. James remembered that flash of negative emotion that passed between Kitty and Brandon at the reunion when Kitty said she might invest in the corporation. Why would Brandon be angry about that? In fact, James wasn't convinced when Brandon had said he "couldn't be bothered" with the investment. Didn't rich people jump at the chance to increase their wealth? Then James thought about how Brandon claimed not to have known that Kitty had been an actress. While he knew Los Angeles was a big town, and the two might not have been there at the same time, didn't it stand to reason that Kitty would mention her own acting career when she met both Brandon and Joel since they were actors themselves?

Acting, that's what those two men were doing when James and Lucy had questioned them.

James pulled into the driveway of the house on Hickory Hill Lane. He cut the engine of the Bronco. His heart swelled when he looked at the glow of lights coming from the windows of the small two-story house. Miss Pickles was silhouetted in an upstairs window, keeping watch over the neighborhood.

Inside, James knew his family was there, waiting for him to come home and complete them. Pop had told him that he was a good father, that he took good care of his family. James prayed it was true. His family was his life, the only thing that ultimately mattered to him. It would be that way forever.

He locked Jane's infinity necklace in the Bronco's glove compartment. He'd give it to her tomorrow on Valentine's Day. But as for the box of candy, James realized too late that he should have left it in his office until tomorrow night. He couldn't leave the chocolates in the truck to freeze, so he picked up the box and carried it into the house.

"Daddy!" Eliot called as he raced toward James. James quickly stuffed the Valentine's box under his arm so that he could catch his son. "How was your day, Eliot?" James asked, putting the boy down.

Snickers dashed to the door and barked. James opened it and let the dog out.

"Great! Mrs. Spalding gave us watercolor paints. We made family portraits. Mommy put mine on the refrigerator. Come see!"

"Let me hang up my coat," James told him.

By the time James had put his winter gear away, he heard Snickers frantically scratching the door and let him in.

He followed Eliot, juggling the Valentine box around his back so he could surprise Jane. She was in the middle of pulling out the skillet pot pie she'd made from the oven. James inhaled the smell of the cheddar biscuits on top of the savory mix of vegetables and spices. Once Jane placed the hot skillet on top of the stove, she turned to him. "Hello there, husband."

"Eliot, let me say hello to your mother," James said, disengaging himself from his son.

"That means you want to kiss her," Eliot pronounced.

James stepped over to his wife and did just that. He noticed she had a hand on her lower back. "Your back hurting, honey?"

"Never mind that. What have you got in your hands?"

"A box of Valentine candy!" Eliot shouted. "Can I have a piece?"

Jane's eyes shone with laughter.

James brought the box around and handed it to her. "I can't get anything past the two of you. Happy Valentine's Day one day early."

"How lovely, James. Is that Milla's handiwork?"

"Yes."

"That means these will be the best Valentine's chocolates I've ever had," Jane said. "Thank you. I have something for you, but you have to wait until tomorrow."

"Come on, Daddy! Look at my picture."

James stood in front of the fridge with Jane behind him. Eliot's painting featured himself, James, Jane, a small round glob that Eliot said was the baby, Snickers, and Miss Pickles. The backdrop showed the yellow house under a large orange sun.

"I'm bigger than you," Jane whispered in his ear.

"That's because you're pregnant," James whispered back.

They both praised Eliot for his artwork, James even saying that the picture was good enough to be framed.

When they'd all but declared their son to be another Rembrandt, Jane asked him to set the table.

While she prepared plates for each of them, James switched on the small television. "Oh, boy, here he is," James said, turning up the volume.

"This is a special report from WSHN and Jim Topling, meteorologist." The aggravating man came on the screen, a map of the East Coast behind him. "Neighbors, what have I been telling you? This storm is a devious gal. She's played another trick on us."

"More like, you can't predict the weather," James said.

"That's right," Topling continued, almost as if he confirmed James's statement, "our snowpocalypse is hovering over Pennsylvania, dumping the area with over fourteen inches of snow so far. The lady can't make up her mind when she'll visit the Shenandoah Valley, but trust me when I say she'll be here soon bringing blizzard-like conditions to our entire viewing area. Meanwhile, gents, it looks like you don't have an excuse not to take *your* lady out for Valentine's Day. Our area will be clear with no chance of snow again until Thursday. Stay tuned for more updates!"

"It annoys me no end that he calls this storm a woman," Jane said.

James switched the television off.

After they'd eaten, they each had a piece of chocolate from Jane's Valentine's box. Milla had provided a handwritten guide to what was inside the chocolates. Jane selected an orange truffle while James picked an Amaretto truffle. Eliot had the caramel. Then James and Jane cleaned up the kitchen, put Eliot to bed, and read to him until he fell asleep.

James changed into his pajamas. Seeing Jane was not in their bedroom, he went downstairs, where he saw her putting dry food out for the dog and cat. When she straightened, her hand went to her lower back again.

"Honey, let's get in bed so I can rub your back for you."

"If I can make it up the stairs. I feel like a whale."

Whales made James think of dolphins. Once he and Jane were snuggled in bed, James poured some almond-scented lotion into his hand and began massaging Jane's lower back. He thought of asking her if she wanted a push present, then decided this wasn't the time. He told her of his trip to the jewelry store, leaving out the part where he bought her the infinity necklace and describing the dolphin ring Bennett bought Gillian.

"That's the type of ring I'd think Gillian would love. What made Bennett decide to finally propose?"

James hesitated, unwilling to tell Jane the tragic story of Uncle Abe when he was trying to relax her so she could sleep. "Bennett told me that he realized he was being a coward. He shared a story from his boyhood. I'll tell you about it another time, okay?"

"M'kay," Jane mumbled.

James soon heard her even breathing and knew she'd fallen asleep. He felt himself unwind and relaxed back to his side of the bed, his head sinking into his pillow. He thought he should lean over and select a book to read from the towering "To Be Read" pile next to his nightstand, but he was so warm and comfortable he couldn't move.

His mind drifted back to Bennett and then to Uncle Abe and his camping trips. James could picture little Bennett running around the campfire, playing with his friends, then scared by his uncle's ghost tales.

Suddenly, an image of another campfire presented itself in James's mind. A young Brandon as Joshie, looking sulky and poking a campfire. The special episode of *Hearth and Home* that Brandon had shot on location at the Richardsons' summer house, Fairbridge. The episode that had been shown again at the reunion. Joy had pointed it out to him with reverence.

His eyes snapped open.

Moving slowly so he wouldn't disturb Jane, James reached for his cell phone. He hated using the Internet on his phone, feeling the screen was too small. With a few passes through Google, though, James had his answer. That episode of *Hearth and Home* had been shot in mid-October, at the same time Kathy Richardson's father had sent her out to Fairbridge, in the same year. Kathy Richardson and Brandon Jenson had met all those years ago, James was sure of it.

He'd caught Brandon Jensen in a lie.

James's mind raced with possibilities. Had Brandon been the one Kathy had run away with to Los Angeles? It certainly made sense. Had he been the one to get her started in acting? Had they been lovers?

James thought about calling Lucy, then hesitated. No matter how quietly he slipped out of bed, he ran the risk of waking Jane. Besides, he wanted to enlist the Fitzgerald twins' wizard-like abilities on the Internet to see what else he could find, then put all the information to Lucy. Maybe Lucy would give it to the judge tomorrow and he'd decide not to rescind Murphy's bail.

With this plan in mind, James fell asleep.

Chapter Twenty-three

Valentine's Day morning, the library had an early rush of returns and checkouts. James saw the Fitzgerald twins had everything under control, so he went into his office and opened his email program.

First he sent Lucy a message: *Putting together new info on Brandon. Could be critical to Murphy's hearing this afternoon. Will be in touch ASAP. James.*

Then James looked at his in-box.

From Bennett:

> *James, I'm engaged! Gillian loves the dolphin ring and it fit her like I had it custom-made. She can't take her eyes off it. I went down on one knee like I told you I would. Shaved my mustache off too, like Gillian wanted, before I proposed. Man, do I feel naked, but Gillian showed me how much she appreciated the gesture. Oh, and get this: Gillian says she has a big surprise for me. It's my Valentine's present. Have to wait until tonight to find out what it is, but she said to dust off my suitcase. About the murder, sorry, but neither of us has had much time to think about it. We both think Brandon and Joel are as fake as Kitty's "diamond." Later, Bennett.*

James felt thrilled for his friends' engagement. He wondered how Bennett looked without his mustache and what Gillian's big surprise was. Sounded like they'd be taking a trip. He dashed off a quick congratulatory email, then scrolled to his next message.

From Lindy:

> *Hi James, I'm writing this before class. Brandon and Joel are both actors, so if they want to keep something from you, they'll lie like experts. One thing I wondered about. Did you or Lucy ask Mr. and Mrs. Anderson if they saw anything out of the ordinary the night Edwards was killed? I'm sure Sheriff Huckabee*

questioned them, but maybe they've remembered something since then. Worth a shot. Luis is so grateful for Bennett's idea of a Mexican restaurant here in Quincy's Gap. Alma loved the idea! Luis is going over to see if he can rent the space today. Gotta run. Talk to you later. Happy Valentine's Day! Lindy.

James wrote back and thanked Lindy for suggesting he speak with Mrs. Anderson. He also said for her to let him know the minute Luis knew something about the restaurant.

With no other emails demanding his immediate attention, James left his office. The twins were chatting with the last of the library patrons. James stood in an attitude of waiting to speak with them.

"What's up, Professor?" Scott asked when he was free.

"I'd like you both to come over to the computer station with me. I need your help," James said.

Francis followed Scott and James to the computer desks. "This sounds serious, Professor."

James nodded. "It is. I know you two are wizards when it comes to finding information online."

"True," Francis said in a matter-of-fact tone.

"I need to know everything I can about two people: Brandon Jensen and Kathy Richardson. Kathy also goes by Kitty Walters."

"This is for the murder investigation, right?" Francis asked.

James nodded.

"Cool," Scott said.

Francis positioned himself at one computer while Scott took the one beside him. James stood behind them where he could see the screens. Holding a notepad in his hand, he said, "I think that Brandon Jensen filmed an episode of *Hearth and Home* at the Red Bird, which was known as Fairbridge at the time, in the middle of October."

Both twins typed on their keyboards. Scott said, "Filmed October fifteenth through October twenty-first, 1990. The episode was called 'We Don't Speak French Here.'"

James jotted down the confirmation of what he'd found last night. He thought for a moment of the young heartthrob and the nineteen-year-old Kathy rambling around Fairbridge together. Not for one second did James believe Kathy hadn't shown Brandon that secret passage. He could picture them laughing as they ran up and down the stairs in a romantic game of hide-and-seek.

"Professor?" Scott said.

"Next," James said, "I Googled when Kathy, or as she was known, Kitty Walters, started acting, but I didn't mark the date."

Francis said, "According to Wikipedia, 1991. Kitty Walters was twenty at the time. She played a waitress on *Roger That!* A cop show that filmed in Los Angeles." He turned and looked at James. "You're trying to establish a history of these two people as what, a couple?"

"That's part of it," James said as he made more notes.

Scott said, "In that case, let's see what we can find out about them."

Francis and Scott tapped away on their keyboards.

Scott said, "Look at this on Google images. It's from an old tabloid article. Dude, the two of them are wasted."

James looked at the photo. Kitty, her blonde hair permed and falling in wild curls down her back, clung to Brandon as the two exited a bar on the Sunset Strip in Hollywood.

"Uh-oh," Francis said. "Better look at this one. It's from a tabloid too, but there's a really grainy photo of them supposedly using a white powder. We all know what that's code for."

James read the headline over the photo: *Joshie's Coke Shame!*

Scott said, "In this article, *Hearth and Home*'s publicist denied that Brandon had ever done drugs. There's a photo of him with the actor who plays his dad on the show. They're at the beach with some of the other cast members and some hot girls playing volleyball."

"I've got another photo of Brandon and Kitty together," Francis said. "It's from an after party the night of the Emmys in 1999. But there's also plenty of images of Brandon with other actresses over the years. Then another one of him and Kitty in 2008 at a twenty-year reunion of sorts of *Hearth and Home*. Nothing official. Looks like it was taken at a restaurant, but they're all there, including dates."

"That actress that's an author doesn't have a date," Scott pointed out.

"She wouldn't," James said. "Somewhat of a loner. Seems that Brandon and Kitty have had an on-and-off relationship since they met. Why would she keep taking him back?"

"Maybe they never broke up. They could have an open relationship," Scott said with an expression of disgust.

"Neither one of them ever got married," Francis reported.

"All right," James said. "I need to know where Brandon lives now. He's in Louisville, but I want the exact address. If you could find out about his finances, that would be helpful too."

"You don't have his social security number, do you?" Scott asked.

"No."

Francis said, "I've got his date of birth. It's here on a fan page someone made along with his birthplace. He's actually from Louisville. Give us a few minutes, Professor. We need to access public records."

"And some not-so-public records," Scott added.

James waited patiently. Now he understood why Brandon had offered Kitty his room so that she wouldn't have to stay in the third-floor suite. It was because they'd been involved for years and were at least friends, if not more. But what was Kitty's relationship with Edwards? There was that look Brandon and Kitty exchanged at the reunion. James guessed they'd argued about Edwards.

"Got Brandon's address," Francis said. He rattled it off.

"Google Map it for me, would you?" James said, knowing what he'd see. Sure enough, when Francis pulled it up, it was Kitty's house in Spring Farm. Brandon had told Lucy he lived in a house with an in-ground pool. He hadn't told her it was Kitty's house. "Drives a BMW?"

While Francis typed, James wondered why Kitty would let Brandon stay in her house rent-free while she lived with Ray Edwards. She must have still cared for him deeply. And surely Brandon wouldn't murder the woman who was letting him live in her house without paying.

"Right, a red 2010 BMW," Francis said.

"Whoa, Professor, listen to this," Scott said. "I've got his credit report. Brandon Jensen's in some deep debt. His credit cards have been maxed out and cut off. He owes them over two hundred thousand dollars. But his major creditor is the Belvedere, an online gambling site. He's in for over six hundred thousand dollars."

James saw a library patron standing at the checkout counter, giving them a frustrated look. "See if you can find anything else. I'll be right back."

While automatically taking care of the man and exchanging pleasantries, one thought kept going through James's head: Brandon desperately needed money. What did he do with the money he got from the show? Maybe he did have a drug problem. Gambling could be an addiction too.

When he rejoined the twins, Francis said, "It says on this fan site run by Joy Carmichael that there's going to be a reboot of *Hearth and Home*."

"That's true. They announced it at the reunion," James said. "Maybe Brandon was planning on paying off his debts with money from the new show."

"Possibly. He could do that if he stopped gambling," Scott said. "But dude needs to clean up his financial mess stat. The tabloids will start to look for stories about the cast before the new show starts. Trash like, 'You Won't Believe What Josh Has Been Up To!' Wouldn't go with the wholesome image of the show for one of the leads to be a known gambling addict."

James looked out the library window, the snow falling barely registering in his mind. He wanted to talk to Brandon Jensen. Now.

"Here's one other thing," Francis said. "The Louisville *Courier-Journal* reported in March of 2012 that a newly formed development company called Edwards-Jensen had been dissolved after a project in Nashville fell through."

That did it. "The two of you will have to hold down the fort," James said. "I'm going to see Brandon Jensen."

"Hold on, Professor," Scott said, standing up. "This guy could be a murderer."

"I'll call Lucy and get her to meet me. Don't worry," James said.

He shrugged into his heavy coat, wrapped a scarf around his neck, and pulled on his gloves. When he opened the library door and stepped outside, he saw the snow coming down briskly in fine flakes. About an inch had accumulated already and it was sticking to the street.

James cleaned the snow off the Bronco, let it warm up, and began his trip down to Cardinal's Rest. He drove carefully, using his windshield wipers to clear the snow so he could see. His mind focused on a confrontation with Brandon. He was grateful he had his notes in case Brandon, in his suave way, denied what James knew to be true. He wondered if he could get Brandon away from the other cast members so they could speak in private. Maybe Brandon would slip and say something incriminating if he felt relaxed and not on his guard.

With these thoughts claiming his attention, James forgot all about calling Lucy.

Chapter Twenty-four

James knocked the snow off his shoes, then entered the Red Bird. No one was around. James walked back to the kitchen. In the rounded sunroom area where the oak table stood, the blinds had been raised over all six double windows, showing an ever-whitening world outside. He found Mrs. Anderson standing by the stove. She looked at James and said, "It's true. A watched pot never boils."

James smiled. "Smells good. What are you cooking?"

"Lentil and vegetable stew with Moroccan spices, although I don't know who in this bunch will eat it." She stirred the spicy mixture. "Seems they only want their own special food."

"Are you here by yourself? Where's Mr. Anderson and the actors?"

"My husband drove into Quincy's Gap for supplies in case this is that big snow Jim Topling keeps promising us. You must have passed him on the road. The cast members are all in their rooms. Yesterday they didn't come downstairs until lunchtime. Seems like that's their new schedule. Of course, that Joy Carmichael runs their lives," she said with a grimace.

"Is Joy here now?"

"Oh, yes. Amber Ross slept late. Joy took her a vile-looking smoothie a few minutes ago."

"Mrs. Anderson, I need to speak with Brandon. What room is he in?"

"Number four, that's on the second floor."

"Thanks." James started to head up the stairs, then remembered Lindy's suggestion. "Mrs. Anderson, I know the sheriff's team questioned you after Ray Edwards's body was found, but I wondered if you remembered anything else about that night."

Mrs. Anderson tapped the spoon on the side of the pot, then set it on the spoon rest. "No, I haven't. It may sound selfish, but Brian and I have been worrying about how these murders are going to affect our business. We barely get by as it is."

James stuffed his gloves into his pockets. "I understand. I've spent plenty of sleepless nights in my time worrying about money."

Her eyes widened and she turned to him. "That's funny. When you said 'sleepless,' I remembered something. You see, I couldn't sleep the other night and wanted a midnight snack. Brandon couldn't sleep either. He had come downstairs for a glass of milk. Poor thing was rummaging around in the pantry looking for a glass when I walked into the kitchen. I poured us each a glass of milk and got out some cookies left over from the reception. Brandon asked me about the profitability of running a bed-and-breakfast. We sat at the kitchen table chatting until he felt like he could go back to sleep."

The pantry. Where the secret passage from the third floor ended. James felt his muscles tense. "Was this the night of the reception?"

"Yes. The night Ray Edwards was murdered. Brandon must have heard something that disturbed his sleep."

If there had been any doubt in James's mind about the identity of the killer, it was gone. "You've been very helpful. I'll go talk to him now."

She turned back to the stove. James unbuttoned his coat and walked fast toward the stairs. He didn't want to encounter the nosy Joy or anyone else. He took the steps two at a time. On the landing, he searched for number four. Finding it, he knocked.

Brandon opened the door. He had on jeans and another expensive-looking sweater, this one in a dark gray. He hadn't shaved and his eyes looked different. It took a second, but then James realized Brandon's pupils were huge. He'd been doing coke. "What can I help you with, James, isn't it?"

"I wanted to talk for a few minutes, if you have the time."

Brandon waved him inside. As soon as the door was shut behind him, James felt a twinge of fear, but he brushed it away. He took in his surroundings. His gaze went to the fireplace mantel first, where a pair of the inn's signature glass cardinals stood. A wood fire crackled and burned brightly. The king-size bed had been covered with a thick red and gold comforter and matching skirt. James wondered if Brandon had gotten his Egyptian cotton sheets.

A wool Oriental rug in shades of red, cream, and blue covered the hardwood floor. Two stuffed chairs with blue velvet upholstery were positioned on either side of a glossy wood table, where Joy's basket of fruit had been placed. A few flecks of white powder were visible on the table next to a credit card and a short straw. From everything James had read on the subject, he knew that using coke normally made a person confident. Hopefully, it would make Brandon careless and loosen his tongue.

"Care to sit down?" Brandon asked, dropping into one of the chairs.

James took the other. "Thanks. I'm sorry about Kitty's death. I know the two of you were close."

Brandon drew in a breath. He didn't meet James's gaze. Instead, he looked toward the fire. "Guess I wasn't going to be able to keep our history a secret now that everything I do is on the Internet."

"Why did you try?"

"Edwards. She didn't want Edwards to know about us. That's what she told me. Tried to convince me she really loved that buffoon. I knew better."

"Oh?" James kept his tone conversational.

"All part of her plan to make me jealous enough that I'd finally ask her to marry me. It didn't work. I'm not the marrying kind. Hard to be faithful to one woman. At least it is for me. You want a drink?"

James saw the glass decanter filled with a light brown liquid and the matching glasses next to it. "Too early for me."

"Not for me," Brandon said and poured a glass. He moved the decanter within reach.

James rose to his feet and went to the window, pretending to look at the snow. With what he had to say next, he felt better standing. "Did you argue about getting married?"

Brandon scoffed. "Are you kidding? All the time."

"Things got heated, I bet."

Brandon took a drink and closed his eyes. "We always made up. Couldn't stay away from each other. Twenty-eight years. Imagine that."

"Must have been the mother of all arguments when you pushed her into the fireplace hearth. You didn't mean to kill her. It was just another fight." James held his breath.

Brandon put his glass down and shot to his feet. "I never meant to hurt Kitty. She fell. It was an accident."

James nodded, his heart beating fast. "I knew you wouldn't hurt her from the time you offered to take the third-floor suite and give her this room."

"I was good to her in all the ways I could be. I loved her, had loved her since we met right here in this house. We were kids, but I fell for her. I never stopped loving her. And now she's gone." The actor paused, then with a smirk he said, "All because two people fell in love."

James recognized the *Hearth and Home* saying. "I know that Kitty loved you. She let you live in her house and helped you plan to get out of debt when you found out about the *Hearth and Home* reboot," James guessed.

"You know about that too?" Brandon asked, his intense gaze causing James to feel another twinge of fear.

James held up a hand. "Hey, we all have things we can't give up. With me, it's overeating. I love food. With you, it's gambling."

"Those bastards at the Belvedere were forcing me into bankruptcy. You know what the tabloids would have made of that? The producers don't care what I do in my private life, but the fans would have. Their dear, sweet Joshie, a hardened gambler," Brandon sneered. "They wouldn't have watched the new *Hearth and Home*. The show would tank. I told Kitty I'd kill myself before I went through that kind of humiliation."

James felt his fear dissipate. In its place, anger rose at Brandon's emotional blackmail tactic. "And the thought of you committing suicide must have frightened Kitty badly. First you hoped you could convince Edwards to let you in on the Honeybee Heaven Farms Corporation, make the money that way, but he said no. The two of you had tried to work together before—"

Brandon pointed at him. "The failure of the Nashville deal wasn't my fault. So I was doing a little coke, who doesn't?"

"Then you had to try something else. Was it Kitty's idea to kill him?"

Brandon didn't answer. A wary look came into his eyes.

James said, "Who made up the forged will? You? Kitty buys herself an engagement ring, she's got the will, and then when Edwards is dead, she'll have the million-dollar insurance payoff. She'll be able to wipe out your debts. A clean slate before news gets around about the new show. Then, if the development went through, she'd make a fortune selling houses. With your income from the new show, neither of you would have to worry about money. That is, as long as you stopped gambling."

"I'd have to marry her and go to counseling. Those were her terms," Brandon said in a cold voice. "I did try to reason with Edwards first. The night of that reception. I asked him again if he'd front me the money to get in on the development deal. But he was drunk and with that woman, Murphy Alistair. He wouldn't listen to me."

"And then the only way was to carry out the plans you and Kitty had made. You waited until Edwards and Murphy went to bed, passed out drunk. Then you used the secret passage you'd learned about all those years ago to get into their suite. You picked up the cardinal and bashed him in the head, leaving Murphy to take the blame. Because," James stated, not bothering to hide his ire, "like all womanizers, you really don't like women at all. That's why it was okay by you if Murphy took the fall and okay by you to be violent when you argued with Kitty. Only this time, you killed her."

Brandon smashed the glass decanter on the side of the table. Liquid spread across the wood. He held the broken glass in front of James's face. "You know what, librarian, you know too much. What difference will a third dead body make?"

James looked at the sharp slice of glass and didn't hesitate. He lurched forward toward the door to the bedroom.

Before he could grasp the doorknob, the door opened inward, revealing Joy Carmichael framed in the doorway. She held a pistol pointed right at James's heart.

In that second, James thought he would die without seeing his baby daughter. Without ever holding Jane in his arms again. Without reading the rest of *The Lion, the Witch, and the Wardrobe* to Eliot. Without seeing his friends again.

He backed into the room. Joy stared into his eyes, and what James saw there, and in the set of her mouth, was grim determination.

Holding the pistol steady and never taking her gaze from James, she said, "Brandon, dear, put what you need into your duffle bag. We're leaving."

Brandon threw open the closet door and began rapidly stuffing clothes into his case.

James said, "He's killed two people, Joy. Ray Edwards and Kitty Walters."

"I know," she said in a voice that lacked concern. "I know everything about my dears."

"Where are we going, Joy?" Brandon asked, pulling on a coat.

"To the airport in Charlottesville, then back to Los Angeles. We'll say you couldn't handle your grief at losing Kitty and needed to go to rehab. The fans will accept that."

"Good thinking," Brandon said. "I don't know what I'd do without you, Joy."

Joy smiled. "You'll always have me. Go ahead and get in the rental car. I'll be right behind you."

Brandon glared at James. "This is your fault. Joy wouldn't have to kill you if you had kept your nose out of my business." He went out the door. James could hear him running down the stairs.

Joy closed the door behind him. "Now, Mr. Henry, you must listen to me."

James looked around wildly for a weapon. Fireplace poker. Too far away. The broken glass decanter. He'd never be able to cut her with it. Maybe if he ran past her, he'd still get shot, but her aim would be off, and the shot wouldn't be fatal. James felt as if his heart would explode any second, saving Joy the trouble of killing him.

"Listen to me, Mr. Henry!" Joy repeated. "I'm not going to kill you. You won't be able to prove that Joshie, I mean Brandon, murdered anyone. I'm leaving with Brandon. The wholesome legacy of *Hearth and Home* must be maintained. For everyone: the cast and all the fans across the world. That's what is most important. Don't forget."

Before James could form another thought, Joy's arm swung toward him in an arc, the gun coming down, closer, closer, then darkness.

Chapter Twenty-five

"Mr. Henry, are you all right?" Mrs. Anderson asked. "Mr. Henry!"

James came awake and stared at her. "Am I bleeding?"

"Not that I can see," she said. "Here, try to sit in this chair. Goodness, is that white powder what I think it is? And what a mess Brandon made with this bottle. Watch where you step."

James slowly sat up. He put his hand to his head but felt no blood or lumps. "I'm not injured?"

Mrs. Anderson examined his head. "No. Did you have a shock? You may have fainted. Let me get a cold cloth." She went into the bathroom and James could hear the water running.

Had he collapsed at the thought of Joy's gun crashing into his head? If so, James didn't know whether to be happy he wasn't seriously injured or embarrassed. He cautiously moved to the chair.

Mrs. Anderson returned and put the cloth on his neck.

"Thanks, I feel better," James said and found that he did. He had to call Lucy. "Mrs. Anderson, did you see Brandon leave?"

"Yes, he and that awful woman, Joy, left in the rental car. They didn't even stop to say anything to me."

"What kind of car was it? Do you have the license plate number?"

"Oh, I don't know much about cars. You'd have to ask my husband when he comes back. The car was black, I know that. We don't write down license plate numbers like the big hotels do."

James stood. "Thanks anyway. I need to leave."

"Are you sure? This snow is worrying. Will you be able to make it back to Quincy's Gap?"

James saw no need to tell her he wasn't going to Quincy's Gap. "Yes, but please have your husband call me the second he returns and tell me what model rental car Joy's driving. It's very important."

"I will," Mrs. Anderson promised.

Joel came out of his room. "What's going on?"

James didn't pause to answer him. He had to stop Brandon and Joy. He ran downstairs and swung open the front door. Snow hit him in the face. The flakes were flying fast. There were about three more inches on the ground than when he'd come in.

Silently cursing Jim Topling and his "no snow on Valentine's Day" forecast, James trudged out to the Bronco. The truck would make it through the snow, he told himself. He turned the engine over. While it warmed up, he called Lucy.

The phone rang and rang until James got her voice mail. He'd have to leave a message. "Lucy! Brandon killed Edwards and Kitty. He admitted it to me. He and Joy are headed for the Charlottesville airport. You've got to stop them or get someone to the airport to pick them up. They're in a dark-colored rental car. I'm waiting on a call from Mr. Anderson at the Red Bird for more information on the car. Call me so I know you got—" The voice mail cut off.

James got on the road that would take him past Quincy's Gap and up to the small town of Elkton. There he would get on the Spotswood Trail, Route 33 East. He didn't know what else to do. His head still felt fuzzy.

The phone rang. "Professor," Scott said, "we got a call from the board telling us to close the library."

"Do it," James said without hesitation. "You and Francis can lock up."

"We'll put a note on the door and call the TV station so they can announce it in their list of closings. Then we're going snow-boarding!"

"Thanks. I don't know what I'd do without the two of you. Be safe," James said and disconnected.

The roads weren't too bad but the snow came down almost like a blizzard. As he drove, he had the Bronco's windshield wipers on high. Even though it wasn't even one o'clock, the day had darkened.

He thought about calling 911. What would he say? *A famous actor admitted to me that he killed two people. He's on his way to Charlottesville with the head of his fan club.* Would the 911 operator believe him? Doubtful.

His phone rang again. James fumbled to tap "Answer." He hated driving and trying to use the cell phone. "Hello."

"Mr. Henry, this is Brian Anderson out at the Red Bird."

"Yes, what about that rental car?"

"It's a Nissan Altima. Got Virginia plates, but we never take down numbers here. I've got Joy Carmichael's credit card number, though, if this is serious. You can understand that I can't give out personal information unless there's an emergency."

"There is, I promise you."

"All right."

James saw the turnoff for Route 33. "Can you do me a favor, Mr. Anderson? Call Deputy Lucy Hanover and give it to her. If she doesn't answer, call the sheriff's office and tell them Brandon Jensen is trying to leave the state. Give them the information on the car and the credit card."

"Okay, wh . . . her . . . ber?"

The call was breaking up. James gave Lucy's number and asked Mr. Anderson to repeat it. He had to do it three times with the bad reception, but when he disconnected, he was sure the innkeeper had the correct information.

James sat forward in his seat, trying to see through the snow, making sure the Bronco stayed on the road. Ten minutes passed. Looking in his rearview mirror, he saw no one behind him. He slowed and tried to call Lucy again.

"James!" she said. "I got your message."

"Lucy, thank God. Brandon told me everything. He and Kitty planned to kill Edwards so they could get Brandon out of debt. Brandon promised to marry Kitty and—"

"Later, James! Mr. Anderson called me. We've got the rental car info from Joy's credit card company and patrol cars are on the way. We figure they're taking Route 33 to Charlottesville. It's the fastest, but Sheriff Huckabee sent Donovan down the secondary roads just in case. Albemarle County is stationing law enforcement at the entrance to Highway 29 from Route 33. Brandon and Joy aren't going to make it to the airport."

"They could be going down to Interstate 64," James said.

"I doubt it. That way is longer. I'm on Route 33 now."

"I'm on Route 33 myself. Lucy, Joy said something strange to me about the show. Lucy? Lucy!"

The call had dropped out.

James tried to decide if he should turn around and go back to Quincy's Gap. It wouldn't be cowardly. Law enforcement had the roads covered, according to Lucy. But he wanted to be there when they caught Brandon and Joy. Besides, he was on a two-lane curving road. If he decided to turn back, he still had to wait for an opportunity to turn around.

Several miles later, he saw a place to turn. He struggled with himself, then figured it would be best to turn around. He had to ease into the turn, as he was at a higher elevation now and the road was slippery.

James's cell phone rang. He didn't dare not answer it. "Yes."

"James," Lucy said in a matter-of-fact tone. "Turn around and go back to Quincy's Gap. We found them. Brandon and Joy are dead."

James jerked the Bronco to a stop. He slid a bit but got the vehicle under control. He sat idling on the side of the road. "What happened?"

"It's bad. I don't want you to see it. State trooper on the scene says the car was likely going a hundred miles an hour, hit the guardrail, and went airborne. It slammed into the cement pole of an overpass. No survivors."

James swallowed hard. He thought about Joy's words. "Lucy, Joy's last words to me were very insistent. She said, 'The wholesome legacy of *Hearth and Home* must be maintained.' Do you think she deliberately made the car run off the road?"

There was a long pause. "It's possible she did, knowing how fanatical she was about the show. There are no skid marks," Lucy added glumly. "But with the snow and the slick conditions . . . I don't know. I have to go. Sheriff Huckabee is staring at me. I'm going to tell him that you'll be in to make a statement as soon as you can with the weather being what it is."

"I'll head back to Quincy's Gap right now and come straight to the courthouse."

"See you there." She disconnected.

James covered his face with his hands. Joy. Obsessed with the show, its legacy, to the bitter end. *Don't forget,* she'd said. She'd killed Brandon and herself rather than see the show tainted, ruined for all its fans by Brandon's actions. James believed her sacrifice would be in vain.

He put his hands on the wheel and looked around to make sure he could turn safely, then gave the Bronco some gas. He noticed the temperature gauge was alarmingly near the hot zone.

The engine cut off.

"What?" James said to no one. "Come on, Bronco, you are not seriously going to start this—or not start—okay, let's not play around. We're in a blizzard here, no thanks to that Jim Topling. I have to get to the courthouse and give that statement so Sheriff Huckabee will release Murphy."

He tried the ignition again.

Nothing.

The truck was dead.

Chapter Twenty-six

James took a deep breath and told himself to remain calm. It wouldn't do him any good to freak out. He exited the truck and opened the hood. Snow flew in a white tunnel all around him. He could make out the trees that were on either side of the road, but the road itself was white. The only tire tracks were his.

His gaze went to the battery and the connecting wires. Everything looked fine to him. *But what do I know?* James thought. *Nothing, that's what.* He needed to call someone. Not for the first time, James regretted not paying what he considered the exorbitant annual fee for a roadside service. There was nothing he could do about it now, though. He had to call a tow truck from Harrisonburg.

Ten minutes later, James had exhausted all of his possibilities. No tow trucks were available due to high demand because of the snow.

There was only one other option: Ace, the mobile mechanic.

Freezing cold, James fumbled in his pocket and pulled out his wallet looking for the man's phone number.

His cell phone rang.

James answered the call without even looking at the caller ID, hoping it was someone calling him back to say they could tow him after all.

"James," Jane said.

"Hi, honey," James said with as much cheer as he could muster. Maybe he could avoid telling her he was, yet again, stuck on the side of the road.

"James, I'm sorry to call you while you're at the library, but I—oh!"

"Jane! Jane, are you all right?" He heard his wife breathing rapidly. "Jane!"

"I'm okay," she said after an agonizingly long few seconds. "It was another contraction. I've been having them since right after you left for work."

James looked at his watch. "That was five hours ago!"

"It's not that uncommon to have false labor. The baby isn't due for another two weeks. I did start to become concerned when the contractions came regularly. Then about fifteen minutes ago, my water broke and — oh!"

James listened with growing horror as his wife groaned in pain. He had to get to her. He had to get to Quincy's Gap right now! But he couldn't because of the Bronco!

"I called the doctor," Jane said when she caught her breath. "He told me to go to the hospital. Can you come pick me up? Eliot's home. They dismissed school early because of the snow. We can drop him off at Jackson and Milla's on the way."

In that moment, James hated himself. Why had he begrudged his family a newer, more reliable vehicle? He should have given up on the truck three repairs ago. He saw now that having the money in savings didn't matter when it came to reliable transportation and his family's safety.

Frantic with worry and desperate to get to his wife, he forced a calm tone. "Honey, the investigation took me out of Quincy's Gap. The murderer has been caught, but it will take me a while to travel back. Call Jackson and Milla. Have Jackson take you to the hospital in his truck while Milla keeps Eliot."

"Wh-where are you, James? Are you far away? With this being my second baby, I don't know how much longer I'll be in labor. You're not going to miss our daughter's entrance into the world, are you?" she asked, her voice rising on the last few words.

"No, no, I'm not! Hang up and call Pop. I'll meet you at the hospital in Harrisonburg. I love you, Jane."

"James, it's not the Bronco, is it?"

James squeezed his eyes shut, mortified and ashamed. "I'll be there, Jane. Just get to the hospital. Please call me when you're there safely, or have Pop call me."

Silence.

James didn't know if the call had dropped or if Jane had disconnected.

"No!" he yelled into the silent woods. His fingers fumbled the phone. It fell into the snow.

James got down on his hands and knees and plucked the phone from the snowy depths, hot tears dropping into the icy whiteness.

He got in the truck and prayed as he turned the key in the ignition.

Nothing.

Digging in his wallet, James thought about calling Lucy and asking her to come and get him. But he discarded this idea as being selfish. Lucy would come and rescue him, he had no doubt, but she'd get in trouble if Sheriff Huckabee found out one of his patrol cars had been used as a taxi. Still, if Ace couldn't come . . .

Like the last time he called the mobile mechanic, the phone rang and rang while James's heart pounded in his chest. Finally, Ace answered. "Yeah."

"Ace, this is James Henry. Remember me? I'm the guy with the Bronco."

"Yeah."

"I need your help! I can't get the Bronco to start and my wife's having a baby!"

"Don't deliver babies."

James dug the fingers of his left hand into his palm. "I understand. Can you get my truck started?"

"Don't know. Have to see it."

"Where are you?"

"Elkton, visiting my girl."

"I'm on Route 33, past Swift Run but before Skyline Drive. You're not that far away."

"Got my dog, Bacon, with me. Too cold outside for her."

"You're exactly right," James said, willing himself not to scream. "Could your girl look after Bacon while you help me out? We could go to the ATM afterward." James thought he would hand the mechanic his debit card and the PIN if he got the Bronco started.

"Be right there."

James let out a huge sigh of relief. Then he realized he was shivering and hadn't even realized how cold he was. He climbed back into the Bronco. He tried the ignition for the heck of it, but nothing happened. James reached into the backseat and grabbed an old wool stadium blanket that his father had passed down to him. He pulled the warm blanket around his shoulders.

He called Jane but got her voice mail. "Honey, I love you, and I'm doing everything possible to get to the hospital. If I don't make it in time for the birth"—James's voice broke—"kiss our daughter for me and tell her I can't wait to hold her." He ended the call.

James sat with his gaze glued to his rearview mirror, willing Ace's truck to come over the horizon. Aloud he said, "Lord, please help me be there for the birth of my daughter. I promise that I'll go to the nearest car dealer in the morning and buy the best vehicle I can with the money I have. Please let me be there for Jane and, yes, for myself. I'll get a job waiting tables at Dolly's Diner on the weekends if tha—"

He heard the rumble of a truck. *Yes, there it was!* Ace's red and white truck was coming up the road behind him!

James jumped outside and waved his arms madly.

The old truck parked close to the Bronco and Ace climbed out. Once again, he wore a T-shirt and jeans without a jacket.

"Thank God you're here!" James cried, so happy he could hug the guy.

Ace's jaw worked and James could hear the familiar rapid sucking sound. He waited for the crack of the sunflower seed. After it came, Ace said, "Hey."

Ace checked under the hood while James stood nearby.

In a surprisingly short time, Ace turned to him and said, "Blown head gasket."

James didn't know that much about cars and trucks, but he did know that Ace wouldn't be able to fix a blown head gasket on the side of a snowy, icy road. "You're sure, huh?"

"Yep. Oil looks like coffee with too much cream."

"No getting the truck on the road now," James said.

"Nope. Call the scrap metal man. He'll tow it away and maybe give you a hundred bucks for it."

"Tell you what, Ace. I have to get to the hospital in Harrisonburg now. I mean right now. My wife's having a baby. I've got to be there. I'm begging you to take me. I'll sign the truck over to you, you have my word. You can do whatever you like with it."

"Snow's getting deep."

"Plus we'll stop at the ATM and I'll give you a hundred dollars. The hospital's only about thirty miles away. I'm asking you man to man to help me out. I've got to be there when my daughter's born. My wife needs me."

To James's shock, tears formed in Ace's eyes. "Know what you mean. My dog, Bacon, she had puppies once. Needed me there.

'Course, I got her fixed since then so that nasty mutt down the road would leave her alone. Come on, let's go."

James held his hands up. "Okay, give me a second. I want to write a note to leave on the truck's dashboard so the police won't impound it."

Ace nodded and walked to his Chevy.

James turned around so fast he slipped in the snow, but he righted himself. He scribbled a brief note and placed it on the left-hand side of the dashboard. He took a look around the Bronco and was about to get out when he remembered Jane's infinity necklace was locked in the glove compartment. He got it, said, "Goodbye, old friend. I'll miss you," to the truck and then climbed into Ace's old Chevy.

On the way, he looked at his phone. The battery was low, but he made two quick calls.

"Milla?"

"James! I tried to call you but the phone didn't even ring."

"Where are you? Is Jane at the hospital? Is she all right? Has the baby come? Is Jackson with Eliot?"

"Calm down, dear. Jackson stayed at your house with Eliot. Since his stroke, he won't set foot in a hospital. I drove Jane to the hospital in my van. She's in labor and delivery. Where are you?"

Labor and delivery! "Does that mean she's having the baby now?" James hollered.

"No, dear, that's the department where women go to have babies. But she doesn't have much longer to go. What's happened?"

James couldn't bring himself to tell her. "I'm on my way, okay? Please tell Jane that I'll be there in about twenty minutes."

"Gonna take more like thirty minutes in this snow," Ace said as they passed Elkton.

"James," Milla said, "Jane and I talked about it. If you're not here in time, I'm going to be in the delivery room with her for support."

James turned his head to the passenger window so that Ace wouldn't see the tears running down his face. "That's a good idea," he managed. "Thank you, Milla."

"When you get here, come straight to labor and delivery. I'll tell the nurses to expect you."

"Tell Jane I love her," James said and disconnected. He got control of his emotions and dialed Lucy.

"Yes, James, I'm freezing and buried in paperwork. Are you coming in to give your statement?"

"Lucy, I don't have time to talk. My phone's battery is low. Jane's at the hospital. The baby's coming. I was stranded, but I'm getting a ride. The Bronco is still on Route 33. I left a note in it. Can you be sure it won't be towed?"

"Yes," Lucy said. "Don't worry about it or about making your statement. Where are you now?"

"Just past Elkton."

"Be safe and good luck," Lucy said.

The minutes crawled by, but James had to admit that Ace was an expert driver. As they came down from the mountainous area, the road had been plowed, and Ace picked up speed.

All of a sudden, Lucy's patrol car swung in front of them, her lights and siren blaring. Lucy held her hand out the window with the thumbs-up sign.

"Dang," Ace said. "We're getting a police escort!"

"Yes," James said, gripping Jane's present, every muscle in his body tense. "We sure are."

"We aren't stopping at the ATM. I trust you," Ace said.

"Thank you," James responded, vowing to make sure that, along with the money, Ace received a healthy gift certificate from Gillian for the Yuppie Puppy.

With Lucy's help, they made great time.

When they pulled into the entrance circle, James didn't even let the Chevy come to a complete stop before he was out the door and running inside. He dashed into the nearest elevator, then realized he'd forgotten what floor labor and delivery were on. Luckily, another visitor riding up was able to tell him.

James hit the labor and delivery area at a run.

"You must be James Henry," an older nurse in pink scrubs said calmly.

James nodded, barely able to catch his breath. He spotted Milla, already wearing scrubs. She smiled and said, "You go, James. I'll wait by the nursery."

"Snap to it, Mr. Henry. Put these on over your clothes." The nurse handed him a pair of blue scrubs and supervised him while he washed his hands.

The next fifteen minutes went by as if they were only two seconds.

Jane, crying at the sight of him. James cradling his wife's head with one hand, his other hand holding hers tightly as he begged her forgiveness for being late. The doctor saying, "The baby's head is crowning!" Jane's groan ending on a scream, then the sweetest sound James had ever heard in his life: his daughter's first cry.

The doctor placed the baby on Jane's chest. James and Jane smiled at one another through their tears. James kissed his wife, then looked at his tiny, perfect little girl with her adorable dark wisps of hair. He'd never seen anything so beautiful in his entire life.

When the nurses took the baby away to be washed and evaluated, James said, "Jane, can I get you anything, honey?"

Jane said, "I would really, really like some ice cream."

Chapter Twenty-seven

James walked out of labor and delivery in a daze. He knew there was a great big goofy smile on his face but it didn't seem to matter.

"James!" Milla called.

James looked around and found himself outside the nursery, where babies slept with the cutest little woven caps on their heads. James wondered if his little girl would get one.

"James, dear," Milla said and then laughed. "Is everything all right?"

"Milla! Oh, yes, Milla, everything is wonderful." James caught her up in a hug. "I'm going to get some ice cream for Jane."

"Do you want me to get it?"

"No, no, I'm going to do it. Why don't you go see my daughter?"

"I will," Milla said and chuckled. "The Mountain Overlook Café is on the first floor. They'll have some ice cream. I've been having a ball watching these babies."

"Excuse me," a male voice said.

James saw a blond-haired man in a James Madison University sweatshirt and jeans. "Yes?"

The man held out his hand. "I'm Peter Hathaway. My wife, Denise, was in Jane's Lamaze class. I guess Jane had her baby early."

"Right," James said proudly, shaking Peter's hand. "A healthy girl. You and Denise had twins, didn't you?"

Peter beamed. "Yeah, getting ready to take them home today," he said, pointing at two babies in blue.

"Aren't they precious!" Milla exclaimed.

James introduced her, then said to Peter, "Jane tells me you want to sell your Ford Explorer. I'd like to buy it if it's still available."

Peter nodded. "Sure is. Denise said she hoped y'all might want it. It's a good vehicle, I promise you. We just need more room. Be glad to work something out with you."

"Thanks." They exchanged phone numbers and arranged to meet in three days' time to finalize the deal.

James took the elevator down to the café. When he walked in the door, he saw Bennett, Gillian, Lindy, and Lucy standing with balloons that read "It's a Girl!"

His friends surrounded him, each one hugging him and offering congratulations. James felt the tears start again and wondered if he'd ever stop crying from happiness.

"I can't believe you all came out in this weather," James said. Lucy must have called the other members of the supper club.

"Of course we did," Lindy said, smiling. "It's stopped snowing and the roads aren't too bad."

"That Jim Topling really screwed up," Bennett said. He looked five years younger without his mustache. "We've got a total of five inches, and the storm's moved east to Richmond. No three feet of snow for us."

"All the better," Gillian said. "Bennett and I are leaving for a *long* weekend getaway on Friday." She smiled.

"We're going to Sanibel Island, Florida. That was Gillian's Valentine gift to me," Bennett said. "I looked it up and you can see groups of dolphins right offshore. Gillian will like that," he said, looking at his sweetheart.

James noticed they were holding hands.

"Not as much as I love the dolphins on my finger," she replied. Gillian's eyelids sparkled with turquoise eyeshadow. "Who knows what might happen down there with the warm sand under our feet and the sun shining down on us. Bennett and I might even *elope*."

Bennett shot James a panicked look, and then they all laughed.

"James," Lindy said, "Luis locked down the deal on the restaurant. Alma is so excited and, I have to admit, so am I. She wants my help picking out what tables and chairs to put in the Mexican Kitchen. That's what she's calling the new restaurant."

"That's great news," James said. "You and Luis get your privacy back, and Quincy's Gap gets its first Mexican restaurant."

"You must want to get back to Jane. We won't keep you," Gillian said. "We'll come back tomorrow afternoon to see the baby. Have you named her yet?"

"No. I'm getting Jane some ice cream. After she eats, maybe we can talk names. She's exhausted, though."

Bennett slapped him on the back. Gillian and Lindy hugged him. Then they left him holding the balloons, standing with Lucy.

"Thanks for giving us an escort, Lucy," James said. "I won't ever forget it."

"It was nothing."

"I do want to give my statement."

"I'll come by the hospital early tomorrow, if that's okay. You are staying the night?"

"They couldn't hoist me out of here with a crane."

Lucy chuckled. "I'll take your statement in the morning then. That way, Murphy can go home tomorrow."

"That would be terrific. I have a feeling that once we leave the hospital, I won't have a spare minute," James said, then asked, "Any plans tonight? It is Valentine's Day."

"I'm on duty. Those are my plans," Lucy said, raising her chin. "I'm happy for you, James."

"Sullie over at the Red Bird?"

Lucy shrugged. "I don't know. He said something to Sheriff Huckabee about going fly fishing somewhere warm this weekend. Guess he figures that Amber and the rest of the actors will clear out as soon as they're given the word tomorrow."

James looked at his friend with concern. "I want you to be happy too, Lucy."

"I am. My idea of happiness is different from yours. I don't see a home and family life in my future," she said and gave him a big smile. "Don't worry about me, James. Go and get Jane's ice cream. I'll see you in the morning."

James watched as she left the café. He hoped that Sullie would have to eat a lot of crow before getting her back.

Upstairs, James carried the white bag with two small containers of chocolate ice cream and two Godiva chocolate bars along with the balloons. He paused on the threshold to Jane's room.

Jane cuddled their daughter, who'd been washed and wrapped up snuggly in a pink blanket. A pink and blue cap covered her hair. Seeing him, Jane said, "Her eyes are open, James. Come look. Who sent the balloons?"

James didn't need to be asked twice. He put the ice cream and the chocolate on the side table next to the bed and wrapped the ribbons to the balloons around the doorknob. "Bennett, Gillian, Lindy, and Lucy gave them to us. They'll be here to visit tomorrow." He kissed Jane, then gave his little girl a kiss on her sweet forehead. She smelled of baby powder and a newborn smell that James couldn't identify but that intoxicated him.

"She was determined to be a Valentine's Day baby," Jane said. "Must be a romantic at heart."

"Speaking of romance," James said. He pulled out the wrapped infinity necklace.

Jane's eyes widened. "Don't tell me you got me a push present. Our little girl is all the present I need."

Relief coursed through James. "I was going to ask you if you wanted a push present. I thought we had a couple more weeks. This is the other part of your Valentine's gift."

"I have your Valentine's presents in my bag. I didn't have time to wrap them, but go get it, please."

James looked inside the bag and found a gray T-shirt and matching socks. Each had due dates stamped on them, like a library card. "These are wonderful. Thank you, honey."

"Will you open this jewelry box for me?" Jane asked.

"How about if I hold our daughter and you open the box," James proposed.

Jane transferred the baby over. James held her tight. He'd never held a newborn before. He stared down at her tiny features. "She has my mother's eyes, Jane."

"Does she? Oh, my, James, you shouldn't have gotten me something so expensive," Jane said, holding up the necklace. The diamonds danced in the light.

James didn't notice at first, though. His eyes were locked on his daughter's. Then he looked at his wife. "It's an infinity necklace. I got it because I'll love you forever."

"What a lovely sentiment. It's beautiful. Now, would you pass our daughter back to me?"

James did so reluctantly. "I bought something else today, but we won't get it for a few days."

Jane settled the baby, and then glanced at him. "Oh? What's that?"

"I spoke with Denise's husband. The Explorer is ours." James held his breath. He figured Jane had every right to tell him "I told you so" and more after he almost missed the birth of their daughter. He was certain she knew the Bronco was toast.

But Jane only nodded. Then she said, "Perfect for exploring our lives as a family of four."

James leaned his cheek against the top of Jane's head. "Thank you, honey," he whispered, grateful for her understanding. Then, in a normal voice, he said, "I want to name our little girl after you."

"Jane is such a plain name. I think we should call her Constance after your mother."

This was something he hadn't expected. James's heart soared. "Constance Jane Henry," he said.

Jane met his gaze, a twinkle in her eyes. "Constance Jane Austen Henry."

James grinned, and then laughed out loud. "That's perfect. Are you sure it's the name you want?"

"I'm sure. It fits our little Valentine's Day girl just right."

"I love you, Jane."

"I love you, James Henry. Now, would you pass me the ice cream, please?"

Recipes

Gillian's Goat Cheese and Spinach Pita Bake

Serves 6

1 (6-ounce) tub sun-dried tomato pesto
6 (6-inch) whole wheat pita breads
2 Roma (plum) tomatoes, chopped
1 bunch spinach, rinsed and chopped
4 fresh mushrooms, sliced
½ cup crumbled goat cheese
2 tablespoons grated Parmesan cheese
3 tablespoons olive oil
Ground black pepper to taste

Preheat the oven to 350 degrees F. Spread tomato pesto onto one side of each pita bread and place them pesto-side up on a baking sheet. Top pitas with tomatoes, spinach, mushrooms, goat cheese, and Parmesan cheese; drizzle with olive oil and season with pepper. Bake in the preheated oven until pita breads are crisp, about 12 minutes. Cut pitas into quarters.

James's (Store-Bought) Greek Style Salad with Chicken

Serves 4

2 cups shredded chicken
½ cup bottled reduced-calorie Greek vinaigrette salad dressing, divided
Lemon zest
½ teaspoon dried oregano, crushed
6 cups torn romaine lettuce
1⅓ cups chopped cucumber (1 medium)
1 cup grape tomatoes, halved
¾ cup chopped yellow sweet pepper (1 medium)
½ cup thinly sliced red onion, rings separated
½ cup crumbled reduced-fat feta cheese (2 ounces)
¼ cup pitted Kalamata olives, halved
Lemon wedges for garnish (optional)

In a medium bowl, combine chicken, ¼ cup vinaigrette, lemon zest, and oregano; set aside.

In a large salad bowl, toss lettuce with the remaining ¼ cup vinaigrette. Spoon 1½ cups lettuce into each of four shallow bowls. Top each with about ⅓ cup cucumber, ¼ cup tomatoes, 3 tablespoons sweet pepper, and 2 tablespoons onion. Add chicken mixture to the center of each. Sprinkle with 2 tablespoons feta and 1 tablespoon olives. If desired, serve with lemon wedges.

Mamma Mia's Light Chicken Marsala

Serves 4

2 large boneless, skinless chicken breasts
Salt and pepper
¼ cup plus 1 teaspoon all-purpose flour
1 tablespoon salted butter
2 teaspoons olive oil
3 garlic cloves, minced
¼ cup finely chopped shallots
1 pound mushrooms
⅓ cup Marsala wine
½ cup fat-free chicken broth
2 tablespoons chopped parsley

Preheat the oven to 200 degrees F.

Slice the chicken breasts in half horizontally to make 4 cutlets. Put each cutlet between two sheets of waxed paper and lightly pound them until they are about ¼ inch thick. Season with salt and pepper.

Place an 18-inch-long length of wax paper on the counter. Put the flour in a shallow dish and lightly dredge the chicken pieces in the flour, shaking off any excess. Put the chicken on the wax paper; reserve the 1 teaspoon remaining flour to use later.

Heat a large nonstick skillet over medium-high heat. Add ½ tablespoon of the butter and 1 teaspoon of the olive oil to the pan and swirl the pan until the butter has melted. Add the chicken and cook until slightly golden on both sides, about 3 minutes per side. Transfer to a baking dish and place in the oven to keep warm.

Add the remaining ½ tablespoon butter and 1 teaspoon olive oil to the skillet. Add the garlic and shallots and cook until soft and golden, about 2 minutes.

Add the mushrooms, season with salt and pepper, and cook, stirring occasionally, until golden, about 5 minutes.

Sprinkle in the reserved 1 teaspoon of flour and cook, stirring, for about 30 seconds.

Add the Marsala wine, chicken broth, and parsley. Cook, stirring and scraping up any browned bits from the bottom of the pan with a wooden spoon, until thickened, about 2 minutes.

Return the chicken to the skillet with the mushrooms, reduce heat to low, cover, and simmer in the sauce to let the flavors blend, about 4 to 5 minutes.

To serve, put a piece of chicken on each of 4 serving plates. Spoon the mushrooms and sauce evenly over the top, and serve hot.

Mrs. Anderson's Lentil and Vegetable Stew with Moroccan Spices

Serves 6

1 teaspoon ground cinnamon
1 teaspoon ground cumin
1 teaspoon salt
½ teaspoon ground ginger
¼ teaspoon ground cloves
¼ teaspoon ground nutmeg
¼ teaspoon ground turmeric
1/8 teaspoon curry powder
1 tablespoon butter
1 sweet onion, chopped
2 cups finely shredded kale
4 (14-ounce) cans vegetable broth
1 (15-ounce) can garbanzo beans, drained
1 (14.5-ounce) can diced tomatoes, undrained
3 large potatoes, peeled and diced
2 sweet potatoes, peeled and diced
4 large carrots, chopped
1 cup dried lentils, rinsed
½ cup chopped dried apricots
1 tablespoon honey
1 teaspoon ground black pepper, to taste

Combine cinnamon, cumin, salt, ginger, cloves, nutmeg, turmeric, and curry powder in a large bowl.

Melt butter in a large pot over medium heat. Cook the onion in the butter until soft and just beginning to brown, 5 to 10 minutes. Stir in kale and spice mixture; cook until kale begins to wilt and spices are fragrant, about 2 minutes.

Pour the vegetable broth into the pot. Stir garbanzo beans, tomatoes, potatoes, sweet potatoes, carrots, lentils, apricots, and honey into the broth; bring to boil, reduce heat to low, and simmer until vegetables and lentils are cooked and tender, about 30 minutes.

Season stew with black pepper.

If you want to thicken the stew, dissolve 1 tablespoon of flour or cornstarch into 1 tablespoon of water; stir into stew and simmer thickened, about 5 minutes.

Milla's Black Bean Soup

Serves 2–3

2 tablespoons extra-virgin olive oil
1 medium red onion, finely chopped
2 cloves garlic, minced
1 tablespoon minced jalapeños
1 tablespoon tomato paste
Freshly ground black pepper
1 teaspoon chili powder
½ teaspoon cumin
3 (15-ounce) cans black beans, with liquid
1 quart low-sodium vegetable broth
1 bay leaf
Sour cream, for garnish
Sliced avocado, for garnish
Chopped fresh cilantro, for garnish

In a large pot over medium heat, heat oil. Add onion and cook until soft and translucent, about 5 minutes. Add garlic and jalapeños and cook until fragrant, about 2 minutes. Add tomato paste, stir to coat vegetables, and cook about a minute more.

Season with pepper, chili powder, and cumin and stir to coat.

Add black beans with their liquid and vegetable broth. Stir soup, add bay leaf, and bring to a boil.

Immediately reduce to a simmer and let simmer until slightly reduced, about 15 minutes. Remove bay leaf.

Using a food processor, blend the soup to desired consistency.

Serve with a dollop of sour cream, sliced avocado, and cilantro.

Lindy's Tuna Garden Pasta Salad

Serves 6

2 cups whole-wheat rotini (6 ounces)
⅓ cup reduced-fat mayonnaise
⅓ cup low-fat plain Greek yogurt
2 tablespoons extra-virgin olive oil
1 tablespoon red-wine vinegar
1 clove garlic, minced
1/8 teaspoon salt
Freshly ground pepper
2 cans tuna packed in water, drained
1 cup grape tomatoes, halved
1 cup diced yellow or red bell pepper
1 cup grated carrots
½ cup chopped pitted Kalamata olives
½ cup chopped green onions
½ cup chopped fresh basil

Bring a large pot of lightly salted water to a boil. Cook pasta, stirring occasionally, until just tender, 8 to 10 minutes, or according to package directions. Drain and rinse under cold running water.

Whisk mayonnaise, yogurt, oil, vinegar, garlic, salt and pepper in a large bowl until smooth. Add the pasta and tuna, and then toss to coat. Add tomatoes, bell pepper, carrots, olives, green onions, and basil; toss to coat well.

Tip: Cover and refrigerate for up to 1 day.

Dolly's Buttermilk Pie

3 eggs
⅔ cup buttermilk
2 cups sugar
1 tablespoon flour
½ cup melted butter
1½ teaspoons vanilla
Pinch of salt
2 unbaked pie shells

Preheat over to 275 degrees F. Beat eggs and combine with buttermilk. Sir in the rest of the ingredients. Pour into 2 unbaked pie shells.

Bake for 10 minutes then increase the temperature to 300 and bake for 50 minutes.

Makes two because Dolly has a lot of customers who love this pie.

The Red Bird's Cranberry Kisses Mocktail

Serves 25

25 orange wedges
75 ounces cranberry juice cocktail
12.5 ounces fresh orange juice
Club soda or Sprite

Add juices to punch bowl. Fill with ice and club soda or Sprite. Pour into individual glasses and garnish with an orange slice.

About the Authors

New York Times bestselling author Ellery Adams grew up on a beach near the Long Island Sound. Having spent her adult life in a series of landlocked towns, she cherishes her memories of open water, violent storms, and the smell of the sea. She now writes full-time from her home in North Carolina, which she shares with her husband, two trolls, and three keyboard-hogging felines. Adams loves coffee, champagne, kickboxing, 1,000-piece jigsaw puzzles, Pinterest, and black jelly beans.

Her traditionally published series include The Secret, Book, and Scone Society Mysteries; The Book Retreat Mysteries; The Books by the Bay Mysteries; and The Charmed Pie Shoppe Mysteries.

Her Indie series include the Supper Club Mysteries, the Hope Street Church Mysteries, and the Antiques & Collectibles Mysteries.

• • •

Rosemary Stevens is the author of the Murder-A-Go-Go retro mystery series set in 1960s New York City, the Beau Brummell mystery series set in Regency England, and four sweet Regency romances in the Cats of Mayfair series. Stevens won the Agatha Award and the RT Reviewers' Choice Award for her first mystery, *Death on a Silver Tray.* She lives in Central Virginia with her family, including two Siamese cats whose wishes she caters to day and night. She loves British detective shows, anything vintage, chocolate, pizza, and Southern food, especially biscuits and gravy, and is perpetually on a diet.

Printed in Great Britain
by Amazon